THE LACED CHAMELEON

Bob Rogers

Dedication

For my wonderful granddaughters…
Deja
Jada
Jinglin
Mecca
Rachel

Acknowledgements

Barbara Perry Grainger undertook the task of editing my manuscript while I continued the annoying habit of rewriting scenes. Special thanks are due Barbara for suggesting the title of this work.

Sister Doris Goudeaux took time to share with me her studies of the history of the Sisters of the Holy Family and the founder, the Venerable Mother Henriette Delille. During the interview, I was enriched and enlightened. I am grateful.

During a recent trip to New Orleans, I had the good fortune to meet Edward Curtis and his lovely wife, Alexander Katherincotti. They told me the history of their home, which was built in 1830 and appeared in the 1991 movie, *Grand Isle*. They invited me in from the street and gave me a tour. Thanks to both of them, what I saw and photographed in their home became the basis for the interior of the house shared by my protagonist.

Many thanks are due Dr. Shelley Kirilenko, author and friend, for guiding me to resources that were most helpful in writing chapters in the point of view of a mass murderer. My friend and classmate, Dr. Leroy Zimmerman (former army colonel, artillery), assisted me with employing resection and related mathematics in the text. I thank Veronica Rogers, KenYatta Rogers, and Marc Rogers for their valued feedback on the story, cover, and title.

Many have made contributions to the success of this project. I am much obliged to each person named for their assistance. Nonetheless, I alone am responsible for any errors found herein.

Bob Rogers
Charlotte, North Carolina
February 2014

Then all of you came to me and said, "Let us send [agents] ahead to spy...and bring back a report...."
Deuteronomy 1:22

List of Lists

Author's Note

In America, race matters. Within the artificial construct of race, color and class have mattered for centuries, and still matter today. Sex between white men and African, Native American, and mixed-race women produced offsprings known as mulattos, quadroons, and octoroons. Mulattos are likely to have as few as one or two white grandparents and an African or Native American parent. Quadroons have three white grandparents, while octoroons have seven white great-grandparents. These arranged unions between white men and women of color existed in antebellum New Orleans society by contract in a recognized extralegal system called *plaçage*. In *The Laced Chameleon*, Francesca Dumas was a quadroon. While in a *plaçage* arrangement, Francesca and her contemporaries were known as *placées*. Race and class matter in Francesca's story.

Though this is a work of fiction, the mores, economic and social options of women of color depicted in New Orleans, and historic events of 1862 are real. Lists of fictional and non-fictional people mentioned in this work are provided for your convenience.

Chapter 1

Shots rang out from upriver. A single bullet fired from a .44 caliber Colt Walker revolver shattered Joachim's right temporal bone, scattering fragments in the lobe, then passing through the hypothalamus, wrecking his autonomic nervous system, stopping his heart, before exiting through his left ear. Francesca heard Joachim make a gurgling sound. She turned toward him in time to see him sag and crumble, then fall into the mud on his back. Francesca screamed.

In an instant, she dropped her umbrella and was on her knees beside Joachim, cradling his head between her hands. She saw blood oozing from the hairline at his right temple. Francesca shrieked, "Oh, mon Dieu, non!"

Minutes before, at almost noon that Friday, the heavy downpour had become a steady light rain. In spite of foul weather on the afternoon of April 25, 1862, a large crowd of New Orleans's citizens remained standing in the mud atop the levee on the east bank of the Mississippi River. Smiling broadly, Francesca and Emily had broken into song when the first of Union Flag Officer David Farragut's warships came into view, rounding Slaughterhouse Bend. Francesca had thought this is better than the Mardi Gras that Mayor Monroe restricted last month. They had waved their umbrellas to and fro in time with the song. A half dozen or so on-lookers had joined them. Emily's mellifluous mezzo-soprano voice soared above the crowd:

> Yankee Doodle went to town
> A-riding on a....

Now, Emily retrieved Francesca's umbrella and knelt beside her, and, using two umbrellas, shielded both of them and Joachim's face from the rain. Francesca wailed and sobbed, repeating, "Non, non, non, non!" Her shoulders shook as tears, mucus, and rain drops streamed down her face.

With her bloody fingertips, Francesca closed Joachim's blue eyes. Her lower lip quivered as she again touched the bullet hole in his bleeding right temple. With his lips barely parted, Joachim's face still showed surprise. Francesca noticed that his blood felt sticky. She no longer heard the crowd moving about her as their screams had ebbed into a low buzz while others attended the wounded. Absent-mindedly, Francesca wiped her hands on the hem of the expensive ankle-length red hoop dress she had worn the previous evening to Joachim's party celebrating his twenty-fifth birthday. As onlookers murmured and gawked, she unfolded his bandana and covered his face and temple. She unbuckled Joachim's gunbelt and felt her corset pinch her waist as she pulled the belt from underneath his body. Then, from his pockets, she removed his watch and purse.

Still on her knees, using the last hole, she strapped Joachim's belt about her small waist under her coat and felt it slip down. But for her hips, his belt and holstered four-shot Allen & Wheelock .31 Pepperbox Model 1857 would have fallen into the mud. The pistol was less than the length of her hand, weighed not as much as a pound and had four fluted barrels that rotated, each of them two and seven-eighths inches long. Francesca cried, "Why? Why? Joachim, who took you away from me? Oh, Joachim, my love, my love, I swear I'm going to find out who did this to you. I promise you, the bastard will pay with his life."

She sniffed and her tears burst forth anew. Presently, Francesca brushed her wet cheeks with the back of her hands. Then, for the first time since she knelt by his side, she looked up. Francesca's friend, Brooke, and Joachim's friend, Louie, held out their hands to help her and Emily stand. In her grief, Francesca appreciated the warmth in Emily's quivering empathetic smile.

Standing in the crowd on the levee beside the river opposite the beginning of Bienville Street and now holding Emily's hand, Francesca blinked back tears and whispered, "See the scum walking toward Front Street?"

Emily and Louie nodded. "Uh-huh."

"Find out if those bastards are the ones who did the shooting. Later, I'll need to find them."

Emily glanced at the men. And then, she protested in a pleading voice. "Fran, I know it's hard, but forget them. They ain't worth the trouble. I'll help you take care of Joachim and get home."

Louie and Brooke agreed. Louie said, "Yes, they're worthless. Of course, you know we could just turn the matter over to the law."

"That is, if you can find a lawman who hasn't run off to Camp Moore with the soldiers," said Brooke.

Silence.

Francesca stared at her friends for almost a minute before noticing several in the crowd gazing at her. Resolute, she set her jaw and shook her head. Her remaining brunette curls bounced and her bangs shifted. "Y'all, that's very kind. I need what I asked you to find out. In the meantime, I'll get men here on the levee to help me move Joachim."

Her friends looked from one to the other. Emily said, "I heard you promise revenge. Now, why do you think you're fit and able to go traipsin' off 'hind gunmen? Don't you 'member, there's a war on? Any ways, what could *you* do if you caught up to them? They could just shoot you, and that would be that. You know there ain't no mo' law to speak of here 'bouts." Emily glanced at the small pistol's bulge under Francesca's coat. "Besides, you know less about guns than I do, which ain't much."

Francesca sucked her teeth. "That's why the bastards ain't dead, yet."

Still holding Emily's hand, Francesca turned for another look at David Farragut's procession of United States Navy warships gliding upstream as more rounded Slaughterhouse Bend. She took a deep breath. Her voice was low, but firm, "Em, I've never been surer of anything in my life. I'll avenge Joachim's murder or die trying. Now, please go before they're out of sight."

Nodding and looking from Brooke to Louie, Emily hugged Francesca and said, "O-okay. W-we're going."

"Thank you, my dear friends."

The muddy hem of Francesca's dress covered Joachim's right knee and the top of his boot. She did not watch her friends depart. She remained close to Joachim's body and continued gazing, as if in a trance, at the warships and the stars and stripes they flew. Though grieving, Francesca wanted to remember the sight of the return of the grand old flag to New Orleans. She whispered to no one in particular, "Thank God, we're back in the Union."

A wet stubble-faced white man wearing a battered fedora, black coat, and wrinkled collarless white shirt stepped from the crowd and tapped Francesca's shoulder. "Er, Miss, I'm sorry to bother you heah in your time o' b'reavement. But I seed what happened. Some thugs just fired on anybody cheering dem Yankees. I'm sho' glad you didn't get hit. Damn shame, there ain't hardly any law ta speak of in these times."

Francesca turned her stern, tear-stained face and looked the short man level in the eye. "Yes? What do you want?"

The man snatched his hat off and fidgeted. He stammered, "W-Why, I-I-I'm sorry Miss. Er, I-I-I didn't mean ta rattle on like that. What I meant ta say was me and my cousin, Jimmy," he pointed, "over yonder, have a wagon at the bottom of the levee. We'll deliver the body for you to the undertaker of your choice."

The rain fell again in torrents. Francesca felt it had been a long time since she had smiled -not the ten minutes that had actually passed since she laughed together with Joachim, Emily, and others on the levee while waiting to welcome the arrival of Farragut and his ships. The ships were an even more formidable sight as they rode high on the river due to a recent freshet that caused the river to be nine feet higher than normal. Their big guns pointed down into the city's streets.

Francesca forced a faint smile as the small man clutched his hat by the crown and held it to his chest. "Sir, I'm sorry that I was a bit gruff."

He nodded. "Yes'm. It's alright. I understand."

"Thank you for your kindness. Please help me take my husband's body to the undertaker Peter Casanave up there on Bourbon Street. Tell him that my husband's father is Edouard Buisson."

The man smoothed back a wet blond and gray lock and donned his hat. "Yes'm, we can do that. Did you say, Pierre Casanave?"

"No, Peter, Monsieur Pierre's son."

"Now, where 'xactly on Bourbon is this heah Casanave undertaker?"

Francesca brushed damp hair from her face and tucked a tress behind her left ear. She pointed over the man's shoulder to the intersection of Water and Bienville Streets. "Go straight up Bienville to Bourbon. Casanave's is on the far corner on the right."

Balancing her umbrella between her shoulder and jaw, Francesca stirred the contents of Joachim's purse and pulled out three Confederate paper notes. She groaned at the irony. The two New Orleans Bank Confederate one dollar notes in her hand were printed by the American Bank Note Company of New York City and in the top center it bore the image of five enslaved black stevedores unloading a schooner. Francesca held out her hand with the two ones and a Central Bank of Alabama Confederate ten dollar note printed in Philadelphia bearing separate images of George Washington and enslaved black cotton pickers. "Oh, I'm sorry to ask, but will you take these Confederate dollars as payment?"

Chapter 2

The pandemonium that began early on Thursday in brilliant sunshine had continued over a misty night and persisted unabated during the rain on Friday. It all started when word arrived that the Yankees had fought their way past Forts Jackson and St. Philip. All over the city on Thursday, church bells had sounded the alarm. On Friday, the smell of smoke still lingering from smoldering cotton bales, ships, and warehouses set ablaze by Confederates, made Francesca cough from time to time as she wandered upriver beside the levee on the cobblestones of Water Street. Even with the coat she wore, Francesca felt chilled and she clutched at its collar. In spite of the umbrella, her hoop dress was wet well above its muddy hem. Because the dress stood out all around from her mid-calf length pantaloons, her undergarments remained mostly dry. Though tired and hungry from being afoot for hours, she trudged along in her soaked and muddy high-top shoes among the crowd watching the warships drop anchor on both sides of the river opposite the city's streets, Canal through Julia.

Francesca's mind drifted back to her first, and last, Christmas with Joachim, just four months ago to the day. Though Emily and her mother, Ada, had pooh-poohed her notion that Christmas Day was her wedding day, that's the way she remembered the signing of her plaçage contract with Joachim. The memory of that happy time before the parlor fireplace caused a lump in her throat. She let go of the coat collar and covered her mouth lest she sob aloud in a crowd of strangers. Francesca swallowed the sob as her tears flowed again. She felt her heartbreak afresh as the wonderful moments of their courtship in the summer of '61 flashed through her mind. Brooke had introduced Ada and Francesca to Joachim last spring at the Orleans Ballroom on Orleans Street where well to do white men went regularly to meet beautiful young octoroons and quadroons. She thought Joachim was handsome, dashing, and exciting to be with in New Orleans's weekend party scenes and balls. She remembered the fun they had taking the new streetcar service from the stop beside their house to concerts and plays. At age twenty-four, Joachim was younger than her other suitors. And besides, he made her feel like a queen.

Francesca dabbed at her wet cheeks with her sleeves. She thought, with the rain, maybe people won't notice. Yet, another memory came to mind. Joachim's promise to send their children to school in New York or Boston was in their plaçage contract, thanks to Ada and Brooke. She continued crying knowing that she would never bear Joachim's child, for her menses had ended on Thursday.

At Girod Street, Francesca glanced at the frantic movement of Confederate formations, commandeered mule drawn wagons, and oxen or horses pulling two-wheeled carts loaded with supplies and plunder from hastily emptied warehouses. Yesterday, she was amused by the panic of Confederates. Today, her emotions floated back and forth from grief caused by the loss of Joachim to somewhat diminished joy that her city had been liberated. For Francesca, the Confederates were reduced to scenery.

Presently, Francesca looked into the throng of angry faces gazing at the warships. She found not one familiar face. Francesca was popular and seldom alone. Her thought of missing Emily and her friends was interrupted by a stabbing hunger pain. She made an audible sigh and heard her voice announce, "I will go home."

Hunger caused Francesca to remember that only a day's rations remained at the house she had shared with Joachim. She had been surprised that Joachim's purse held only $43.00 in

Confederate dollars and two books of streetcar tickets worth about ten cents per ticket. She knew she would need a plan, and soon. Her future looked as bleak as the skies. Francesca decided, "I'll survive. She was reminded of her hero from Alexandre Dumas' novel, *The Count of Monte Cristo*. If Edmond Dantes survived, so can I."

Tears blurred her vision causing her to miss, her turn at Julia Street. She wiped her eyes and found herself at St. Joseph Street. She took a deep breath and turned northwest on St. Joseph toward her streetcar stop at Tivoli Circle, heading away from the river. Several blocks ahead she could see a column of wagons turning from Camp Street onto St. Joseph and making rapid progress toward the railhead of the New Orleans, Jackson and Great Northern Railroad. Ragged formations of soldiers, some of whom were so inebriated that they staggered, followed the wagons. Francesca's smile at the sight of fleeing Confederates vanished and she stopped abruptly to ponder the thought, Joachim's murderer could be escaping with the fucking Secesh, running like rats for the trains.

* * *

Francesca sucked her teeth and began walking again, this time away from her streetcar stop and toward City Hall on St. Charles Avenue. Aloud, she said, "I don't know who he is or where he is. I don't know how, but I'll find the scum."

It had not occurred to her until now to seek help from the police, for Francesca had heard many stories about how ineffective and corrupt the New Orleans police force was. Besides, many policemen had volunteered to fill the regiments requested by Louisiana's Governor Moore and sent to fight for Confederate armies in Arkansas, Tennessee, and Virginia. On wooden sidewalks, she remained close to buildings and out of the oncoming traffic moving with dispatch toward the railhead.

Four blocks later, she stood in front of New Orleans' magnificent nine year old City Hall. Here, she paused and considered retreat. Looking up three stories at the figure of a woman in the center of the pediment representing justice, Francesca thought what would Edmond Dantes do? The pediment was supported by six massive marble columns whose capitals curled like those seen in paintings of the Acropolis in Athens. She took a deep breath and darted across the street to the building, weaving among cantering horses pulling carriages, wagons, and carts bearing soldiers and the rich.

Francesca stood inside the great hall, near the door, trying to control her nerves and breathing. Presently, she found the desk sergeant; an old man who she judged was born in the eighteenth century. He referred her to Detective Philipe Rousseau. She found herself wondering who was older, the man at the desk or Detective Rousseau. His white hair was thin and he was bald and pink on the top of his head.

With one hand, Philipe Rousseau held papers at his side while he used the other to smooth the silver hair above his ear. Philipe looked at her from head to muddy dress hem. Flushing, Francesca said, "Sir, I'm sorry to barge in like this from out of nowhere. I must look a fright."

Philipe Rousseau smiled and the handles of his silver handlebar mustache moved upward at the corners of his mouth. He said, "Let's sit over here and be comfortable. Alright, now, tell me who you are and what brings you our station."

As Francesca poured out her story in English and French, Philipe Rousseau made notes. From time to time, uncontrollable sobs interrupted her speaking. The effect of reliving her trauma surprised Francesca. She wished for better control, but could not muster it. Philipe waited each time Francesca stopped for her to begin again. He made no attempt to comfort her.

When she finished, Philipe said, "I'm sorry. But I must ask you a few questions."

Francesca's eye brows rose. Her voice was pleading. "Why must you interrogate me?"

Philipe waved his pencil back and forth. "Oh, no, Mlle. Dumas. My questions will wrap up our interview. This is not an interrogation. We interrogate suspects. You're not a suspect; that much is quite clear to me."

Francesca leaned back in her uncomfortable wooden chair. "Oh."

"Did you see who shot Monsieur Buisson?"

"No, sir."

"Was anyone near you hit?"

"I'm not sure, but I think so from the screams. I didn't see anyone on the ground."

"How many shots did you hear?"

"I don't know."

"Half dozen?"

"More."

"A dozen?"

"Less."

"How close was the sound of the shots?"

"I don't know."

"You told me where you stood. From which direction did the shots come?"

"I think from upriver."

"How many shooters?"

"I don't know."

"Did you hear rifle fire or pistols?"

"I don't know."

"Close your eyes. Did all the shots sound the same?"

Francesca tilted her head to the right and frowned. "They all sounded the same except the last one."

"In what way was the sound of the last shot different?"

"It was louder."

"Was that the shot that struck Monsieur Buisson?"

"I don't know."

"Okay. You can open your eyes. Mme. Dumas, I'm going to be perfectly candid with you. Though your loved one was the son of a prominent banker, I'm afraid we have no resources left for a case like this. The body and witnesses are gone from the scene and you haven't given me the first lead. Unless someone who knows the perpetrators walks in here and gives us something we can go on, there is nothing we can do. I could make promises, but I won't."

Philipe stood. "Besides, the way I hear it, the perpetrators may have been common Confederate sympathizers. We are at war. Mlle. Dumas, I'm very sorry about your loss."

As Philipe walked away, Francesca sucked her teeth and clinched her fists on her lap. She remained seat and cried silent tears.

* * *

At St. Charles Avenue and Tivoli Circle, Francesca was greeted by an unusual sight. Downtown bound streetcars sat idle at Tivoli Circle with no mules to pull them, for they had been commandeered by absconding Confederate soldiers. With the thought of walking the twenty-three blocks home from Tivoli Circle, her breathing quickened as she trudged along Prytania Street past abandoned uptown bound streetcars toward the sound of braying. Ahead, a queue of expensively dressed women was waiting, tickets in hand, to board the only streetcar in sight with a mule hitched to it. She rummaged through Joachim's purse and pulled out a pasty, sticky, well-used shinplaster that reeked of rotting meat for the female conductor. Francesca tried to smile at the thought that this was her first memory of ever being happy to see a brown mule.

* * *

Francesca sneezed. She blinked the tears from her swollen eyes. With her left hand, Francesca unlatched the yard gate in front of the house at Conery and Prytania Streets. She passed under the sprawling limbs of a large live oak and by the small Crepe Myrtle she had planted in March to reach Joachim's house, the place she had called home since December. The unbearable thought that Joachim would not join her caused new sobs. Yet, she was glad to be away from the too kind woman who was her streetcar seat-mate. The stranger had tried to comfort Francesca during their ride, but had made matters worse.

She struggled to remove her wet shoes on the veranda before entering the house Joachim had provided for her. Suddenly, the front door opened. Startled, Francesca's eyes widened and she dropped a shoe. A plump, apron-clad dark-skinned woman of about thirty-five smiled at her from the doorway. Francesca sneezed again, then stammered, "W-who're you?"

Beaming, the woman opened the door wider. "Why, I'm Edna Black, Missus Maria's house servant. You must be Francesca, Joachim's partner."

Francesca frowned. "H-how did y-you know....? Y-you don't know, do you?"

"How do I know who you are?'

"No. Y-you don't know..." Francesca sneezed.

She saw Edna's brow crease. In a scolding tone to match her frown, Edna said, "Com'on in the house outta this damp weather, Chile, 'fore you catch yo' death." Smiling and cheerful again, Edna continued. "Now, o'course, I don't really know you. I just know nobody but a missus would take off her shoes on a veranda and not knock. Guess you wonder how cum I'm here? Well, Missus Maria done sent me over to tidy up for y'all."

Francesca looked into the kind face and ached to talk with someone, anyone. If not Emily, maybe this pleasant woman would do. With a full throated sob and new tears, Francesca seized Edna in a fierce embrace. She screamed, "You don't know! You don't know!"

Her forehead furrowed, Edna dropped her feather duster and hugged the distraught Francesca with both arms. Patting Francesca's back, Edna softly asked, "Chile, what is this thing I don't know?"

Francesca tried to catch her breath. She was gasping between sobs. Finally, she blurted, "Joachim's dead! He's gone. My Joachim's gone! What am I gonna do? Oh, Mary, Mother of God, what can I do?"

Edna hugged tighter. "Oh, my Lawd, Chile. My, Lawd. I'm so sorry." Edna rocked Francesca gently from side to side. "Honey, I'm so very sorry 'bout yo' loss."

Francesca's teeth clattered.

Edna walked her upstairs to the bedroom, removing and dropping clothes and they went. "Let's get you outta these wet things and into a hot bath."

Edna left Francesca on the bed under two quilts and went to the kitchen to heat water.

While Edna prepared the bath, Francesca, prayed, "Mary, Mother of God, thank you for sending someone in my time of need."

* * *

After Francesca's bath in a zinc coated tub of about four feet long with lion paw feet, she told Edna the details of

Joachim's death. Francesca guessed that Joachim must be in his coffin by now, so she covered her sixty-four inch one-hundred-thirteen pound frame in black mourning clothes. She let her bangs hang, but braided the rest of her brunette hair, tying the two mid-back length braids around her head like a crown. As they talked, she rubbed oil on her bare white shoulders, resting her brown eyes on the small round dark birthmark at her left shoulder like it was the first time she had seen it. Edna helped her cover the mirrors and drape the front door according to mourning custom. They shared a supper of yams, bread, and dried beef. Edna made sassafras tea as the gloom outside brought an early onset of night.

Francesca asked, "Miss Edna, do you think the Buissons will let me stay in this house for a time?"

Edna dropped her head. And then, she looked into Francesca's brown eyes. "You can call me just plain Edna. But, to answer your question, I don't know."

"What do you think?"

Edna hesitated. "Well, I don't really know. But, since you insist on an answer, I think they will ask you to leave."

Francesca sipped her tea and nodded thoughtfully. "Logical. Deep down, I suppose I knew that. What more can a black woman expect? But now, I'll be prepared."

Edna tilted her head in a quizzical gaze. "I know you've got African blood. But you look white."

"I guess that's because my ma is mulatto and my pa is French."

"Are you free?"

Francesca saw a pained expression on Edna's face that said she wished she had not asked. Francesca smiled. "Edna, it's okay to ask. You're my friend." Her weak smile faded and her face turned serious. "No, I'm not free. I'm just another enslaved quadroon. My pa owns me and Ma."

Edna nodded, smiled, and stood. "Well, I need to get back. Wid dis bad weather and all, I think you oughta stay in tonight. Do you want me to give Missus Maria the bad news?"

Francesca leaned forward in her chair. "But, you didn't finish telling me about your girls, yet."

"That'll have to wait for another time."

Now, Francesca realized she didn't want Edna to leave, though she didn't say so. She thought for a long moment and decided to take the easy way out. And then, she stood. "Yes, please tell Madame Buisson."

Chapter 3

"Son, by the grace of the Almighty, you're back here in time to take charge of the family cause. Me and yo' ma are dependin' on you to make it happen." Sixty-one year old Paul Dodson could say no more. Red-faced, he rocked back and forth on his horse, reeling from a dry hacking cough.

Thirty-four year old Troy's narrowed eyes and creased brow showed grave concern for his father who was nearly twice his age. "Pa, you know I'll do my best. Don't you think you oughta see Doc Peters about that cough? It's been with you ever since I got back."

Between coughs and spitting, Paul managed to say, "Don't mention that ol' quack to me again."

When his coughing ceased, Paul said, "I still believe 'twas a miracle that saved you on that battlefield and brought you back home to Belle Chasse." The older man raised his sweat-stained wide brimmed hat and smoothed his silver hair.

Troy's horse raised her head from grazing and snorted. Father and son sat their horses on the track leading from the barns to the first cane field. They watched Matt, Troy's younger brother; assign the day's tasks to enslaved men and women preparing for work in the dim light of early morning that Thursday, April 10, 1862.

Troy laughed and said, "Have it your way, Pa. But, you know I still think it was ol' Jean Pierre, at the risk of his own skin, who dragged me from harm's way."

"Never you mind, it's that same Providence that will see us own this place and the means of production 'fore I pass on. Just you mark my words."

Troy thought, *yes, and someday it'll be mine.* To his father he said, "Well, Pa, the morning's wearing on. I'd best be getting on to Slaughter House Point. I'm following your advice to get in and see that banker at a good hour. So, I'll need to catch an early ferry."

"Yeah, son. You run along and bring home a deal that make ol' Theodore salivate. Make me and your ma proud."

* * *

As Troy rode toward Algiers, he remembered his teenage years when Judah Benjamin owned Belle Chasse Plantation. He was young, about the age Troy was now. After Benjamin emerged from a flamboyant life and the dregs about Rampart Street to become a successful attorney, he married a beautiful young girl who was Troy's age. In no time, Benjamin owned a townhouse on Bourbon Street, bought Belle Chasse, and built one of the grandest Greek Revival houses anywhere near New Orleans. Troy still admired the whitewashed two-storied structure supported by tall square columns with its wraparound verandas on both levels columns. Oh, and the parties Benjamin held! Benjamin's still a worthy hero. Troy smiled. *Now, that's what I want before I'm nearly as old as Pa.* Benjamin was the go-to fellow for planters far and wide seeking to duplicate his successful sugar cane planting and process methods. *I can see myself bringing those days back. And, by Jove, I will!*

The contacts I'm making by working for General Mansfield Lovell should help me and Pa gain respect in Plaquemines Parish, New Orleans, and beyond. Colonel Hebert's letter of introduction has already been a big help. With a little luck, I oughta be able to make General Lovell's close connections to Mayor Monroe and Governor Moore count. In due time, I'll make Mr. Benjamin remember me.

Troy's face turned grim when he remembered how his father had just missed taking advantage of Benjamin's misfortune. He thought how he had felt bad for his hero when Benjamin, now just three weeks into his new job in Richmond as Secretary of State for the Confederate States of America, was forced to sell Belle Chasse and its three-hundred acres, including about a hundred-fifty slaves, at a loss. Troy slapped his thigh. As he recalled, Benjamin had to sell in 1850 to pay off the debt of a friend who defaulted on a loan Benjamin had co-signed. He shook his head in awe at the memory that Benjamin didn't just recover, but went on to serve two terms in the United States Senate. Theodore J. Packwood, one of Benjamin's partners, had outbid his pa for the purchase of Belle Chasse and that was that. Troy's eyes brimmed with bitter tears as he recalled the derision of community people who scoffed at the notion that the overseer class, folks like him and his pa, had the temerity to even attempt to enter the planter class.

Aloud, Troy said into his horse's hearing, "Well now, we'll just see about that!" With a snarl on his lips, he spurred the animal, hard. "Com'on, git up there!"

His horse responded with a grunt and by vaulting from a canter to a gallop.

* * *

Troy disembarked from the Canal Street Steam Ferry and walked along Water and Custom House Streets to Citizens Bank at the intersection with Royale, arriving minutes before nine o'clock. In one of his new finely tailored suits, black string tie, and matching black boots, Troy felt the part of the gentleman planter and businessman he aspired to become. He threw his shoulders back and walked tall as a clerk showed him to the office of Edouard Buisson, who received him with grace. After minutes of pleasantries, Monsieur Buisson said, "Mr. Dodson, a thousand pardons, but because an urgent government matter has thrust itself upon me just yesterday, I must spend unplanned time on getting it resolved. Of course, this is highly unusual, especially after my letter confirming our meeting. However, I have arranged for another officer to assist you. Please do forgive me."

Troy's ire went up. "So my business is not important to you."

"Oh, contraire, Mr. Dodson, we see the business you bring today reaching into a bright future for your Belle Chasse Plantation and our bank. We are well aware of Judah Benjamin's success at Belle Chasse. We'd like to help you reach even greater success. Now, please come with me. Let me introduce you to one of our real estate stars. This officer is none other than my esteemed son."

* * *

A seething Troy Dodson used his fork to pick at and rearrange the food on his plate in the City Hotel's restaurant. From his portfolio, he withdrew paper and a pencil. In his two hour meeting with Monsieur Joachim Buisson, they had agreed that the likely total sales price for Belle Chasse Plantation and its one hundred forty-seven slaves would be approximately one hundred ten thousand nine hundred twenty dollars. Early in the meeting, Troy had offered ten percent down. Too late, he realized the estimated purchase price would require the Dodsons to raise another forty-five hundred dollars. He wondered where the hell that would come from. He knew they had nothing they could sell that would raise the difference. With his brow furrowed and sweating, Troy fought off the urge to tell Joachim that he needed more lenient terms and to explain what hard workers the Dodsons were. His pride won. He did not ask. Worse, Joachim's final word was that Citizens Bank could not do a deal on Belle Chasse for less than twenty percent down. Aloud, he said, "Damn that little Yankee-loving bastard!"

Troy looked about to see if anyone had noticed his outburst. Seeing no one looking his way, he muttered, "Somehow, the sniveling little sonovabitch must know I can't raise twenty-three thousand dollars."

* * *

Troy sat in his room figuring until one o'clock the next morning. He slept fitfully and was out of sorts when he rose. He managed to collect himself at breakfast.

Troy presented his new proposal with fresh confidence to Joachim. "Monsieur Buisson, let's make eighteen of the slaves a part of the deal, added to my down payment with the mortgage and say that'll close the deal. That sum will easily reach the estimated sales price we made yesterday."

Joachim stood and paced behind his desk with one hand rubbing his chin. Troy watched as his new found confidence eroded. His anxious mind wondered, w*hat now?*

At length, Joachim returned to his desk, opened a side drawer, and flipped thru a large ledger. He began shaking his head. With a finger on a number to hold his place, he looked up at Troy. "I see a problem here with diminishing returns."

An annoyed Troy said, "Speak plainly, Monsieur Buisson."

"Alright. There are presently one hundred forty-seven slaves at Belle Chasse. Selling eighteen slaves will not close the gap for you."

"Why, that's more than fourteen thousand dollars I'm adding to my down payment! Of course, the deal closes."

Joachim shook his head and said, "I don't think so. Eighteen would fetch perhaps a just bit more than ten thousand. But the real concern I have is will there be enough labor left to produce harvests required to make the mortgage payments?"

"I don't agree with your slave prices."

"Mr. Dodson, I think your assumptions are perhaps a bit optimistic, at best, on the speculative side, given the falling prices of slaves auctioned right here in the city at Mr. Thomas Foster's depot since the loss of Forts Henry and Donelson this year. Not factored in is the certain negative impact of catastrophic Confederate losses this week at the Battle of Shiloh. Nor, can we estimate future influence of battlefield losses on markets."

Troy leapt from his seat and hit Joachim's desk with his fist. Tremendous pain in both temples and behind his left eye caused him to close his eyes and massage both temples. His caged thoughts were hot with fury, what does a profiteering Unionist like him know about battles or the better than even chances of our armies to drive out the invaders? He forced himself to take a deep breath. He had a blinding headache. After a moment, Troy turned and left Joachim's office without a hand shake or farewell.

On the street, Troy said several times, "Confounded! Hellfire! Damn his black soul!"

* * *

Back at Belle Chasse Friday afternoon, Troy told his father and Packwood that the officers at Citizens Bank were considering his proposal and would reach a decision before the end of the month.

The next day he returned to work for General Lovell at the general's headquarters on Camp Street across from Lafayette Square. Within an hour of his return, General Lovell sent Troy off on a small steamer to check again the readiness of Forts Jackson and St. Philip to defend against an attack by the Union Navy. He wore a collarless brown shirt and the coarse butternut trousers like the ones he had worn during his stint as an infantryman in the Confederate Army. His nearly sixteen inch long Colt Walker .44 six shooter was strapped to his right thigh.

As he had predicted to General Lovell, the Union fleet opened fire on the two forts the next week. He also predicted the forts would hold off the Yankees. Saturday, April 19, the day after the Federal's siege began, Troy returned to Belle Chasse to collect clothing and his soldier's accoutrements. While there, Packwood summoned him without his father and intimated that the day before he had received an unsolicited bid from a team of investors.

With a forced smile, Troy said, "Well now, that's very interesting. Can you tell me who these folks are?"

Packwood answered, "Of course, I can. The bidders are James E. Zunts, a part owner of the City Hotel at Camp and Common Streets and Joachim Buisson, an officer at Citizens Bank on Royale Street. Their bid is an even one hundred thirteen thousand. With you in mind, I'm delaying them. I told them I'd let them know my decision by Monday, the twenty-eighth instant."

* * *

Standing at the stern of a small Confederate steamer on another reconnaissance Wednesday morning, April 23, Troy raised his head from staring into the brown waters of the Mississippi River as a grim grin changed his countenance. He had settled upon a new plan to acquire Belle Chasse. Upon his return, he made his report to General Lovell: The forts may not hold after all unless we deploy our powerful ironclad, the *CSS Mississippi*, tonight and destroy the Yankee mortar schooners laying siege.

Using his influence as a Confederate agent, Troy had collected personal information and built a dossier on Joachim Buisson, James E. Zunts, and Sarpy Lille, an officer in the

Union Bank of New Orleans. Putting his plan into action the same afternoon, he coerced Zunts to sign an agreement and join as his bid partner alongside Union Bank should the bid Zunts made with Buisson be turned down by Packwood or withdrawn.

By evening, Troy was in Lafayette Cemetery peering through his binoculars into the windows of Joachim Buisson's house across Prytania Street. He tried to ignore the sound from the Federals' six-day old continuous bombardment of the forts. Troy scoffed as he remembered General Duncan's telegram from Fort Jackson to General Lovell at the end of the day; "We can hold them at bay. We can stand it if they can." He shook his head and said aloud, "Stay focused on Buisson. The fate of New Orleans is not my affair." Troy reassured himself. Again, he thought it is clear; the only path to success is to kill Buisson. He smiled. Then, of course, his bid is withdrawn. *I must be patient and be present when the right moment presents itself to remove the haughty young Monsieur Joachim Buisson.* He repeated several times: *Discipline. I will wait and watch for a clear opportunity.* He fondled the grip of his powerful Colt Walker .44.

Before mid-morning on Thursday, New Orleans was sent into a panic when the ringing of a prearranged twelve bell signal by the city's churches announced that the invading enemy had managed to pass the forts. Troy's immediate thought was that his plan for the day was doomed. He slapped his holster and said, "Hellfire!"

Instead of stalking Joachim, Troy went to General Lovell for orders. With Troy and several staffers, Lovell decided to take his steamer downriver and assess the situation himself. Lovell ordered the captain to retreat to New Orleans when they were nearly captured by the *USS Varuna*. Before they escaped the Federal warship, Troy thought hellfire, there goes Belle Chasse!

Back in New Orleans, General Lovell instructed Troy and his staff to order troops to burn anything that could be used by the enemy and evacuate. For the rest of the day, Troy fought his way to and fro on a commandeered horse through the throngs of marching soldiers, and terrified women and children to oversee fires being set to tens of thousands of bales of cotton and warehouses. He encountered Negroes and poor whites with wheelbarrows and pails salvaging high priced staples that were being destroyed, including molasses and sugar. Toward evening, dark clouds rolled in from the south and west, but that did not deter the mayhem in the streets.

With his duty done and Lovell in lengthy meetings with Governor Moore, and Mayor Monroe explaining why his foot soldiers would not be able to defend the city against a fleet of warships, Troy took his leave. The last words he heard from Lovell to the governor and mayor were, "Dammit, I've told you several times that our *CSS Mississippi* is still under construction. There is no way we can have her engage the enemy."

A cold heavy mist fell as he retired to his room at the City Hotel where he discovered a birthday party in progress in honor of Joachim Buisson. Troy learned from the desk clerk that Joachim and his friends would be at the hotel until Saturday. He thought that's more than enough time to find an opportunity. Troy was confident but did not sleep well because, with the change in weather, pain returned in his left thigh where he was struck by shrapnel during the Battle of Oak Hills.

Dressed in a business suit and wide-brimmed white hat covering part of his face at breakfast, Troy watched Joachim and his friends as they decided to go to the levee in the rain to await the arrival of the Union warships. He checked the load in his Colt Walker .44, turned up his collar, and followed. Determined not to limp, Troy endured the pain in his thigh and walked as much as possible like a soldier marching.

Around noon, the heavy rain gave way to a farmer's shower. As the first of the Federal warships were sighted rounding Slaughterhouse Bend, sparse, but distinct cheers arose from Unionists in the crowd gathered on the levee. When some revelers broke into "Yankee Doodle," gunfire erupted to Troy's right; he thought *my opportunity has arrived. Act. Dammit, be quick!* In a continuous fluid motion, Troy brushed aside his coattail, drew, cocked the .44, aimed, fired a single bullet into the side of Joachim Buisson's head from thirty-five feet, and holstered his revolver.

Chapter 4

In Saturday morning's sunlight streaming through the dining room window, Francesca sat with an unpainted red cedar pencil and a used envelope behind the remains of her breakfast. There were only tiny bits of her fried eggs and grits left clinging to her plate under a few bread crumbs. As was her habit while contemplating any matter, Francesca used the index and fore fingers of her left hand to curl and uncurl a tress above her left ear. For the third time, she counted the Confederate notes in Joachim's purse. Returning the Confederate currency and soft brown leather draw-string purse to their place inside her corset between her small breasts, Francesca began a list of items to buy, if she could still find them, while people may still accept Confederate dollars. She thought, what is the best use, right now, of $31.00? At the rate prices were rising, would the things on her list still be affordable next week? Or could they be found at any price? And, when the money is gone, what then?

On the same envelope, Francesca wrote the names of people she thought could or would help her. After thirty minutes, she still had only five names: Ada De Mortie, Emily Jenkins, Brooke Bouffard, François Dumas, and Edouard Buisson. With a heavy sigh, she dropped the pencil into the lap of her black dress.

She put her arms on the table and lay her head down to sleep. Francesca had been awake since four o'clock and was now afraid to sleep lest she have the same dream from which she awoke twice, heart racing and in a sweat. In her dream, she saw Joachim shot and fall. The dream ended each time with the gunman running her down and placing his revolver to her head.

The cord beside the transom above the front door swished and the doorbell rang angrily, driving the thought of dreams from her head. Startled, Francesca felt the hair on her neck move. She stood and her left hand flew to cover her mouth. Her pencil clattered onto the hardwood floor. The visitor gave the pear-shaped wooden handle attached to the cord on the outside another firm yank. The bell rang again. She wished Joachim was there to confront the caller. She blinked and thought what would Edmond Dantes do? He would handle it. *But he was much stronger and more athletic than me.*

The thought did not linger. She shouted, "Bonjour, un moment!"

Francesca ran up to the bedroom and strapped Joachim's pistol above her left hip and covered it with a black shawl that she draped around her shoulders. She thought, Em is right, *I've gotta learn how to use this thing. Dear Mary, Mother of God, please do not let me need to use it.*

At the front door, Francesca reached for the latch and paused. She took a deep breath, put her left hand under the shawl, and opened the door with her right. Instead of Joachim's killers, she was relieved to find a tall slim thirty-something white woman dressed in expensive mourning clothes standing on the veranda eyeing her from head to foot under a frowning brow, arms folded and tapping one foot. Francesca felt like a side of beef must feel hanging in the market.

Francesca mimicked the posture she saw and folded her arms. With a confident smile she did not feel, Francesca said, "Bonjour. Vous devez être Mme. Buisson." Francesca moved aside and curtsied. "S'il vous plaît venez po." Once she spoke, Francesca thought she saw surprise in the woman's face and the foot tapping ceased.

The woman stepped inside and glanced about the front hallway as she spoke. "Bonjour. Je vous remercie. Oui, je suis Mme. Buisson."

"I'm Fran…"

Still examining what she could see of the house and with ice in her voice, Mrs. Maria Buisson cut her off, "I am well aware of who *you* are."

Francesca maintained her forced smile. Standing under the front hall chandelier, she gestured toward the parlor. "Please sit here in the parlor. I will make tea for us."

Maria's hand went half way up and Francesca saw "no" on her lips. Maria closed her mouth, exhaled, and dropped her hand. Francesca pretended not to notice. Maria elected to sit upon a bowed seat upholstered bergeres chair with scrolled wooden arm tips and said, "Thank you. Tea would be lovely."

* * *

Though she had only sassafras tea and no sugar, Francesca brought it to the parlor in a fine tea service, just as she had practiced at Mère Henriette Delille's small parochial school in a house on St. Bernard Avenue. She tried to keep smiling though the tremor in her hands angered her.

"Aha! So that's why I could not find my mother's tea service!"

Francesca, startled by this news, recovered and served tea while changing the subject. "Mrs. Buisson, I'm sorry that when we finally meet it is under these sad circumstances."

In an aloof voice, chin raised, Maria sounded detached. "Yes. Otherwise, it is possible that we *never* would have met. So-o-o, tell me, do you know the Buisson and Bouligny families?"

"I remember what Joachim told me. He said that his uncle, John Bouligny, was serving in the U.S. House of Representatives when Louisiana seceded and chose to stay and live in Washington."

Maria hissed. "Yes, the damned Unionist!"

Francesca ignored the epithet. "He also told me that John's uncle, Charles Bouligny, served in the U.S. Senate. All I recall about Buissons is that Joachim, like his father, is an officer at Citizen's Bank."

"I don't suppose the little Unionist told you that our cousin, Pierre Benjamin Buisson, serves 'the cause' in our Confederate States of America as a brigadier general."

Francesca shook her head. Uncomfortable in the presence of a supporter of the "peculiar institution" of slavery, she shifted her feet about and tried to think of a way to change the conversation.

Maria asked, "Now tell me, what's noteworthy about your family? How have they served Louisiana?" Running on and not pausing for Francesca to respond, Maria clucked. "I learned that your father, François, is a hopeless drunk, a gambler, and runs a pathetic little restaurant in Vieux Carré. Is there anything else I should know?"

Francesca blinked and silently seethed. Again, she shook her head and stared into her cup.

Maria sipped her tea and changed the subject. "Frankly, my dear, I must tell you, though Joachim was only my step-son, I completely disapprove of plaçage *arrangements*."

Angered, Francesca felt tightness in her chest and about her head. She took a deep breath and spoke in an even tone. "Actually, Joachim and I had much more than an arrangement. I loved him, and he loved me."

Maria made a small backhanded slap gesture. "Ha! What do *you* know of love? How old are you anyway? Seventeen? Maybe, eighteen? Certainly, you're old enough for sex and making babies, but not old enough to know the difference between sex, love, and exploitation. You, and your kind, give sex in exchange for room and board, plus a relative life of ease, in other words, the kept woman." Maria raised her chin and looked down her nose at Francesca and spat her next words. "Or, perhaps, I should say *concubine*."

Francesca flushed bright pink and felt the tears coming. She willed the tears back but her forehead still felt warm. *I can cry later.* She sipped her tea as if Maria had not spoken. She tried to sound aloof. "Last year, Joachim and I had a wonderful courtship. We were in love. Though he's gone, I will love him for a very long time. If we could have married under the law, we would have. Plaçage is what we could do for now. Oh, by the way, I'll be nineteen this year, in just a few months."

Maria set her tea cup into her saucer with a crash. "When I walked in here, I was pleasantly surprised by your command of two languages, apparent education, housekeeping, and manners. I expected much less. For a moment, I thought maybe this one is more than just another pretty face with a great body. Now, you have confirmed my original beliefs. Plaçage girls are just that, *girls*. They have no idea that they're being exploited for sex. Love has *nothing* to do with it. *Nothing!* Open your eyes, *child*, and look around! How many of these *arrangements* have you seen where the white man does not eventually marry a white woman, whether he keeps his plaçage girl or not? I prematurely gave you *far* too much credit."

Again, Francesca blinked. She thought, *though I don't like her, this rings true. But, true or not, I don't like what I'm hearing, no, not one bit. It sounds too much like something Mère Delille said.* She blinked again and tried desperately not to sound hollow. She insisted, "Joachim and I are, I-I-I mean, were in love."

Maria sneered, moved forward to the edge of her chair, and looked at Francesca with narrowed eyes. "Why, you little fool! Did Joachim love you enough to introduce you to his family and his betrothed?"

This time, Francesca was completely unprepared for what she heard. She felt stabbing pain in her temples. Her tears burst forth before she could attempt to control them. Because her vision was blurred, she set her cup and saucer down at an angle, spilling her tea as the cup overturned onto the parlor's marble top center table. Francesca leapt from her seat, hit another bergeres chair with her knee, recovered, and ran from the room. The stairs were a blur, so she stumbled forward using the hand rail. She threw herself onto her tall four-post mahogany bed without noticing that her speed caused the mosquito net hanging from the canopy to billow as she continued sobbing loudly. Francesca buried her face in one pillow and pulled another over her head. The pain inside her head would not subside. The ache and anguish she felt was deep in her chest and acute, like a hand in fire that could not be removed before the burn registered. This new hurt was worse than seeing Joachim gunned down. It was far worse than anything she could remember or imagine. For now, the hurt absorbed her whole mind as she gradually curled into a fetal position. She shut out all else, even Maria.

After Francesca had cried for what felt to her like hours, actually only forty minutes, she sat on the edge of her bed wiping her eyes. She felt fatigued. When she could see again, there was Maria in the doorway, leaning against the jamb, arms folded. Francesca's first thought was to shoot Maria. But then, she thought, *Maria is only the messenger. Besides, by the time I figure out how to work the damn gun, she'd be upon me, and I'd have no gun.*

With a slight grin, more a smirk, Maria asked, "Can you talk?"

Francesca nodded.

"Okay, there are three more things I need to mention before I depart. One. Which undertaker has Joachim's body?"

42

Francesca coughed and cleared her throat. "Peter Casanave on Bourbon Street."

At the mention of Casanave, a black undertaker, Maria paused and scowled, but made no remark. She said, "Two. You are not to attend the funeral or have any contact with my family. And three. You can keep gifts Joachim may have given you, but you are to remove yourself and your personal belongings, and *only* your personal belongings, from this house within the hour. Understood?"

It was almost ten in the morning.

Slowly, Francesca stood and plodded to within five feet of Maria. With a quizzical look on her face, Maria stood up straight, arms still folded. Francesca maintained eye contact, conveying hatred. With her right hand, she removed her shawl and let it fall to the deep red and white ornate carpet. With her pistol exposed and left hand by her side, Francesca was surprised when she heard herself speaking in a stern voice, without hysterics, "Mme. Buisson, je pense que la fin de la journée est assez tôt. Pas vous?" (Mrs. Buisson, I think the end of the day is soon enough. Don't you?)

Maria's eyes widened as she retreated backwards from the doorway. Gone was her haughtiness. Maria's voice went up and down, from flat to squeaky to flat again. "W-why, er sure, Francesca, t-the end of the day is quite soon enough. A-actually, t-tomorrow will be fine."

Francesca stood rooted to the spot staring at the door and listening to the sound of Maria's shoes on the stairs. Momentarily, she heard the front door open, and then, it slammed shut again.

Chapter 5

For a time, the only sound in the house was the tick-tock of the 1860 inlaid French Morez movement clock that hung on the wall above the mantle, striking the hours and half hours. The black and gold picture frame clock was two feet tall. When it stopped at 11:53 a.m., Francesca let go of the hair above her left ear and looked up from her seat on the floor of the parlor. She smiled and thought, *time's up for me, too.* She remembered that Joachim had last wound the clock a week before, back when Confederate General Lovell, in charge of the defense of New Orleans, and the local rags still believed the two forts downriver would defeat the Union Navy.

Gazing at the clock, Francesca thought, this day reminds me of the time they threw poor Edmond Dantes into the sea bound in a burial sack. It is time to sink or cut free and swim. *I will follow Edmond. I am done with crying. I will live.*

In the bedroom, Francesca spread a sheet on the floor. In the center, she placed clothes she had brought with her to Joachim's house the previous December. She left all the expensive clothes Joachim had given her hanging in the large polished mahogany crown wardrobe or neatly folded in two drawers, visible when the wardrobe doors were open. Francesca let the wardrobe doors and drawers remain open for Maria to see. She arranged a display of jewelry gifts on the marble top cherry wood commode beside the fine china wash bowl and pitcher, with several necklaces hanging from the supports of the five foot tall free standing mahogany framed mirror.

By half past noon, Francesca was hungry. She thought, *I'd better finish this little job off and get on to Mama's.* She sat down at the dining room table and wrote notes she would post on the front door upon her exit for Emily and Brooke, inviting them to visit at her mother's home. She stood and took a step before she returned to her seat. She sat and wrote another note, this one to Maria:

> Chère Mme. Buisson, trouver de l'argent pour le drap de lit j'ai pris dans un pot dans le placard. Je suis également quitter tous les dons de Joachim. Francesca Dumas. (Dear Mrs. Buisson, find money for the bed sheet I took in a jar in the cupboard. I am also leaving all of Joachim's gifts. Francesca Dumas.)

She placed the note for Maria in the parlor on Maria's mother's tea service. As she laid the note in place, the doorbell rang. Startled, Francesca's left hand moved to her pistol. "Qui?"

"It's me, Edna."

Francesca took a deep breath and ran, smiling, to admit her new friend. "Coming!"

* * *

They ate pork sausage patties generously covered with blackberry jam stuffed inside Edna's large flakey warm biscuits from the center table in the parlor with their legs crossed like high society women, sipping sassafras tea. "Miss Edna, I mean, Edna, I'm so glad to see you." Francesca laughed. "And your food! I was starved after all that packing."

"Now, what all packin' is dis you're talkin' 'bout, chile? From what I see, yo' thumb is firmly in Missus Maria's eye by yo' leavin' behind all that fine jewelry and them fancy clothes Joachim done bought fo' you!"

Laughter.

Smiling, Francesca tilted her head and put a hand on her hip. "Oh, I wouldn't want the Buissons to have nothing to sell when all those Confederate dollars of theirs turns into confetti!"

Raucous laughter.

"Chile, you the quickest 'widow' I ever seed recoverin' from her b'revement."

"That's because you never met a 'widow' who found out the day after her man died that the double dealing scoundrel was betrothed to another."

More raucous laughter.

When they recovered, both fell silent. Francesca felt the need was more urgent than ever to spend the contents of Joachim's purse, quickly. What to do for income next week? Next month? She mused, *Maybe, in a month or so, I'll get Brooke to line up a new partner for me. This time, I'll remember what Maria said. Love ain't got nothing to do with it. I'll do as she expected, I'll exploit. Period. We'll be even. He'll get what he wants and I'll live by my wits. I will live.*

Presently, Francesca realized that she was staring at her tea cup. She looked up. "Since this is your market day, if you don't mind, I'll go with you and pick up some things for Ma."

"Cos' not. You come on along and we can talk. I'll be happy to have you. But, 'fore we go, tell me. Were you just now thinkin' 'bout yo' money sit'ation? 'Bout how you gone eat, live indoors, and sich?"

Francesca's face brightened. "Why, yes! You're right! That's exactly what I was thinking."

Edna's face turned serious. "Though we've known each other for only a minute, I'ma tell you like I'd tell my own Rebecca or Rachel, if'n they were yo' color." Edna leaned forward. Her voice became somber. "Plaçage was invented to trap young pretty girls dat are de color dey are 'cause some white man done ravished dey mamas and gra'mas. Dis plaçage thing ain't no good for yo' heart or yo' head."

Francesca thought these are Mère Delille's words exactly. Could it be that they know each other? Francesca's sigh was audible. She clasped her hands in her lap. "Edna, I must live on my own. Mama can't support me. Papa is always in debt with his damned gambling. We don't have a farm. I can't sew, cook, or do house work. White people use slave women for those jobs. Now, of course, you realize, no white man can marry me, even if one wanted to do so. I've never had any luck to even get a free black man to do more than look at me. And, Lord knows, I've tried. After looking and declaring that I'm beautiful, they tell me I 'look like trouble.' And, since I can't buy one, slave men are out of the question. Don't you see? My choices are very, very narrow." She wrung her hands. "I don't know any other way. I have to use what I have."

Edna slowly shook her head and dropped her chin. Francesca saw sadness on her face. For the first time, the thought occurred to her, maybe Mère Delille was right. Maybe…

Edna blinked and brightened. She interrupted Francesca's thought. "Honey, times are changin' real quick dese days! A woman your color has a better and better chance to make something of herself."

With two fingers in her hair, Francesca tilted her head to one side. You know what; this woman treats me better than my own ma. But, right now, she ain't making any sense. Francesca rubbed her chin thoughtfully. "Give me a for instance. How would I go about making something of me?"

Edna had a satisfied grin on her face. "Well, I'm happy you didn't tell me what I half expected, that I'd lost my mind."

Francesca stretched and yawned, holding both fists above her head. "Oh, no. Not at all. I really believe you have my best interest at heart."

"Gimme a lil' time and, I'll give you a for instance." Edna stood. "Meanwhile, let's head on down to de market."

"Which one?"

Edna chuckled. "With Missus Maria's purse in my pocket, I like de French Market. 'Sides, it's on the way to yo' ma's place."

* * *

Francesca tacked her open faced notes for Emily and Brooke to the front door. Then, they boarded a Prytania and Camp streetcar beside the house headed upriver. The house faced Conery Street, which was only one block long, and across Prytania was Lafayette Cemetery. Francesca was almost certain the Buissons would bury Joachim there.

Though she sat on the streetcar's left side oak bench with her back to the cemetery and thought she had been resolute about declaring an end to tears, she felt like crying again. She thought why is this? *Joachim deceived me, though he never actually said he loved me. I was a fool to assume he did just because of the gentle way he treated me, oh, and all those damned gifts. My feelings are confused.* She wanted to shake and clear her head, but did not, lest Edna inquire. Instead, she stared at the ceiling and held her tears back.

At Toledano Street, the tracks made a turn toward the river. Four blocks down Toledano, they made another left turn onto Magazine Street and started downriver toward the center of the city. Francesca took little notice of the mansions they passed. She wanted to talk and avoid thinking about Joachim. Edna sat on the same bench, which ran the length of the car. Francesca's bundle, tied by the four corners, was between them, crowned by Edna's brown and worn shopping basket.

Again, Francesca was reminded of Joachim as the streetcar passed through the block between Fourth and Third Streets. He had told her that his house, acquired in a sweet deal from his bank following a foreclosure, was built in 1841 on the same architectural plan as the thirty-two year old house she saw through the open window in front of her.

Presently, Francesca asked, "How old is Rebecca?"

A sigh came from Edna. "Bec just turned seventeen last month. Oh, and Rai will be fifteen in a coupla weeks."

Francesca smiled. "Why, they could be my little sisters. I wish I could meet them."

Edna turned her face away.

Francesca saw the pain before Edna turned. She thought, *now look what I've done. I've caused my friend to remember the greatest hurt of her life because I'm trying to escape from my pain.* She reached across the bundle and basket and touched Edna's shoulder. "Oh, Edna, I'm so sorry. I've made you feel bad."

Edna put her hand over Francesca's. "I'm okay. My hard grievin' was done long, long ago. But the dull ache is still deep in here." She slapped her chest. "It returns several times every day. I fear it will follow me to my grave. Now, don't you try to take on my agony atop yo' present troubles."

Francesca's eyes watered. "I'm so glad I met you. I can't wait to introduce you to Mama and my friend, Emily."

"I'd like that."

Both women sat with their arms folded, staring at the floor. Francesca was deep in thought, trying to imagine her mother being sold and taken from her at Rachel's age four years before.

Edna cleared her throat and spoke in a low voice. "Lawd, Lawd dat was a time. Nobody oughta hafta go through dat kinda hurt. And jes lak that." Edna snapped her fingers. "The ol' widow missus up and snatched me from my family. She sold me off, and then my babies and husband saw me led away in chains. Poor lil' Rai ran after the shuffle, blinded by her tears, runnin', stumblin', and fallin' tryin' her level best to catch up to the shuffle. It nearly tore my heart out to see lil' Rai like that." Edna sniffed, her eyes brimmed with water that almost spilled over. "I wanted to yank and pull at my chains. But I couldn't do that 'cause it would hurt the peoples in front and behind me."

Speaking as gently as she could, Francesca asked, "What's a shuffle?"

"Oh, that's a bunch o' slaves chained together by their necks and connected to the back o' a speculator's wagon. We walked all the way from Smith County, Mississippi to N'Awlins by way o' Natchez. That is 'cept ol' Lucille. She had walked from Columbus, Georgia, but died on the road after Natchez. One night, she jes gave up and passed on in her sleep." Edna paused. After a long sigh, she continued. "Once here, they put us in a pen and fatten us up, like hogs, to be sold again. That sellin' was nothing. It was that first one that tore up my family, broke my heart, and wrecked my life."

Francesca patted Edna's shoulder. And then, she caught the eye of a fashionably dressed white woman sitting across from them. The woman had been listening to Edna. The eye contact was less than half a second, for the woman then found the floor to be very interesting.

* * *

Frantic shouting began outside Francesca's streetcar window. She turned on her seat and saw Confederate soldiers and fat huffing old men hurrying away from the doors below the six massive middle columns of the grand St. Charles Hotel. For a third day, they scurried toward the railhead. Minutes later, their streetcar reached the end of the line at the base of the Henry Clay monument, where St. Charles Avenue met Royal and Common Streets.

They entered the heart of the Vieux Carré walking northeast along Royal Street. Five blocks on, Francesca pointed out her father's restaurant at the corner of Royal and Toulouse Streets. One block later, Edna guided them onto St. Peter Street toward the river. They entered Jackson Square's southwest gate. Near the center of the square facing the statue of Andrew Jackson on a horse, Francesca looked to her left at the edifice of the St. Louis Cathedral with its three majestic spires and was again reminded of Joachim. They had met in the Orleans Ballroom in the block directly behind the cathedral. She thought, Hail Mary, Mother of God, please guide my mind. The live oaks in the square flexed their gnarled mighty limbs like the muscles of champion wrestlers. The new light green leaves of spring on other trees and shrubs brightened Francesca's feelings. They exited the square on Decatur Street.

Francesca pointed across Decatur. "Hey, Edna, look. There's the new coffeehouse Joachim told me about. It's called Café Du Monde and was opened just two weeks ago. He said their café au lait and beignets are so-o-o good! Let me treat you to these delights and toast our new friendship."

Edna's face shone with an impish grin. "I've got a better idea. Let's let Missus Buisson treat us!"

Francesca laughed, showing perfectly even teeth. "Edna, you're a mess! I'm so glad I met you."

Leaving Café Du Monde behind, they entered the French Market and shopped until Edna had filled her basket with spinach, strawberries, leeks, kale, scallions, and collard greens. Francesca stuffed a few items into her bundle for her mother, including: asparagus, carrots, mint, parsley, and rosemary. Edna declared that, though the price of most foods were up since last week, before the invasion, the prices for flour, molasses, and sugar had reached levels for which she wouldn't even pay with Mme. Buisson's money. Satisfied with their bounty, they promised to meet the next Saturday at the Café Du Monde and said their good-byes at Decatur Street and Ursulines Avenue.

Francesca boarded an omnibus service that traveled Ursulines through Faubourg Tremé up to Hagan Avenue. She paid the driver with two shinplaster streetcar tickets and he climbed the spokes of the rear wheel and placed her bundle in the cargo rack atop the vehicle. Francesca boarded with five other passengers. The only door was in the center of the rear end of the bus, which was drawn by four large bay horses. She thought the bus looked a bit like an intercity stagecoach from the front. It even had the same high box seat for the driver, but no side doors.

Crossing Chartres Street one block later, Francesca spotted a man who she thought could be one of the shooters. *Damn, here I go again.* She shook her head. *Now, I'm seeing things.* Given her changing feelings about Joachim, she felt less like honoring her pledge to the dead man to avenge his murder. But she also felt guilty because she considered reneging on her promise. She watched the man walk along Chartres toward Dumaine Street until he was out of sight. Twenty blocks later at Ursulines Avenue and Rocheblave Street, Francesca left the bus and let herself into her mother's house. As she expected, her mother was not at home, but was probably working at the restaurant.

The sunny day, Saturday, April 26, 1862, was fading. Francesca poured a cup of sweet tea and dragged a grass-bottom ladder back chair outside and sat on the front veranda facing the shotgun house across the street where Emily lived with her parents, free blacks, Laura and Anthony Jenkins. Before Francesca's chair was warm, Laura ran across Ursulines wearing a troubled face.

Francesca smiled and waved. "Hello, Auntie Laura! How are you?"

Laura, a mulatto who was a well-known seamstress, paused to catch her breath. "Chile, this minute, I'm right poorly. I sho' am glad to see you! Is Emily inside?"

Concerned, Francesca sat her cup on the floor. "No, Auntie Laura, I thought Em was with you. Why, I was coming over for a visit soon's I finished my tea."

Wringing her hands, Laura stopped at the steps to the veranda. A tear trickled down one cheek. Then, Francesca saw Tony, the shoemaker, standing across the street, fists thrust deep in his pockets. His medium brown complexioned jaws were clinched as he stared at his wife and Francesca. Though the day was warm, Francesca felt a sudden chill in her spine and deep foreboding.

With panic in her voice and an outstretched hand, Laura gestured toward Francesca. "Fran, I thought she was with you. Em didn't come home last night."

Chapter 6

Laura and Tony rearranged the ladder back chairs on Ada's veranda so that they sat facing Francesca. Their backs were to Saturday's setting sun.

Francesca was now burdened with the weight of both bereavement and guilt. She knew that Emily was always in daily touch with her parents and that more than twenty-four hours had passed since she sent Emily off to find and follow the gunmen. Laura and Tony allowed Emily out only when accompanied by Brooke and Francesca, both of whom were "married" and one year Emily's senior. Trying to suppress the panic rising in her bosom, Francesca wrung her hands. She thought, *Mary, Mother of God, this is the biggest mess I've made in my life. Please forgive me. What can I say?* In a contrite voice, she said, "Auntie Laura, I don't know where Em could be. Whatever has happened is my fault entirely. I have to tell you that when I last saw Em was when we were fired upon yesterday at about mid-day."

Laura's eyes widened and her hands flew to cover her mouth. "What? Oh, my God! Was Em hit?"

"No, ma'am."

Tony exhaled and was stern when he said, "Now, Fran, it's not like you to take Em into places like Congo Square. I know you have better judgment than that." Tony struck his knee with his fist. "So where did y'all go?"

Francesca took a deep breath and said, "Yes, sir. I'll tell you where we were and when and what happened; which is all I know."

She told them the same story Detective Rousseau had heard the day before and let them know that no help would be coming from the police, especially, not to find a mulatto girl.

When Francesca finished, the sun had set and she felt drained; as if she could sleep for two days.

Laura massaged her face with both hands. Tony looked sheepish and with a faint smile he said, "Fran, I'm sorry about raising my voice a bit ago. I apologize."

Laura reached out and touched Francesca's hand and said, "Fran, my dear, I'm going to apologize, too. I'm apologizing for the unsaid evil that was in my mind."

Francesca's spirits brightened and she no longer felt like sleeping. "Your apologies are not necessary. I can only imagine how both of you must have felt, and, feel even at this moment. But, right now, I promise you, I will find Em and bring her home.

"Uncle Tony, before it's too dark. I need you to show me how to shoot my new gun."

The sun had set minutes before at about half past seven. Tony stood abruptly and said, "Okay. Let's get movin'."

Still seated, Laura clapped her hands once and said, "Lawd, Chile, I always said you're a wonder. I heard your promise, but we ain't gone hold you to it. We gone git busy ourselves trying to find our baby. What with this gun business, I know you're serious. But don't expect too much of yourself."

* * *

By first dark, Tony and Francesca were in Ada's backyard where Francesca pulled the trigger and missed a paper target on the ground at fifteen feet. Tony corrected her stance. On her second attempt, using both hands, she squeezed the trigger like Tony told her and hit the target. Tony had pointed out only the basics of safely firing her pistol. They hurried to his backyard shoe shop where Tony made a gift to Francesca of a leather shoulder bag he had made for a well to do customer. He explained that the sturdy leather bag, the size of a single saddlebag, would be the best way for her to carry her small pistol without notice and that otherwise the gun would wear a hole in a cloth bag.

Giving instructions all the while, Tony walked with Francesca to the omnibus stop and waited in the glow of a nearby gas streetlamp to see her off on the last bus to the center of the city at eight o'clock. While they stood waiting, Tony told her for the third time: "Don't use your gun unless your life is threatened. Don't pull your gun until you must use it. Don't point your gun and shout orders or make threats; shoot immediately into the bad fellow's chest. Remember, right now, you only have two balls left in your pistol."

Blinking, Francesca was somber. "Yes, sir."

* * *

Brooke Bouffard Williams's house at Carondelet and Philip Streets was dark. Hoping Brooke may have only retired early, Francesca pulled the doorbell cord three times. No response came from within. Dispirited and tired, she sat on the front steps of the home Brooke shared with her planter investor husband, Bernard Williams. She knew Bernard had traveled to Baton Rouge to look at a plantation he was interested in purchasing. Francesca held her head in both hands and thought *dear Mary, Mother of God, what have I done to my friends? Please, not Brooke, too. What would Bernard….?* What would Edmond Dantes do?

She stifled a yawn and stood lest she fall asleep on the veranda. Francesca reckoned it must be at least half past nine.

A new thought occurred to Francesca. Her mouth dropped open and her eyes widened. *Mary, Mother of God, suppose the scum are looking for me!* Glancing up and down the deserted streets, she shivered. Aloud, Francesca said, "Edmond would do something; not stand about! What? *What?* I must find a place to rest and start again tomorrow."

She set off in the darkness for Joachim's house, eight zigzaging blocks away, looking carefully at every bush and tree she approached and periodically, glancing over her shoulder. Her sweating left hand was inside her leather bag resting on the polished walnut wooden grip of her pistol. As expected, Joachim's house was dark. Francesca knelt by the steps and hoped she did not encounter a snake or black widow spider as she removed a loose brick from the back of the steps. The key was not there. She felt along the ground. Nothing. Forgetting how far she had crawled, she tried to stand and crashed her head against a joist with a thud. She let out a half muffled cry. Her headache was instant. Before she could get to her feet, a startled raccoon bolted from under the veranda and ran around the corner of the house. In spite of herself, Francesca screamed.

Thoroughly disgusted, Francesca sat on the steps. She weighed the risk and the energy needed to walk eighteen blocks to the kitchen house in back of the Buisson mansion where Edna slept. Then, the sound of scurrying feet came from within the front hallway. Hair rose on the back of her neck and her bladder felt full. She turned and looked at the front door. Only then did she notice that her notes had been removed. She took a deep breath and fought the trembling overtaking her body.

Francesca leapt to her feet and made a step toward Prytania Street, decided she would be seen in the light of the streetlamp, turned and darted behind the ancient live oak in the front yard. There she stayed with her back to Conery Street for almost an hour. During that time, only one carriage passed on Prytania. To avoid being seen, she was perfectly still in her black mourning clothes, making herself one with the trunk of the old tree. It was almost eleven o'clock and a nearly full moon was rising over the downriver edge of Lafayette Cemetery; threatening to take away her hiding place. Displaying a gallows smile, she thought, it's a good thing that Uncle Tony taught me to fear the living; not the dead.

Again and again, she thought who could be in "my" house? And for the tenth time she tried to decide where she would sleep lest she fall asleep beside the tree. In the quiet of the night, she heard the steps again. This time, the sound was close to the door and accompanied by sniffing and soft crying. A woman? What would Edmond do?

Retreating, Francesca tiptoed to the gate and held it open with her right hand, ready to flee. She removed her pistol and held it in her left hand. Then, she remembered what Tony said and put it back in her bag, but held onto the pistol's grip. She cleared her throat and called out. "Brooke?"

The door opened. In the dim light, a woman appeared. The woman sniffed and said, "Fran?"

* * *

In the front hallway, the two friends held each other in a second embrace. This time, the hugging was less fierce and their cheekbones did not collide again. Presently, they went arm in arm into the parlor. They tried several times to talk, but each time they would start at the same time. Then, both stopped trying and laughed.

Grinning, Francesca raised her hand as if in school and spoke first while Brooke beamed, then giggled. Francesca said, "I am so thankful that I found you! First, I went to your house, and then came here. Let me tell you, I surely did not expect to find you here!"

"I thought here was safer than home. You know, in case I was followed."

"Where did you sleep last night?"

"In the streetcar barn."

"Huh?"

"Wasn't that smart? They have a night watchman, you know."

"No, I didn't know…."

Francesca dropped heavily onto a chair and continued with a furrowed brow before Brooke could respond. "But now I must turn to a most serious matter. Em didn't come home last night."

"I know."

"What?"

"A man stole her while she was tending Louie's wound."

Francesca leapt to her feet. Her jaw was agape and she held her aching head with her hands. "What man? Wounded how? Who? Where?"

Tears returned to Brooke's now somber face. "I don't know. I'm so sorry. I'll never forgive myself."

"For what?"

"I didn't go after the man who stole her." Brooke broke into sobs and could not continue.

Though she wanted to hear details immediately, Francesca did not push. She patted Brooke's shoulder and held her hand. "Try to calm down. I'm sure there's nothing anyone could blame you for not doing against such a man."

When Brooke's sobs ceased, Francesca resumed her seat. Detective Rousseau's image flashed through Francesca's mind. Gently, she said, "Brooke, I need you to take your time and tell me the whole story of everything you saw and heard beginning with the minute you last saw me on the levee."

Brooke took a deep breath and said, "Okay, I'll try."

Francesca listened with rapt attention, at one point stopping Brooke to find paper and pencil for note taking. "Okay, now, did you say the five men appeared not to be together? Why do you think that?"

"They didn't talk to the man who later took Em. They laughed about shooting into the crowd. I don't think the man walking behind them laughed at all. Besides, they split up without a farewell from that man, just each other. Four of them seemed familiar with each other."

"Where did they split up?"

"Two continued on St. Joe toward Tivoli Circle while three turned left at Peters Street. I followed the two on St. Joe. Em and Louie followed the three on Peters."

Francesca put her pencil on the parlor's center table. "Well, how did you come to see Em taken?"

"I heard a shot…"

"What?"

"Yes. I had walked less than a block, but I had to find out if our friends had been hurt. So I ran back to Peters and turned the corner. Two of the men we followed had mounted horses and were riding away. Though I didn't see Em and Louie, I continued. While I was still on Peters, I heard Em scream. It was short scream. It sounded as if she had been forced to keep quiet."

Brooke paused. Francesca retrieved her pencil. "Go on."

"I turned onto Delord Street where I thought Em's scream came from. In the distance, the man who seemed not a comrade of the others was walking Em by the scruff of her neck toward Tivoli Circle. That's the last time I saw her."

"Where was Louie?"

"Wait. I'm getting to Louie. I heard a groan in the alley way between Peters and Pearl Streets. That's when I found Louie. He was trashing about in the grass next to a stable and bleeding with a ball in his shoulder."

Francesca slumped in her chair and covered her face with her hands. "Mary, Mother of God, what have I wrought?"

* * *

While Brooke bathed upstairs, Fran sat in the parlor making a list of all the questions asked of her by Detective Rousseau that she could remember. When Brooke returned, Francesca wrote Brooke's answers.

Francesca asked a few questions of her own. "Did the shot you heard on Peters Street sound like that last shot fired on the levee?"

Brooke frowned. "I can't say for sure, but I think so. That's a hard question. I see why you asked, but I don't really know for sure." She smiled. "So since when did you go to police school?"

"Yesterday. Oh, and, by the way, I graduated before I left City Hall."

They had a short laugh. Francesca thought what would 'Ol' Baldy' say?

Brooke announced, "I'm hungry."

"Me, too. You must've found out that there's no food in this house. And, oh yes, Mme. Buisson evicted me this morning, er, yesterday morning. Oh, I can't think now. Don't you reckon it's two o'clock Sunday morning by now?"

"I think it must be closer to three."

"I'll drink a cup of water and sleep right here. You can have the bedroom. I'll never sleep there again."

"Wait." Brooke sat beside Francesca on the canapé. "What're you going to do for money, now that Joachim is gone?"

Francesca made a big sigh. "Both the short and long answers are simply, I don't know."

"I know several of Bernard's friends who'd *love* to have you. I can introduce you."

Francesca no longer felt sleepy. Her eyes rolled upward and she made a face that wrinkled her nose. She felt the edge of a new and unfamiliar sense of unease. She struggled to bring it to the surface and respond to Brooke, but could not. She thought *I need; indeed, I must grab hold of and understand what just happened in my spirit.* Frowning, she sat back in her seat and folded her arms, realizing that the words *"have you"* and *"have me"* were repeating and ringing in her aching head like the lyrics of a song sung to dissonant music. Perhaps, the words were a trigger...

Francesca saw Brooke examining her face but ignored her.

Brooke said, "Fran, are you okay?"

"No. My mind is confused. Since Joachim's deception, I've been troubled off and on about what I've been taught about plaçage and how I'm to live. I think I need to give this plaçage thing more thought; a long and deliberative going-over."

Brooke looked perplexed. "Fran, I'm sorry I didn't tell you about Joachim's betrothal. I apologize again. But now what can you do? You were born a quadroon. Plaçage is the door for you to a comfortable and good life. Without money, but with your beauty, what's to deliberate about?"

"I don't know if plaçage is good for me or not." Francesca thought of Edna. "Enough talk. Com'on, I'll get a couple of quilts for us."

In the bed room, Francesca knelt and withdrew a small polished wooden box from underneath the bed. She opened the box and caressed the green velvet lining in the space made for Joachim's Pepperbox pistol. The box had sections for balls, a gunpowder flask, cleaning rod, and a ball mold. There were a dozen balls in the box. She thought *I'll get Tony to teach me how to load my gun.*

Francesca was leaving the room with a quilt and her box when Brooke said, "Fran, a woman needs a man to make a life in this world. I'm sure we can find another good man for you. With your good looks and body, that won't be a problem."

From the doorway, Francesca said, "Will it be another with a wife or a betrothed?" She thought she saw Brooke wince.

"From birth, all we are given is our bodies. We must make good use of everything we have to make a life."

Francesca sighed. "That could also be an argument for prostitution. But you don't have to think of that. You're white and you have a husband."

"It's the same thing."

"Oh, no it ain't."

"Fran, you're white enough to get a husband. In another city, no one would be the wiser."

"Huh?"

Brooke rushed to the doorway. With a hand on Francesca's folded arms, Brooke took a deep breath. Her voice trembled as she said, "I-I-I'm going to trust you with a serious and u-u-unrepeatable secret to help you understand that a woman has to do what she must to avoid a miserable life of poverty. I may not be as white as you think. Fran, m-m-my father's grandmother was a mulatto."

Chapter 7

Joachim Buisson was laid to rest in Lafayette Cemetery on Sunday afternoon, April 27. Francesca led Brooke on a trek to the Buisson mansion on Louisiana Avenue and Magazine Street. They timed their arrival for about the time they guessed the funeral would begin at the St. Stephen Catholic Church on Napoleon Avenue near Chestnut Street. Between the two, they had not enough money for a single meal. Francesca remarked, "I'm streetcar ticket rich and cash poor!" In the kitchen house behind the mansion, Edna fed the two famished friends red beans and rice with bits of chicken liver and other sumptuous foods from pots prepared for the returning funeral party.

Francesca bade Brooke farewell after the long streetcar ride into the city on the St. Charles Avenue line. Walking toward the levee to meet Bernard's steamer, Brooke left Francesca at Canal Street waiting for another streetcar. At nearly half past five, Francesca arrived at Doctor Stone's Infirmary, a hospital that took patients of all races. From the front entrance, she noticed a small herd of cows across Claiborne Avenue grazing on new spring grass under the watchful eye of a young barefoot white man. She thought cows so close to the city....

Then, she stopped and took a second look at the man. She *thought I wonder what it would be like to live somewhere in a small house with a man like him and make babies.* Again, her mind went back to Brooke's astonishing revelation. She thought *could I pass? How would it feel to pretend that I'm someone else; someone white?* Francesca cocked her head to one side as she thought *how could I be anybody but me? Does this mean that I've thought all along that I'm just another mulatto like ma and not recognize that that's what I thought? I love Em like a sister. Her parents are the finest couple I know. Could it be that Auntie Laura has been the person I've always*

64

wanted to be like? This is hard..... Brooke may be right to think that I could pass, but what then? That man over there would expect me to be white, not just look white. What does being white mean? I fear eventually he would see through my lie. Oh, my, the day is waning. I'll have to think about this later.

Francesca entered the hospital.

Inside the men's ward, Louie greeted her from his perch propped in a sitting position by three pillows at the head of his bed. "Well, you're a sight for sore eyes."

"Humph! I didn't expect you to recognize me in two day old wrinkled mourning clothes with my hair tied about my head."

"Oh, I'd know that funny mug of yours anywhere; no matter what ol' rag you wore."

Grinning, Francesca wagged a finger at Louie. "Watch out! While you have one arm tied up in that sling, I could cuff you, but good."

The two men in beds across the aisle laughed with Louie. He said, "It's good of you to visit."

"Maybe you should decide that when I'm finished with you. Anyway, you don't look too bad for a fellow with a hole in his shoulder."

Smiling, Louie said, "Yeah, Doctor Stone said he thinks I can go home next week."

Francesca drew a chair close to Louie's bed and turned her back to the men across the aisle. She started with a finger across her lips signaling quiet. Just above a whisper she said, "I need to hear what happened as best you can remember since I last saw you. I'll need to ask a few questions when you finish. Can you hear me okay?"

Louie's eye brows rose. He lowered his voice. "Er, yes. I hear you okay."

She explained that no help would come from the police and that she had spoken with Brooke. He nodded. Next, she placed her paper atop her wooden box and held a pencil in her left hand. "Please start your story at the levee."

* * *

Because she had no more paper, Francesca wrote Louie's answers to what she now called 'Ol' Baldy's' questions next to Brooke's answers. She smiled as she thought *I wonder whether anyone calls Detective Rousseau, 'Ol' Baldy'?* Tapping her pencil against her box, she reviewed Louie's responses again.

"Louie, I need a description of this man. Did you see his face?"

"I don't know what a real policeman would ask, but you sure sound like the real thing."

"I'm the only police officer assigned to your case, Emily, and Joachim's. Jokes aside, I shudder to think that I am the only person asking questions. By the way, don't give me credit. Most of these are the same questions that detective asked me. I feel like I'm back in Sister Juliet's algebra class, applying a formula to variables, only I don't know which formula to use and I have to find the variables myself."

"Well, officer, I'm happy with your dedication. Soon's I'm oughta here, I'll join you in this detecting variables business."

Francesca smiled. "Oh, thank you!"

She glanced down at her notes. When she raised her face, it was somber again. She locked onto Louie's blue eyes and said, "Okay. Back to business. Describe the man who shot you."

"He was a couple of inches less than six feet and wore a black suit. From a distance, it looked expensive. His boots were muddy, but I could see they were black. I think he walked as if he may have had a pebble or something in his left boot."

Louie paused. Francesca waited. "Well, go on."

"That's all I know."

She shifted in her chair and repositioned her shoulder bag atop her box, then began tapping again. "Louie, surely you know more than this."

"Huh?"

Francesca said, "Close your eyes and keep them closed." She paused for almost a minute. "Okay. You're on Peters Street following this fellow and two other men. Before he turns the corner onto Delord Street, you see his back clearly. Yes or no?"

"Yes."

"What color is his hat?"

"Well, upon my word! You're something! Of course, he's wearing a hat! It was raining! His hat was white."

"Keep your voice down."

"Okay, okay."

"Was his coattail split?"

"Yes."

"What was he carrying?"

"Nothing."

"Did he wear riding gloves?"

"No."

"Did you see his gun?"

"Er, kind of. I mean, I saw his holster."

"Tell me what you saw."

"The top, I mean, the grip was hidden under his coat. Hmmm." Louie paused and tilted his head to the right.

"What?"

"His holster was brown, but longer than any I've seen. The bottom end was tied to his thigh just above his knee."

"What else?"

"That's the last I saw of him until he snatched Em. Even then, I didn't see his face. Em was bent over me trying to stop my bleeding. He grabbed her from behind and clamped a hand over her mouth. I was dizzy and could barely see Em, let alone see him. In an instant, they were gone."

"Didn't you see him before he shot you?"

"No. He must've realized we were following him. He bushwhacked us, but good."

"Did you hear his voice?"

"No. He never said a word."

"Okay. Open your eyes."

"You were right. I knew more'n I remembered at first. Did I do good?"

Francesca was scribbling rapidly and did not look up, but said, "Yes. You did just fine."

Louie spoke in his usual volume. "Before you go, there's an unrelated thing I meant to mention."

"Yes."

"My purse was stolen last night. The thief also took the purses of my new friends there across the way."

"Didn't the night watchman catch the thief?"

"Nope. There ain't no night watchman."

Francesca laughed and said, "This is no laughing matter, but as soon's I get back to headquarters, I'll ask the chief to assign someone to investigate!"

Chapter 8

Wearing a dry suit and black string tie, Troy found General Lovell near the end of Friday, April 25 at the St. Charles Hotel in conference again with Governor Moore and Mayor Monroe. The group had grown to include several members of the New Orleans Common Council. They were interrupted by the frequent arrival telegrams. Troy sat in a corner of the meeting room and waited. During one disruption, General Lovell spotted Troy and waved for him to join them. Lovell looked him up and down, and then said, "Troy, I saw you enter the room, but in that fancy get-up, I didn't recognize you. I apologize. Gentlemen, allow me to introduce Mr. Troy Dodson. This young man is a wounded veteran of our victory in the Battle of Oak Hills and one of my most reliable staffers."

The graying group applauded and a chorus of "Cheers!" and "Salute!" rang out.

General Lovell pulled Troy aside and said, "Troy, I'm leaving for Camp Moore, forthwith. I want you to stay behind and pass on information of both high and routine value. First, comb through our headquarters again and make sure nothing of value to the enemy was left behind."

"Yes, sir. God's speed, sir."

* * *

Troy limped along Camp Street in the glow of occasional streetlamps. His thigh and knee ached. The pain, his proximity to Canal Street, and General Lovell's mention of the battle caused Troy's mind to drift back to the previous spring.

Following secession, January 26, 1861, and a short life as a sovereign nation, Louisiana joined the Confederacy in March. Troy answered one of the governor's calls for men to join the

Confederate Army. By the time he decided to join, Louisiana had already sent ten infantry and three artillery regiments east to fight in Virginia.

Troy had arrived in New Orleans not long after Mardi Gras in 1861. By April, he was promoted to corporal in Company A of the Third Regiment, Louisiana Infantry, because of his excellent marksmanship and his age.

Troy alternately used his bandana to wipe sweat and flap at large mosquitoes. "Damn. This has got to be the hottest April I can remember."

Jean Pierre, a soldier from Plaquemine in Iberville Parish, said, "Well, Troy, if that be the case, this must be the hottest April since the Almighty created dirt!"

The soldiers, sitting in a semicircle around their supper cook fire, broke into hysterical laughter. Smoke wafted out the open side of their circle carrying the scent of bacon and beans. Troy thought why am I irritated by Jean Pierre's remark? He's only funning me. Troy forced himself to join the laughter.

Jean Pierre said, "I guess y'all know ol' Troy joined our company 'cause comin' from Plaquemines Parish he thought he could find out from us upriver folks what plaquemine means since our town is named Plaquemine. The po' boy been eatin' plaquemines all his life and didn't know some peoples calls'em persimmons."

More laughter. Troy's ire rose, but he managed to smile.

The next evening at supper before the same soldiers sitting on the ground, Sergeant William Tunnard asked, "Why did you fellows answer the governor's call to fight?"

The soldier beside Tunnard spoke first. "Now, that's one pure d silly question. I'm heah to do my part! I'ma help drive the bloody Yankees outta our country."

Several raised fists and said, "Hear, hear!"

Troy poked at the fire and added a handful of twigs. "I've noticed in several New Orleans newspapers some vague-ass talk about our freedoms being threatened. But what do y'all think this fight is really all about?"

Tunnard said, "Hold on a sec. I'll tell you." He retrieved and unfolded a tattered page torn from a newspaper. "I think our vice president made real plain what this war is about in his speech last month. What he said was this thing is about our 'peculiar institution of African slavery.' More to the point.... Wait, let me not mess this up, so I'll read it: '*The proper status of the negro in our form of civilization was the immediate cause of the late rupture and present revolution*'."

Jean Pierre removed from his mouth a weed he was chewing and said, "Now, I find that to be a *real* interestin' reason for dying." He leaned back on an elbow. "By the fuckin' way, who is this damn vice president that I had no say in electing?"

Troy said, "The real fact of the matter is we're in this fight to keep our rights. The main thing is keeping our means of production. Like it or not, niggers are key cogs in our incomes and way of life."

Another soldier wearing a puzzled face asked, "So w-why do the Yankees wanna take away our niggers?"

Jean Pierre interrupted. "William, you've got the paper. I still wanna know who this asshole is who thinks I should grab a gun and go march off to die for the '*proper status*' of niggas. So, answer me, who the hell is he?"

Tunnard said, "JP, the vice president of our Confederate States is Mr. Alexander Stephens."

"Where the hell did he come from?"

"Georgia."

Troy turned to Jean Pierre. "So, tell me, why are you here about to march off and fight?"

Jean Pierre sat up. "Simple. My brother died at the hands of Yankees. I don't know which ones did it, but I'm heah to kill off a few of'em, all nice and legal like in this heah war."

Tunnard put a hand on his hip. "Then what?"

"Then, I'll take my scrawny scaly ass on back to Iberville Parish."

Laughter erupted.

Presently, Jean Pierre continued. "Say, which one's o' y'all owns any niggas?" He looked about the group. Each soldier searched the faces of his comrades. No one said a word. Jean Pierre smirked and nodded. "Uh-huh. Thought so." He leaned back and resumed chewing his weed.

Remembering there was no one present from anywhere near Plaquemines Parish, Troy said, "JP, I, for one, will soon own more'n a hundred niggers and many acres for them to work."

Tunnard said, "Troy, I think planters, and what your family is doing, sustain the flow of cash for most everyone in our new country. That includes craftsmen, livestock breeders, shipbuilders, shopkeepers, and countless others."

A few soldiers nodded. Others exchanged bewildered looks.

Jean Pierre sat up again. "Lookit, some o' y'all, like ol' William and ol' persimmon Troy, might have a dog in this heah hunt. But I ain't, and I know it. Me and my folks are po' dirt farmers just tryin' ta live. What some high muckety-muck in far off Georgia like this heah Alex fellow has ta say don't mean shit where I come from.

"The thing is for y'all that don't know why 'tis you joined up, you oughta. I figure a man oughta know why he's dying."

They argued until time for lights out. The next night the debate was about women. Another night, it was about what a dastardly swampy mosquito-infested nightmare of a hell-hole Camp Walker was.

The Third Regiment, Louisiana Infantry was sworn and mustered into the Confederate Army on May 17, 1861. Some soldiers were disappointed that their marching orders did not send them to join other Louisiana regiments fighting in Virginia. Instead, they marched out of Camp Walker three days later at four in the afternoon down Canal Street to waiting steamers that transported them upriver to Arkansas. New Orleans turned out and gave them a big sendoff. Troy smiled when girls with flowers darted into their ranks and surprised him and his comrades by kissing them as they marched to the wharfs.

After nearly two months of small skirmishes and much marching about the Arkansas countryside, Troy was ready for the big battle he felt sure would come any day. Orders came on August 8 for an attack on Union forces near Springfield, Missouri, which was led by a man Troy hated, a Connecticut Yankee, General Nathaniel Lyon of St. Louis Arsenal infamy. The attack was delayed by a day, and rain arrived August 9 prompting yet another delay. Troy thought we have hurried again only to wait.

As a gray dawn broke over the valley along Wilson's Creek where several Confederate regiments were camped, Troy and comrades were folding tents and awaiting orders to march. Before he could think about breakfast, gunfire and the commotion of Confederate ambulances and supply wagons driven rapidly toward them caused the soldiers to drop tents and packs to grab rifles and form a line. To no one in particular, Troy said, "Hellfire! That bloody Lyon is upon us!"

Thus began the Battle of Oak Hills. Their volunteer regiment moved to defend against regular United States Infantry troops. The covering Federal artillery fire from Union

Captain James Totten's battery was heavy and murderous. After an hour of furious fighting, the Union regulars yielded and left the field to the Confederate volunteers. Troy thought not bad for raw barely trained fellows like us.

Without a break, the regiment formed again and was marched down the valley to counter an attack by Union Colonel Sigel's command that had routed Confederate cavalry. The advancing gray-uniformed Confederate Third Louisiana was mistaken by Union forces in blue to be a sister unit, Third Iowa, which also wore gray uniforms. By ten o'clock, Troy was feeling so hungry, clumsy, light-headed, and dehydrated, that even murky creek water tasted good. As his company climbed the rocky hillside above Wilson's Creek to charge with fixed bayonets, Troy expected to be shot down at any minute. To Jean Pierre, he said, "Surely, they see us coming. On these blasted rocks, I feel like a fish in a barrel."

"Yeah, I can see that they see us. But I, for one, will never understand the ways of damned Yankees."

With a blood curdling rebel yell, Third Louisiana charged. Colonel Sigel's surprised Union force fled, losing more than two hundred killed in the cornfield they crossed and along the road leading away from the five artillery pieces they abandoned. While chasing the fleeing enemy, Troy tripped on a broken down cornstalk and fell. He felt pain from a hard object under his ribs and rolled over. He quickly tucked his discovery into his waist band. A fleeing Union officer had dropped his empty .44 Colt Walker revolver.

By noon, Troy's hunger burned. Third Louisiana was ordered back across Wilson's Creek to charge Captain Totten's battery, the artillery unit that had decimated its ranks earlier in the day. During this hard fought see-saw engagement, a jagged piece of shrapnel ripped through Troy's left thigh just above his knee, but missed his femur and femoral artery. At midday on that bright hot August 10, silver flashing stars filled his sky. The last thing Troy remembered was the ground rushing up to meet his face.

When he regained consciousness, he was on the front porch of the Ray family's farmhouse near the site of their morning battle. The house was overflowing with wounded from both sides. He was greeted by Dr. George W. Kendall who said, "Don't worry, lad. I'll not take your leg. It'll take months, but think a fit fellow like you will heal in time."

Troy did not try to raise his head. "Thanks, Doc. How did I get here?"

A clever and brave soldier by the name of Jean Pierre brought you here on his back, with a tourniquet in place. I should have a friend so faithful."

Troy was surprised. He never thought he had a friend, much less one who would rescue him from a battlefield. Tears welled but did not spill. His right hand went to his waistband.

Dr. Kendall said, "I suppose you're looking for this." He held up a revolver. "Jean Pierre insisted that I keep it for you, lest someone steals it. This is a fine and powerful gun. I'll take good care of it for you."

* * *

From the steps of General Lovell's former headquarters, Troy looked back at Canal Street, five blocks away, remembered marching off to war and shook his head. Inside, he discarded his memories and headed for the basement.

"I brought you some vittles."

"Let me out. I need to pee."

"Gal, you'd better watch your mouth. Educated or not, you ain't a free nigger no more. Your ass is mine now. You'd better quick learn to say 'please' and 'sir'. Now, eat your supper while it's warm. Then, I'll take you to the outhouse."

"Yes, sir."

Emily took the warm food Troy had brought from the St. Charles Hotel's restaurant. Four hours earlier, Troy had locked her in the basement of General Lovell's deserted headquarters, across Lafayette Square from City Hall.

While Troy stood outside the privy in the dark that Friday evening waiting for Emily to come out, he tried for the third time to estimate her value at a Thomas Foster slave auction. He thought *she's a young strong mulatto and might fetch near a thousand dollars if I sell her right away. I wonder if a pregnant wench is worth a premium.... But on the other hand, maybe she would be useful to Ma running the household staff. He snapped his fingers. Dammit, I keep forgetting. I've got to remember; I can't sell her until get my hands on a notary and create a fake bill of sale and deed.*

Chapter 9

Francesca entered the kitchen and stopped to stare at Ada sitting beside the table. Francesca had seen that forlorn look before. She said, "Ma, what's wrong?"

Ada took a sip of her sassafras tea. "Is this the last day of the month?"

"No, ma'am. Today is Tuesday, April 29. Why? What's wrong?"

Ada cried.

Francesca sat beside her mother and held her. After Ada's sobs subsided, Francesca said, "Ma, talk to me. What's wrong? Is it Papa?"

Ada nodded and cried again.

With hands akimbo, Francesca asked, "Ma, did he hurt you?"

Shaking her head, Ada sniffed and blew her nose. After two deep breaths, she shook her head again and said, "No. François went and…." She cried again.

"Ma, you're not hurt." Francesca hugged Ada tighter. "That's all that matters. Cheer up and let's get some breakfast in you." She stood and patted Ada's shoulder.

Ada blurted, "He's done gone and mortgaged us!"

Francesca had lifted a lid on their four-hole cast iron wood burning cook stove. Upon hearing this news, her mouth flew open and she dropped the lid with a clatter back onto the stove. "W-what? W-w-when?"

Francesca felt nauseous and slumped onto a chair.

"My baby, my poor baby." Ada stood beside Francesca stroking her only child's hair. "I waited two days to tell you, because you got more'n enough gone wrong in your life, what with Joachim and Em."

Francesca's voice was barely above a whisper when she said, "It's okay, Ma." She patted Ada's hand resting on her shoulder. "This is not a total surprise, knowing Papa's love of gambling. It is about gambling, isn't it?"

Ada nodded and said, "Yes."

They sat in silence for a time holding hands. At length, Francesca stood. "I'll make breakfast."

* * *

Dressed for work at the restaurant, Ada paused at the front door and adjusted her shawl. She cleared her throat and said, "Fran there is one more thing. Perhaps, it's the most important of all; for it could stop you from finding Em."

With a dish rag in her hand, Francesca plodded through the shotgun house to her mother. "What, Ma?"

"Two men came to see your father at the restaurant on Sunday. One looked like a banker; the other was a well-dressed thug. I overheard them from the kitchen. The banker-looking fellow did all the talking. He demanded payment in full for money François had borrowed to pay old gambling debts. The man gave François until the end of the month, or he will foreclose."

"This month?"

"Yes. It seems François also mortgaged this house and it is included in the threat to foreclose."

"Can't Papa borrow the money to pay the debt?"

Ada's eyes watered. "No, child. Last week, both Citizens Bank and Union Bank turned him down.

"It seems he made the mortgage months ago and was to pay in March. But, in March, François lost even more money. The restaurant is operating day to day off cash receipts and the backs of unpaid fishermen, butchers, and farmers. That's where the food we ate this morning came from. The foreclosure will happen as surely as I stand here."

Francesca's eyes widened. "Ma, we've gotta run!"

"But, Fran, where can we go?"

"We can't stand around and be captured! We could end up auctioned and who knows where."

"Baby, I know and I'm as scared as you are. But the question remains. Where can we go?"

Staring at the floor, Francesca sucked her teeth and twisted a tress above her left ear. Presently, she raised her head and said, "Ma, you go on to work. I'll come by the restaurant this afternoon. Once outside, we must make a plan."

"I knew I could count on you!"

* * *

Francesca made the decision while she bathed. She would not be deterred. She would not leave New Orleans and abandon Emily. Francesca smiled as she thought Edmond Dantes would not renege on a promise, much less fail his best friend. With a stern face she decided, *I won't either.* Wearing her mother's best black dress, decorated with lace and ruffles, Francesca applied make-up and styled her hair for the first time in days. Next, she borrowed from Laura a locket on a chain, a black see-thru shawl with tassels, and a matching hat.

Feeling elegant and full of confidence, Francesca strode into Citizen's Bank at half past ten and announced to the office manager that she had a confidential message for Monsieur Edouard Buisson. She smiled at the office manager and said, "You can tell him that Mademoiselle Francesca Dumas is waiting to see him."

"Mademoiselle Dumas, I assure you, Monsieur Buisson is quite busy and will not be able to see you today. I shall be happy to help you make an appointment for some time next week."

Francesca's smile vanished and the gap between her eyebrows narrowed. Looking into the short man's eyes, she stood as straight and as tall as her sixty-four inch body would reach. Her right hand rested on her hip. With her left, she pointed to the center of the man's chest. In calm and even tones, she said, "Monsieur, vous allez maintenant dire à M. Buisson que mademoiselle Dumas est ici avec un message pour lui. (Mister, you will go now and tell Monsieur Buisson that Mademoiselle Dumas is here with a message for him.)"

The man blinked twice and stammered, "Oui, M-mademoiselle Dumas." He hurried off to deliver her announcement.

Edouard Buisson's greeting was effusive and he appeared ill at ease. "Ah, Mlle. Dumas it is so very good to meet you. I've heard so much about you. Do come into my office and be comfortable."

"Sir, the pleasure is all mine." Francesca did a curtsy, but did not smile.

Settling into his chair behind his large mahogany desk, Edouard's expression changed and his voice deepened; his smile was gone. "I trust your confidential message is not about money or my late son's house. I understand that Maria made matters quite clear to you."

Francesca leaned forward in her chair and put one hand on Edouard's desk. Without blinking, she said, "I hope Mme. Buisson also let you know that not only did I vacate Joachim's house, likewise, I returned every gift he ever gave me. You should also know that I decided to keep his small purse, watch, and pistol." She saw his eyebrows rise as he leaned back and away from her. "Moreover, sir, under no circumstance would I accept a cent from you."

Edouard flushed. He made a deep sigh and said, "Well, I...."

Francesca interrupted. "Now, let's get down to the matter of my visit. As you guessed, I do not have a message for you. However, as I deem you to be a wise and influential man, what I need from you is advice and confidential non-monetary assistance."

She stared at what appeared to be a surprised face wearing a forced smile. Edouard regained his composure, tugged at his jacket's lapels, and said, "Well, Mademoiselle Dumas, I'm willing to help, if I can."

Francesca ignored him. "I'm sure you know that my father is a notorious gambler and loser...." When she had explained the details of the mortgage, Edouard leaned forward and put his elbows on his desk, interlacing his fingers under his chin. Again she ignored him. "Further, I have reason to believe that the man who murdered Joachim is the same man who shot Louie Laveau and stole my friend, Emily."

"Yes. Lamentably, we've not had the opportunity to meet until after the unfortunate loss of my beloved son. I understand from the police that unknown men opened fire on the levee in direction of Unionists singing 'Yankee Doodle'. Poor Joachim...." Edouard sniffed and blew his nose. "Forgive me. Poor Joachim was an ambitious fellow and at the time he passed, he was looking forward to owning a west bank plantation." Edouard paused again, this time staring at his desk, but not seeming to see.

Francesca sneered and thought *oh, the poor thing. Joachim never mentioned buying a plantation to me. He wanted a plantation for his betrothed! Spare me.* She glowered at Edouard.

He looked up and into her face, flushed, and changed the subject. "The police seem not to have a clue to go on and, unhappily, they have dropped the matter. How did you come to believe you know who murdered my son?"

"Sir, how I came to my conclusion does not matter. Anyway, I don't know his name, but I believe I know who to look for."

Edouard took a long look at Francesca over folded hands. She felt he was sizing her up, or resizing her. He nodded.

Francesca said, "Monsieur Buisson, let me be clear; foreclosure notwithstanding, I have no intention of departing from New Orleans and leaving unresolved the matters of murder, wounding an innocent man, and stealing my friend.

"So let's get back to the business at hand. Sir, here's where you come in. First, I need to leave your office with a letter of recommendation for my mother as an experienced restaurant chef. I want you to address your letter to Monsieur Antoine Alciatore and let him know that a room in his boarding house is acceptable as part of her wages. Second, I want your opinion and advice on my scheme to hide my mother less than two blocks away from my father's restaurant."

Smiling and shaking his head, Edouard stood and pulled at his salt and pepper handlebar moustache. "Mlle. Dumas, I do declare if you were a man, I'd hire you straight away as an officer in this bank!"

Francesca folded her arms and gave Edouard another icy stare.

Flushed again, he cleared his throat and said, "Er, hmm, well, eh, you know what I mean."

"I do." Francesca did not smile.

"Well, eh, what I meant to say is, your plan sounds well thought out. I especially like the part about hiding your mother in plain sight. Yes, regrettably, I do know your father, but I'm happy to say I also know Monsieur Alciatore. Mlle. Dumas, you will have your letter. Furthermore, I will visit with

Monsieur Alciatore forthwith and make clear what we require of him."

At the mention of '*we*', Francesca felt a rush of warmth for Edouard, but kept her poker face and determined demeanor. "Merci, Monsieur Buisson."

* * *

Inside City Hall's front entrance, a large wall hanging clock struck one. Francesca had not eaten since breakfast. Facing the ancient desk sergeant, Francesca insisted she would not speak to anyone but Detective Rousseau. Seated on a hard chair near the desk sergeant, she watched the parade of people and the odd policeman arrive and depart. Several wanted to see Rousseau. The clock struck two. Her hunger seared.

A few minutes before half past two, Rousseau walked in at a brisk pace. He carried his suit jacket and small composition book in one hand. Francesca stood. The desk sergeant pointed and said, "Mlle. Dumas, the man holding the fedora will be the first to speak with Detective Rousseau."

Francesca resumed her seat. "Yes, sir."

Rousseau stopped and looked at Francesca. She could not read his look. Rousseau spoke without looking away from her. "Monsieur, I apologize. But I'll have to ask you to wait. I need to talk with this lady. Mlle. Dumas, please come with me."

They sat in a small sparsely furnished room that had only a table and three chairs, not Philipe's office. He hung his jacket on the back of a chair and opened his composition book on the table. Without a greeting or a smile, he said, "Where were you last night?"

Francesca frowned and tilted her head to the right. After hesitating and thinking why is he behaving this way, she said, "Good afternoon, Detective Rousseau. It is good to see you, sir."

"Answer my question."

Now, her eyes widened. The scene unfolding in the small room felt not unlike Ada interrogating her when she was a child. She thought this is indeed an interrogation! She clasped her hands on her lap lest they tremble.

"Mlle. Dumas, I don't have all day. Answer my question."

"Y-yes, sir. I-I was at my mother's house."

"Were you there all night without going out?"

"No, sir. Not that it's any of your business, but I did go to the outhouse."

"No place else?"

"No, sir."

"Was anyone else there all of the time you were there?"

"Yes, sir. My mother was there."

Rousseau scribbled in his book. Then, he turned back two pages. Next he asked, "When were you last at Dr. Stone's Infirmary?"

Francesca let her surprise show. "Day before yesterday."

Rousseau ignored her. "With whom did you visit?"

"Louis Laveau."

"Are you related to Monsieur Laveau?"

Does he think I'm white? He does. "No, sir. Why?"

"Mlle. Dumas, I ask the questions here. You will answer my questions. Did you visit anyone else at the infirmary?"

Surprised again by Rousseau's demeanor, Francesca lowered her voice and decided to say as little as possible. "No."

"How do you know Monsieur Laveau?"

"He is my friend."

Rousseau put his pencil in his book and closed it. He covered his moustache, mouth, and chin with his hand. Staring without blinking, his eyes remained fixed on Francesca's eyes. Though she felt ill-at-ease and wanted to squirm in her seat, Francesca sat still and stared back, avoiding the urge to blink.

After a whole minute, Rousseau said, "Monsieur Laveau is dead."

Francesca's hands flew to cover her mouth. Her sudden intake of air made a loud gasp. Francesca shrieked, "Oh, mon Dieu, non!" Her tears flowed as she muttered, "Dear Mary, Mother of God, please give me strength. I don't know if I can take anymore...."

She folded her arms on the table and lay her head down. Now, she understood Rousseau's questions. Struggling to stop her sobs, Francesca thought *I must collect myself and learn what I can from Detective Rousseau.*

When Francesca had dried her face, she turned to face Rousseau again. "Please forgive me. I've had one bad thing after another enter my life since last Friday."

"Mlle. Dumas, I'm sorry about your losses. A thousand pardons for interrogating you, but it's my job."

"Thank you, sir. I understand."

"I learned that you made notes while you were there. Isn't that unusual behavior for a visiting friend in a hospital?"

She frowned. "Are you continuing....?"

Smiling, Rousseau cut her off. "Oh, no, Mlle. Dumas, I'm sorry. This is now a friendly chat."

They laughed. Francesca sniffed.

"Well....?'

"Oh. Er, yes, sir. I interviewed Louie."

From her handbag, she put her scraps of paper on the table. Rousseau laughed when he saw that with Brooke and Louie, Francesca had mimicked his earlier interview with her.

She cried again when she told Rousseau that Emily had been stolen. Rousseau grabbed his composition book and began scribbling at a frantic pace.

He looked up from his notes and asked, "Do you think the killer will recognize you?"

"Though he must have seen me at a distance on the levee, I don't think so. I certainly won't wear that dress again. But, now I believe my friend, Brooke, had good reason to fear that he may want to do her harm."

"I agree. Now that I know about your friend being stolen, at least one motive for the killer is becoming clearer. He would have had the same reason to silence Monsieur Laveau."

"Why would he not just take Louie prisoner like Em?"

"He wouldn't be able to sell a white man."

Francesca thought oh my, this is complex work. *I never would have thought of that. Can I do this? I'm not Edmond Dantes, or Philipe Rousseau.* She blinked and nodded.

"Mlle. Dumas, you are a brave and dedicated young woman. I'm sure Mlle. Emily Jenkins does not have a better friend any place." He sighed. "Overworked or not, I'm taking this investigation on. Mind you, I'm not advising you to do this, but if you continue investigating, beware; your life could be in danger."

"Yes, sir. Thank you, sir."

He smiled. "I get the sense that you would continue even if I asked you not to do so. Are you armed?"

"Yes, sir. You're right. I would continue, no matter what you said." She smiled and patted her leather handbag. "And, yes, I'm armed."

"When we first met, I vastly underestimated you. I like your perseverance. Do your best work, but be careful.

"We need to find a motive for one to murder Monsieur Buisson, if this was indeed more than a random shooting. That key could help us find the killer. Please stop in periodically and let's compare notes."

"Thank you, sir. I will."

* * *

When they met behind François' restaurant at four o'clock, Ada gave Francesca two sausage biscuits.

Chapter 10

"Papa, let me remind you. Even the rum you drank this morning should not be enough to cloud such an important promise as manumission for two women you once loved."

Rubbing his salt and pepper stubble, François protested. "I still love both of you."

Ada continued crying.

Francesca leaned forward in her chair so that her face was closer to her father across the restaurant table. "Well, Papa, you sure have a strange way of showing your love. Do you remember that you promised to free both of us and give Ma the house on St. Phillips Street in honor of my eighteenth birthday?"

He blinked his blood-shot eyes, reached into his uncombed hair, and scratched his scalp. "Er, yes."

"Papa, last September 7 came and went. Why didn't you keep your promise?"

François scratched again. "Er, hmmm, well, I-I, er, that bank forced me to produce collateral for a loan I needed for the restaurant."

Ada said, "Liar! Last summer, you and your gambling almost lost the restaurant."

He slammed his fist against the table causing salt and pepper containers and his nearly empty glass of rum to bounce. "Woman, you'd better control your sass. I may be broke and broken, but I can still...."

Francesca stood and interrupted. She held out her hands to her parents. "Please, please, let's not bicker. Papa, the truth is you used your family as collateral last year. Now, you've done it again. Forget manumission. I don't believe you will ever free us. My question today is; have you made an arrangement to postpone foreclosure this afternoon?"

François' red eyes widened. "How did you know about that?" He turned and glared at Ada.

"Papa, how I know is not the question. The question remains, have you done anything to stall the foreclosure?"

François studied his shoe laces.

"Papa, talk to us. Please say something. We need to know what's to happen. Please?"

Francesca paced between the tables. At midmorning the restaurant was not yet open for customers.

François did not respond. Before Francesca could blink, Ada leapt from her seat and delivered a fist to François' right ear, sending him and his chair sprawling onto the floor.

"Ma!"

Ada kicked François' leg and back several times.

"Ma! Stop it!"

Ada stripped off her apron and threw it at François. "Child, there's no need a goin' on beggin' this sorry ass excuse of a man to say anything. I'm damned tired o' cryin' over him. His silence means just what you said yesterday, we've gotta run. Let's go! And I do mean quickly! That thug and his banker-looking boss could show up here any minute with chains and irons."

They left him on the floor crying. As Francesca passed through the rear door, she heard François wailing. "Who's going to cook dinner?"

Ada slammed the door.

* * *

Francesca squirmed in a plush bergeres arm chair as Antoine Alciatore sat behind his elegant desk. She saw him read, then study Edouard Buisson's letter. She looked over at Ada's apparent calm and smiled. She thought *Ma is new woman today and more like Edmond Dantes than I ever knew.*

Presently, Alciatore smiled and stood. He gestured toward his office door and said, "Welcome to Pension Alciatore. My friend, Monsieur Buisson, has spoken very highly of both you. Mme. Dumas and Mlle. Dumas, please allow me to personally show you to your room. Mme. Dumas, I do hope you will enjoy a long and pleasant association with our family."

* * *

In front of Citizen's Bank, Francesca stepped onto Royal Street's cobblestones to avoid colliding with two small white children playing chase on the sidewalk. She glanced and smiled at the mother leaning against the building. Three blocks on, she arrived at the telegraph office inside the St. Charles Hotel. The lobby clock struck one while Francesca was hiring a messenger to deliver her sealed note to Brooke. She paid one devalued Confederate dollar for the messenger's services, a round trip of forty-eight blocks. Now, she had only two dollars left.

> Mme. Brooke Bouffard Williams, Carondolet Street at Philip Street.

> Dear Brooke, I regret to inform you that our friend was found murdered in his hospital bed on yesterday morning. Please remain in your abode. F.D.

Francesca walked out with the messenger and watched him safely tuck her envelop into a canvas pouch secured to his body by a shoulder strap passing diagonally over his body. She bade farewell and watched him stride away toward Carondolet Street on his two wheeled velocipede.

* * *

The children who Francesca saw playing chase on the sidewalk, were huddled against their mother crying. The mother sat on the edge of the wooden walk holding and comforting a small girl about three years old. The boy, whose age Francesca guessed at five, was sniffing and trying to retie his shoe. Crying and whining, he said, "Ma, I can't do it. I need help."

The mother said, "Wait! Can't you see I'm holding your sister?"

Francesca said, "Hello, little man. May I tie your shoe?"

Startled, the boy looked up at Francesca. He looked at his mother. She nodded. The boy nodded. Instead of thanking Francesca when his shoe was tied, he turned again to his mother and said, "Ma, I'm awful hungry!"

His mother hissed, "Shut up!"

The girl cried louder.

Francesca now saw the three through new lenses. They were hungry. She sat beside the woman and said, "Hello, Mademoiselle. I'm Francesca Dumas. How are you?"

The woman looked at Francesca with terror in her wide gray eyes. Francesca's smile remained as she offered her hand.

The woman hesitated, but extended a dirty bony hand. "I'm alright. My name is Annabelle Cocks. I'm pleased to meet you."

Though the boy looked skinny to Francesca, she said, "That's a fine looking young man you have there."

"Thank you."

After getting acquainted with the children, Francesca blinked and hoped for the right words. In her cheeriest voice, she said, "Hey, Able, I'm looking for a good man like you. How about me and you stepping out together for a bite?" She thought *so what if it takes my last dollars.*

The boy, whose name was Able, looked at Francesca with wide eyes and his mouth hanging open. Annabelle said, "N-no, we can't. W-we just met and…."

Francesca said, "Nonsense. I won't take no for an answer. It's all settled. The four of us are going to march into the St. Charles Hotel and eat our fill."

They found the dining room at the St. Charles was still closed after General Lovell's second hasty departure from New Orleans the previous evening. The buzz in the lobby was mostly angst among well to do citizens about the arrival of Federal troops expected the following day. Sitting beside Able and across the table from Annabelle one block away at the City Hotel's restaurant, Francesca examined the woman's face for the third time. She thought *the blonde hair is the same though the face is different now. But I'm sure I've seen her somewhere.* At length, Francesca asked, "Annabelle, were you a student at Mère Delille's Catholic School on St. Bernard Avenue?"

Annabelle flashed a bright smile. "Call me Anna. Yes, I was there until 1853. I left when I was twelve because my father sent me to the Mechanics Institute in New York. You look familiar, too."

"Ah, ha! I knew it! I was there until I was fourteen and left in '57 when my father put me to work waiting tables.

"Oh, call me Fran."

"Okay, Fran. So that makes me two years older than you."

Francesca thought Anna looked much older. They talked like reunited sisters though, because of their age difference at the time, they were not playmates. They spoke of their fond memories of Mère Delille and Sister Juliette Gaudin. While they ate, the conversation drifted to life after school. And then, Anna's eyes became sad. She looked everywhere except at Francesca.

Able, who had been eating with both hands, said, "Ma, what's wrong?"

Anna, whose eyes now brimmed with tears, deflected Able's interested when she forced a painful looking smile and said, "Oh, it's just that your ol' ma is so happy you're eating."

Satisfied, Able turned his attention back to his desert.

Anna blinked and her tears spilled onto her cheeks.

Francesca reached out and touched Anna's hand.

Looking into Francesca's eyes, she said, "Parlons français. (Let's speak French.)" Anna made a quick nod toward Able, whose attention was still on his desert. "Il ne comprend pas le français. (He does not understand French.)"

Dreading what was to come and shifting in her seat for a reason she could not fathom, Francesca said, "Okay."

After a deep sigh, Anna continued in French. "It appears you are among the few who do not know who I am. In a way, I'm grateful for that. But, on the other hand, if you knew, perhaps you'd not befriend me." She paused.

Francesca thought what should I say? She resisted the urge to twist a tress and did not remove her hand as she pondered what to say. Unable to find the right words, she said nothing.

When Anna continued, she said, "Fran, I need a friend. To the people who know me, I'm at worse an outcast, or at best, a soul to be pitied. I hope the old school memories rekindled at this table can be the basis for..... But first, I must let you know why I am scorned, or pitied, and without friends."

Still uncertain of what to say, Francesca smiled and said, "Oh, I'm sure we can be friends."

Now, Anna was dry-eyed. "I hope so. But we will see.

"When I was fifteen, I lost my virginity in a New York hotel room. That was the end of my schooling. My rapist brought me back to his bed in New Orleans. When I was sixteen, I gave birth to the boy sitting beside you. A couple of years after my son was born, this man tired of raping me and told me to marry his protégé. I refused. He beat me in his home. Then, he beat me bloody in the streets in full view of passersby until I agreed to marry his protégé, an octoroon passing for white."

Francesca bit her lip, but otherwise hid her reaction. She thought now is not the time.

Anna continued. "This second man is the father of my daughter. He was happy to have me, though I was miserable and hostile.

"A few days ago, this second man learned my story and that it was known by many people in New Orleans. So he threw me and my children into the streets with nothing but the clothes we're wearing."

Tears welled in Francesca's eyes and she covered her mouth with one hand. "Oh, mon Dieu!"

"Fran, he was like everyone else when he learned, only worse." Anna took hold of Francesca's hand. "Do you know, or know of, Judge John G. Cocks?"

Dread rose in Francesca. She shook her head and said, "No. I don't know him, but I have heard his name." Francesca did not dare ask Anna why she asked.

Anna's gaze was steady as she said, "The good Judge John G. Cocks is my father. And he owns me."

"B-but, you're white. Y-you can't be a slave. I don't understand."

"Not only am I Judge Cocks' daughter and slave; he is also my son's father and grandfather."

Chapter 11

\On the end of the kitchen table nearest her wood-burning cook stove, Laura set out yeast, sugar, salt, milk, flour, eggs, dried apple slices, and lard. On the stove, Francesca moved aside the kettle and a large pot and added a short log to the fire.

Laura said, "Fran, baby, put in more wood than that. Warm water is okay, but I need to do more'n melt that lard. I need it *hot*."

"Yes, ma'am. I surely want to do my part well so's *we* can turn out the most scrumptious apple beignet breakfast in Tremé!"

Laura and Tony laughed.

Tony had brought Francesca's pistol accoutrements' box in from his backyard workshop. They sat together at the other end of the table unloading and reloading her pistol until she could do it quickly and flawlessly. Tony said, "Fran, drop these balls into this little purse. This'll keep'em from rollin' all over your handbag."

"What about the powder flask?"

"Just hold yo' hoss. You and that Em are so much alike. I got that covered." Grinning, Tony whispered loud enough for Laura to hear. "I stole this here cloth make-up pouch from your auntie."

Laura, who now had flour nearly up to her elbows, said, "I'll freely give anything to the detective who's gonna bring my baby home!"

Laughing, Francesca said, "Upon my word, Uncle Tony, you do have everything covered."

Anna and her children arrived from Ada's old house and they ate together. Able declared, "Auntie Laura makes the best beignets in the whole world!"

Anna tussled his hair and said, "Com'on, boy. We've got our washing to do, first us, then our clothes."

"Aw, Ma!"

The adults laughed.

While she washed breakfast dishes, Francesca said, "It's pretty clear to me now that my friends followed the right man from the levee."

Tony said, "From your investigation, we can focus on him and forget the other four."

Laura sat in a corner with her chin propped on the knuckles of one hand. "I sure hope that detective is right about the motive to sell Em and not the many worse things that come to my mind. Why do you suppose he thinks that?"

Tony said, "I think he's just guessing. In any case, what me'n you can do is put the word out around the dealers' depots and them fancy hotel auction places and offer a reward for a report of any new girl coming in who looks like our Em."

Francesca stopped washing and absent-mindedly held a plate in mid-air. She was frowning and pensive before she said, "It was gruesome. I really want to forget. But I can't. After handling the balls for my pistol, I've been thinking about that hole in Joachim's temple. Though I couldn't see the hole clearly because of the blood, I have to say the balls in my bag are much too small to have made that hole."

Tony slapped the tabletop with his palm. "By Jove, I think you're onto something! Sounds as though you're looking for a man with a large caliber pistol."

Tony explained caliber, bullets, cartridges, and gunpowder.

Francesca slowly began drying dishes. She stopped and said, "So bullets are small round balls or large round balls."

Tony said, "You're right about different sizes. But bullets also have different shapes. Some even have more than one shape, like a dome on one end, like a tin can in the middle, and flat on the other end."

Laura held her face with both hands. "Would a bullet pass through a man?"

"That certainly is possible depending on the distance between the target and the shooter, the powder charge, and the weight of the bullet."

Francesca said, "Uncle Tony, wait…."

Tony interrupted laughing and waving. "No. I'm done. I'm afraid I've told you all I know or have heard about bullets. I don't want to tell you more'n I know. I think you should go back and have another talk with your detective friend about these new thoughts."

Laura said, "Wait." She left the kitchen and returned with a sewing basket. "Fran, I'm sorry, but speaking of gruesome, I have a gruesome idea."

Laura set a red tomato-shaped pin cushion on the table. As Francesca and Tony moved closer, she pinned two small buttons the sides. "These are my target's ears." Next, Laura plunged a long knitting needle completely through the pin cushion above the 'ears'.

Covering her mouth with both hands, Francesca gasped.

Laura touched Francesca's arm and said, "Dear, I didn't mean to upset you. I…."

Francesca said, "Your demonstration hasn't upset me. You've shown me something I didn't remember in my grief and failed to share with Detective Rousseau. When I knelt and cradled Joachim's head, *both* of my hands became bloody."

* * *

With dinner money from Laura and Tony in her purse and armed with two wooden toothed rakes, Francesca, Able, and Anna set out for the levee on an omnibus. They left little

Arianna with Laura. Francesca gave Able two of Ada's three prong forks to use as tools while she and Anna used Ada and Tony's rakes to comb for the bullet that killed Joachim. At mid-morning, Thursday, May 1, they arrived at the head of Bienville Street. Francesca used resection between Slaughterhouse Point on the west bank and the intersection of Bienville and Water Streets on the east bank to approximate where Joachim had stood the previous Friday.

First, Francesca showed Able a lead ball and let him hold it in his hand. Then, Francesca drew and erased lines in the dirt surface of the levee until she was satisfied with where her lines intersected. She drew a large 'X' on the spot. Next, she drew two rectangles to represent where they stood, almost side by side. Finally, she drew dashed lines to estimate possible trajectories for the path of the bullet.

"Anna, I wish I had paid attention when Sister Juliette taught us how to find the length of a line in a right triangle."

"At least you remembered you need to solve a right triangle to keep us from raking the whole levee all the way to Slaughterhouse Bend!"

They laughed.

Anna said, "I think I remember ol' man Pythagoras from the Mechanics Institute, not Sister Juliette. Actually, we're going to need to guess the length of two sides. The result of our calculation is going to be double silly, or maybe, silly squared."

Laughing, Francesca said, "Okay, Mlle. Smart Pantaloons, help me. Time's a wasting."

"Okay. Let's start with a point in mid-air. Then, we'll guess the hypotenuse. How tall was Joachim?"

Fifteen minutes later, they had sketched a large area to rake. It was half past one when Able, working inward from the outer boundary on his knees with his two forks, held up a small muddy gray object. The lead cylinder was domed on one end and flat on the other. He asked, "What's this?"

* * *

Waiting in Dr. Stone's office while he made his afternoon rounds, Francesca turned the bullet over several times in her palm, examining all sides of the lump of lead. She had sent Anna and Able back to Ada's house with the tools. In the excitement over her discovery, Francesca could barely sit still. Though she could not fathom how close, she, nonetheless, felt closer to finding Emily.

Wearing a pleasant smile, Dr. Stone entered his office, "Good afternoon, Mlle. Dumas. I am happy to see you again. You look healthy. What can I do for you?"

Francesca stood and said, "Yes, sir. Thank you, Dr. Stone. I'm fine. I'm here to trouble your memory about my friend, the late Monsieur Louis Laveau."

"I see. I remember him quite well. Please sit."

"Thank you, sir. In your opinion, was Louie murdered?"

Dr. Stone frowned and grabbed his beard. "A policeman asked me the same question. Why do you ask? You can't be with the police."

"Sir, you're right. I'm not with the police. But Detective Rousseau is aware that I'm looking into links between the deaths of my friends and the disappearance of yet another friend."

Dr. Stone's eyes widened. "Oh, this is most unusual. Detective Rousseau didn't mention other victims."

"He didn't know at the time you met him."

"Well, the answer to your question in one word is yes. Someone entered the ward sometime after midnight and held a chloroform soaked cloth over poor Monsieur Laveau's nose to quiet him and finally to suffocate him. That someone left the cloth behind."

"Sir, please permit me ask a silly novice question. What is chloroform?"

Dr. Stone explained. Francesca made notes.

Then, he asked, "How do you suppose Monsieur Laveau's demise is related to another victim?"

"The victims, as you call them, were friends. Here is another possible link between the two murders." Francesca handed him the bullet.

Dr. Stone turned it over in his palm. "Is this the one I gave Rousseau?"

"Oh, no, sir. I believe this is the one that killed Monsieur Joachim Buisson. My friends and I found it this afternoon near where Joa...., I mean Monsieur Buisson was shot."

"They sure look the same, as if they both struck bone. We know for certain that is the case with the one I extracted from Monsieur Laveau's shoulder." Dr. Stone held the bullet between two fingers. "You see, this one, like the other, has a slightly miss-shaped head."

Francesca tugged at her chin. "Hmmm. How does one distinguish....?"

Dr. Stone laughed. "Experience, my dear lady, experience. By the time you've dug out as many bullets as I have from the bodies of the good citizens of New Orleans, believe me, you'll know."

Francesca made more notes.

"Is there anything else I can help you with?"

"Oh, yes, sir. There is. I was wondering, do you still have any personal effects that belonged to Monsieur Laveau?"

"I'll check. Please follow me."

Francesca departed for City Hall carrying papers from the pockets of the suit Louie was wearing when he was shot.

* * *

Philipe Rousseau crushed the lighted end of his cigar in a porcelain ashtray on his desk. He placed the chewed end back into the corner of his mouth. He said, "Mlle. Dumas, I know you're anxious to find your missing friend. Therefore, I must apologize for not making progress since I last saw you."

"Sir, progress would be good, but it's okay. I feel we're closer."

A faint blue haze persisted in the room though Philipe had extinguished his cigar. He had smoked while listening to Francesca's report. Now, she watched him pace behind his desk.

"Mlle. Dumas, we're probably correct in believing that Monsieur Laveau was killed because the perpetrator desired to eliminate a man he mistakenly thought was a witness. So, now with these two bullets and Dr. Stone's opinion, I support your theory that Monsieur Buisson was murdered and not a victim of a random shooting."

"Thank you, sir." Francesca tried to think of what question she should ask. Why was Rousseau not working the case as he promised? What should be done next to find Emily? She could not decide if there was something else she needed to know, so she sat with her hands folded atop her handbag.

"What we need to know right now is why Monsieur Buisson was killed. That will get us closer still to the perpetrator."

Frowning, Francesca asked, "How can we learn that?"

"The people, other than the shooter, who know why he was killed are not conscious of the fact that they know. The knowledge is out there." Philipe made a sweeping gesture toward the window. "You might call this 'crowd knowledge'.

It's our job to tease the bits and pieces out of them and put the puzzle together."

"So who do we ask and what do we ask?"

"Let's determine who first. That may contribute to what. At the top of the list should be the people in whom Monsieur Buisson confided. Okay, name these people and make a list. Ready?"

"Yes, sir." She thought *I've found a great ally. What if Detective Rousseau had not agreed to help? I think he is my Edmond Dantes!*

"Okay, you're first on the list."

Francesca's face displayed incredulousness. She said, "*Me?*"

"Of course. You belong at the top of the list. You're young, but you will learn that a man is likely to tell his mate much more than he'll ever tell anyone else, even his parents."

Francesca flushed. "But, sir, only I thought of me as his mate, no one else thought that. You see, it was only when he died that I learned from his stepmother that he had a betrothed. I think his betrothed better fits what you had in mind."

Philipe's face turned sad and he stopped pacing to gaze at Francesca. Presently, he said, "I apologize. I see your point. But I'm going to ask you a few questions anyway."

"Yes, sir."

"Who were the people Monsieur Buisson spoke unkindly of, worse, who did he hate?"

Francesca blinked. She thought, *oh, my. He is tough. Now, I get it. I think I know what should be asked to collect this 'crowd knowledge'.* She said, "I don't think he hated his stepmother, but at times he did speak unkindly of her."

As Philipe's questions continued, Francesca was surprised when she realized how few facts she actually knew about

Joachim's life. Philipe noticed her discomfort and apologized again.

"Because of the upheaval going on in the department this week regarding the flight of our army and the arrival today of the Yankee soldiers, I have been in meetings non-stop. That's why I've made no progress in this investigation. These damn meetings go on and on, day after day and nothing is accomplished. In the end, we're going to do what the Yankees tell us to do. It's simple. They fought and overcame our forces. They won. So they're going to be in charge.... Oh, sorry. I digress."

Francesca thought I never dreamed I could or would work with a Confederate sympathizer. Detective Rousseau is both smart and honorable. "Sir, my ma told me to vent is good."

Philipe smiled. "Can you keep our investigation moving by interviewing Monsieur Buisson's parents?"

"Oh, no, sir. I would rather never lay eyes on Mme. Buisson again in life."

Philipe laughed. He said, "You may have to put aside your antipathy and lay eyes *and* questions on Mme. Buisson."

Though smiling, she hesitated. "Maybe, I can. But first, I think I should talk with Monsieur Buisson and Mr. Williams. Then, we can decide if we need any information from Mme. Buisson."

"Fair enough. I'm going to make a detective out of you, yet.

Though you're a Unionist, it is pleasant to work with you."

Francesca flushed and kept her eyes on the notes she was writing. "When are the Yankees disembarking?"

"Oh, I should've known you'd be in the admiring crowd when they march off their ships." Philipe pulled out his pocket watch. "I heard the parade will start in about thirty minutes from now."

* * *

From the top step at the front of City Hall, Francesca and Philipe watched Federal soldiers step lively to the sound of a regimental band playing "Yankee Doodle" as they marched up Poydras Street and turned on St. Charles Avenue toward Vieux Carré. When the end of the long procession of blue clad soldiers appeared, an officer, who Francesca had noticed watching them, bounded up the steps and directly to Philipe.

The officer said, "I'm looking for the chief of police. Is his office located in your city hall?"

Philipe said, "Yes, you've come to the right place."

The officer glanced again at Francesca. He said to Philipe, "Thank you, sir." He stepped away, but turned back. "Oh, I apologize. Somehow, I forgot my manners. Please allow me to introduce myself. I'm Major George Stone, General Butler's Chief of Staff."

Philipe said, "I'm Detective Philipe Rousseau, New Orleans Police Department." He gestured toward Francesca. "And, this is my friend and protégé, Mademoiselle Francesca Dumas. Major, I'm sorry to say, but even at this late hour, I still have more work to do. So, if you two will excuse me, I'll get back to the salt mine."

"I'm pleased to meet both of you. Detective Rousseau, may your tasks be few and your burdens light. Mademoiselle." George bowed and kissed the back of her right hand.

Francesca did a curtsy and said, "Welcome to New Orleans, sir. I have hoped and waited many months for the arrival of our dear star spangled banner."

George's eye brows rose. "Well, that's a nice surprise. Thank you. Can you spare a few minutes of your time to tell me a bit about your fair city?"

Francesca thought *just as I suspected. He probably already knew where the police chief's office is located. Now, what was that 'number two look' Brooke said I should watch for? Oh, yes. A sustained stare and tilting the head to the right means he's interested in more than a one night lay. Or, was it.... Oh, I can't remember these things. Perhaps, I should have taken notes. Never mind. I can't very well refer to my notes at a time like this. My, but he does look good in that blue uniform, adorned with all those shiny brass buttons. And every hair in his moustache is in place. Does that mean he keeps his rooms neat?*

"Sir, it will be my pleasure to spend a few minutes telling you about my wonderful city...."

Two hours later, George was introducing Francesca to members of Major General Benjamin Franklin Butler's staff in their temporary commandeered office space in the ladies parlor of the St. Charles Hotel, the finest hotel in the city. Brigadier General Shipley and Captain Puffer sat with them upon a canapé.

General Shipley wanted to know about the late New Orleans economy and matters related to Confederate currency. Francesca laughed and said, "My late husband left me practically destitute. So, if you replace Confederate notes with United States notes tomorrow or next month, it won't matter much to me."

George said, "But you're such an obviously refined and educated lady, it makes sense to inquire of you about economic and social matters in New Orleans."

Francesca turned in her seat and looked George in the eye and said, "Sir, poverty has no respect whatsoever for education and manners, even for race or former class status."

Captain Puffer cleared his throat and said, "Hear, hear, and amen. Well said Mlle. Dumas. But speaking of social matters, I heard Major Stone say you're somehow connected to the police department. I'm interested because I was once a policeman. What do you think of the department here?"

"Well, sir, I'm connected only because I've been meeting with Detective Rousseau. Why? Because the department is shorthanded and unable to investigate the murder of my late husband, I'm doing it myself. Otherwise, I know nothing about the department. Speaking of our society, it is scandalous that there is no law for the police to enforce against a man, a judge, who holds his own daughter in slavery, rapes her, and fathers a child with her."

Jaws went agape and eye brows arched. The three men searched the faces of their colleagues. Presently, George said, "Mlle. Dumas, may I impose and ask you to return here tomorrow and tell the story of this judge and his daughter to Mrs. Butler?"

"I'll do better than that; I'll bring the daughter and she can tell Mrs. Butler herself."

Chapter 12

Since sunrise Friday morning, May 2, Laura had toiled in her sewing room creating a new skirt for Anna to wear in her "audience" with the wife of the commanding general of United States Army's new Department of the Gulf. Anna was already wearing a blouse that Laura lent her. From time to time, Anna was a living mannequin as Laura adjusted her measurements.

Francesca made breakfast, and then made the mid-day dinner. In between, she made occasional notes of questions she thought she would ask Edouard Buisson. By the time the second meal was finished, she had but two questions left after crossing off several. She thought merde. This is much more difficult than solving a right triangle. *How can I possibly know what to ask in order to get Monsieur Buisson to tell me what he doesn't know that he knows? I thought I knew, but now, I know I don't. Mary, Mother of God. Please pray for me. I need help to find Emily. Please.*

When Francesca and Anna arrived at the St. Charles and found Major Stone, it was almost four o'clock. He ushered them to an ornate room off the ladies parlor which Mrs. Butler had designated to entertain her guests. Francesca thought George's introduction of them to Mrs. Butler was overwrought and overdone. At the end of his monologue, he said, "Mlle. Dumas and Mlle. Cocks, please allow me to present a living legend, an acclaimed actress for her many performances before packed audiences in none other than Boston, New York, Charleston, and Cincinnati, and now first lady of the great city of New Orleans; Mrs. Sarah Hildreth Butler, wife of...."

Smiling, Sarah waved George toward the open doorway and said, "George, enough already! You're boring my guests. Oh, and thanks again for inviting Mlle. Dumas and Mlle. Cocks.

"Ladies, I am delighted to meet both of you."

Francesca and Anna did curtsies and in chorus said, "The pleasure is all ours."

"I would offer tea, but the hotel staff quit yesterday. I guess they were afraid of us Yankees. I'm so relieved you aren't."

Francesca was studying Sarah's pleasant round face and thinking how Sarah's smile made her countenance light up. *I think we'll get on fine. Let's see.* "Mrs. Butler, we know how to make tea. Let's go make some."

Immediately, Sarah agreed and the threesome headed for the kitchen. Francesca smiled and thought *yes, I thought so. My guess is, even though refined and elegant, she's comfortable with all classes.*

At length, Anna told her story, punctuated here and there by Sarah's refrain as she continued saying, "Oh, my, Lord!"

* * *

When Anna finished, Sarah said, "This is horrible! This man must be punished. Please wait while I see my husband."

Sarah returned and walked them to General Butler's office down the hall. General Shipley and Major Stone were waiting with Butler. Francesca thought the combination of General Butler's wide bald spot on top his head, shoulder length hair from the sides of his head, and his drooping left eyelid made him look like a living, but comic caricature. She hoped that he thought she was smiling because of his warm reception. Soon she thought General Butler, a Massachusetts attorney before the war, was resolute and kind.

When he had heard Anna's story, he shook his head and covered his mustache, mouth, and chin with his hand. He tilted his head and blinked several times, but otherwise his gaze on Anna was steady. Mrs. Butler and his staff officers remained silent. While the room was quiet, Francesca glanced from Anna to General Butler and back again. She squirmed in her chair.

At length, Butler sighed and said, "This is too much to believe on the testimony of one witness. Does anyone else know of these things?"

Anna said, "Yes, sir. These things that happened to me are known by nearly everyone in New Orleans."

Butler nodded to General Shipley and said to Anna, "I will have your case investigated. Please come again in three days."

Chapter 13

At the streetcar stop where Louisiana Avenue crosses St. Charles Avenue, Francesca sat on a tree stump in the shade of a large oak tree reviewing her worn and tattered notes looking for some new pattern to emerge. Every so often, she would glance down Louisiana Avenue toward the river, watching for Edna's approach. Saturday morning, the third of May, was warm. An early morning breeze had died. An uncomfortably hot day had begun. She hoped Edna would appear before her single red rose wilted. She laid her commandeered flower beside her in the grass.

A new question for her planned interview with Edouard Buisson surfaced. Francesca scribbled furiously lest she lose the thought: Please provide a list of contacts for Joachim's deals that failed or went bad. She read and reworded the statement several times and beamed when her wordsmith work was finished.

"Well, good mornin' Mlle. Scholar!" A smiling Edna stood two feet in front of Francesca with her hands akimbo, shopping basket hanging from one wrist.

Startled, Francesca bolted upright on her stump. She quickly laid her papers on the grass and her handbag atop them. She stood and hugged Edna. "Oh, Good morning! Happy Birthday!" She scooped the rose from the ground and presented it to Edna with a dramatic flourish.

They laughed in their embrace.

"I know your birthday isn't until tomorrow, but I wanted to give you something now since Sunday is your busy day with the Buissons."

At the mention of her "employer's" name, Edna rolled her eyes. "Thank you so much for remembering. You are the first person to remember my birthday since I was snatched from my family." Now tears welled in Edna's eyes though her broad smile persisted.

They allowed many streetcars to pass them by. They remained under the tree while Francesca sat on the grass and told Edna, perched upon the stump, all the news of the week. She began with finding Brooke, then Louie, Detective Rousseau, Edouard Buisson, her parents, Anna, and ended with her recurring dream.

"Edna, the dream feels so real. Every time, I awake sweating and trembling. Each time, I see Joachim shot and fall. Then the gunman sees me see him and he runs me down."

Edna shook her head and said, "Lawd, Chile, there ain't many people who've had in a lifetime the excitement you've had in eight days!

"Now tell me something. Can you see the man's face?"

Francesca frowned and broke eye contact as she pondered. "No, I can't see his face."

"I think your dream is giving you a message. I believe the bad man you're looking for is ruthless and dangerous. I worry, but I won't ask you to stop. I know you won't until you find your Emily. I think the dream means you should be prepared to meet the very devil hisself when you find the man who stole Emily."

"Hmmm. My dream seems more frightening the way you interpret it." Staring at a dandelion blossom, Francesca nodded. Then she looked at Edna and said, "Thank you. God willing, I'll be ready. He has already given me you, Tony, and Detective Rousseau. I'll be fine."

"I'm sure you will." Edna slapped her thighs and stood. "Let's go shopping."

Francesca looked down at the weed again. "Today, I only came to visit with you. I'm not going shopping."

Edna's quizzical look turned into a broad smile. She patted her handbag. "Never mind about money. You're comin' with me. Mme. Buisson will treat us to beignets and café au lait again this day."

Grinning, Francesca leapt to her feet. "Last one on the next streetcar is a rotten egg!"

* * *

Sitting on a bench in Jackson Square, Edna reminded Francesca that she had promised to think about "for instances." She told Francesca she had a few. "First, there is so many peoples who can't read or figure, you could be a teacher. Second, there is the opportunity to create a seamstress business with your Aunt Laura and Emily. Third, you could let your Uncle Tony teach you to make leather things to sell, like ladies shoes, handbags, and purses. Fourth, you and Emily could start your own laundry business servin' military peoples and others. Fifth, I just thought of this one today, you could offer private detective services to mostly women, but also to men. So these are just a few alternatives to plaçage.

"Out of this tragedy, you've found out that you're a capable woman whose good looks ain't got diddley to do with the wonderful progress you've made in this investigation."

Edna sighed. "If you remember nothing else I say in life, remember this, you don't have to be no slave to a man, no damn toy, neither."

Her face placid, Francesca sat with her jaw in one hand, elbow on her knee. For a time, she said nothing. She thought *why couldn't I have thought of these possibilities? Now, the last person I would have thought could give such insightful advice would be a black enslaved woman sold away from her family. Why did I have low expectations of her? Or of anyone who is dark skinned and enslaved? My own slavery isn't so different as to make me not the same. Mary, Mother of God, please forgive me.*

Presently, Francesca said, "Edna, thank you for giving me very real possibilities to think about. I don't know why I couldn't have recognized these. Most of all, thank you for giving me a new way of seeing myself."

"Chile, I understand. You ain't lived very long. You know what you've seen and been taught all o' your short life."

Francesca thought *my God; I have been so stupid to think I'd only find wisdom among the so-called people of letters.* "When we're free, can we make a business together?"

Edna turned to look into Francesca's eyes. She said, "Why, that's the highest compliment anyone's given me since my John. Thank you. I'd be happy to work side by side with you."

They embraced.

* * *

At a corner table in Café du Monde, Francesca sat deep in thought, nibbling an apple beignet she had dipped in brown sugar on her plate. She thought *the key to finding Em is Detective Rousseau's crowd knowledge idea. But I can't run to him every time I'm stymied like a child running to her papa. I've got to do a better and quicker job of running ideas to ground. She sucked her teeth. Today, I'm making but little progress, what with only one new question for M. Buisson. Some detective I am! Merde.*

With a big grin, Edna waved her hand across Francesca's vision and said, "Hello. Is anyone at home over there?"

Francesca laid her half eaten beignet on her plate. Smiling, she stretched and yawned before she said, "I'm sorry. My mind drifted back to the task of finding dear Em."

"You told me...." Edna turned to see what had grabbed Francesca's attention. Outside of the window, a tall handsome broad-shouldered black man in a crisp well-tailored coachman's uniform held the door of a carriage open for an elegantly dressed middle age white woman. Edna turned back to Francesca and smiled.

Francesca flushed, and then laughed. "Uh-huh! You caught me! You read my thoughts correctly. Yes, I'ma save my money so I can *buy him*. What a great living piece o' man flesh he is! Quick! Hold me before I go snatch'im up and run off with'im right now!"

Holding her sides, Edna laughed until she cried.

While Edna was dabbing her eyes, Francesca pretended to be an aristocratic lady and put on airs. She held her cup by its handle with her thumb and forefinger while extending the other three into the ether. She said in her best imitation British accent, "Yes, my dear? Now, what was it you were saying before I was so rudely interrupted?"

Edna laughed again, but managed to say, "You told me the next person you plan to interview is M. Buisson. Did you change your mind?"

Francesca dropped her airs and sipped her café au lait. She said, "No. But it won't be much of an interview because I have so few questions."

Edna looked about, and then leaned forward, motioning for Francesca to do the same. Edna whispered, "Here are a couple of things you may want to ponder. M. Buisson and several foreigners are moving silver or gold, I forget which, from the bank to some consulate before the Yankees can lay hands on it."

Francesca's eyes widened and she leaned even closer, her midriff pressing against the table.

Edna continued. "Another thing is, if I were you, I'd think foreclosures and see where it might lead. I've heard this favorite subject again and again over supper with outsiders and with M. Joachim. Them bank peoples get rich off the misfortunes of others."

Francesca's hand covered her mouth. "Oh, my. How did you learn all this?"

A sinister smile crossed Edna's lips, turning into a lip curling snarl. "Don't I look like a potted fiddle leaf fig, or maybe an areca palm, set in the corner of a dining room? Chile, can't you see a'tall? Didn't you know I'm a stupid potted plant to the Buissons and all who dine with them?"

Francesca covered her mouth to stifle her giggles.

"Fran, something else you might have already looked into is M. Joachim's papers. Didn't he carry a satchel to and from work like his pa?"

Francesca face was serious. She said, "Oh, my. Yes, he did. I never thought of that. This is very good. Thank you so much."

Edna sat back in her chair. "By the way, it wasn't all business in that dining room. You mentioned that poor Annabelle Cocks. They had mighty big fun for a long while laughin' about that disgustin' ol' Judge Cocks."

* * *

Francesca bade farewell to Edna and disembarked from the St. Charles Avenue line streetcar at the Jackson Avenue stop. Two blocks later, she arrived at Brooke's home well ahead of time for supper and was greeted at the door by Bernard.

"Ah, ha! So the woman who frightened my poor wife into hiding has arrived on our veranda!"

Francesca laughed. "Good afternoon to you, too, Bernie!"

"Oops! Sorry. Where are my manners? Good afternoon. Now, with your display of civility, you don't sound as forbidding and formidable as your cryptic note. Please tell me you're here to release sweet Brooke from hiding. Can she go to Antoine's with us tonight? Please."

Francesca felt like throwing her head back and letting go with a belly laugh. Instead, she decided Bernard was not taking her warning to Brooke seriously. She entered the front hallway with her arms folded. Francesca looked up into Bernard's blue eyes, made her face stern, and said, "No."

She held his eyes in her unsmiling gaze as Bernard appeared ready to continue his banter. She saw his expression change.

In the parlor, he said, "You're really serious, aren't you?"

"Yes." She paused and took a deep breath. "I want you to know I am certain that Brooke is in grave danger. Please pardon the pun."

"What? Oh, yes. Sure. Excuse me. I'll get Brooke."

Over mint juleps, Francesca recounted the week's news for Brooke and Bernard. Deciding they did not need to know all, she left out important clues and conclusions. Brooke nodded but asked no questions as Francesca spoke of her collaboration with Detective Rousseau. Bernard's face showed surprise.

When Francesca's monologue was finished, Brooke was pale. She fidgeted with her nails in her lap. Finally, she said, "Fran, I'm very grateful for all you're doing. I hope you and your detective friend will catch this mad man soon. I had hoped to attend Louie's funeral tomorrow. But now, I'm sure I won't."

Francesca heaved a sigh of resignation. "I won't go either. Though it is not likely, but possible, the killer may remember me from the levee. To make matters worse, I don't yet know what he looks like."

Bernard smiled and said, "Fran, I've learned more about you in this hour than I thought I knew from all the many months since Joachim introduced us. I salute you." He held up his silver mint julep cup.

At a quarter before six, the doorbell rang. While Bernard admitted a guest, Brooke said, "Oh, my. In the excitement of being confirmed as a possible target of a murderer, I forgot to tell you that Bernie and I invited his friend, Mark Donohue, to join us for an evening at Antoine's. Bernie was so sure there was nothing to your warning note that he went ahead and made plans."

Francesca's ire flared. She saw recognition of her anger in Brooke's face. Brooke said, "Oh, Fran, I'm so sorry. I should have persuaded Bernie to wait until...."

The two men entered the room and Bernard introduced Mark. He went on to explain to Mark why they would dine in instead of going to Antoine's.

Mark whistled.

* * *

Brooke's servants were clearing the dining room. Distracted, Francesca sat on a bergeres chair and smiled, shook her head, and decided that the thin dark woman was the fiddle leaf fig and robust cook must be the areca palm. She thought *I would love to listen to them in the kitchen.* Across the parlor table sat Mark on a divan. She noticed that his lips were moving, but had no idea what he was saying. She thought *I should catch his next words so I can close.*

Mark was saying, "And that's not all. Several west bank plantations may go up for sale after this year's harvest. It's possible I could expand in that way."

"Why, Mr. Donohue, it's all very impressive. I can see that you're a refined and successful gentleman. I shall look forward to seeing you again."

Mark stood.

Francesca thought oh, good. He got it.

She walked Mark to the front door and bade him farewell. As soon as the door closed, Francesca heard footsteps rapidly descending the stairs. They met at the landing. Francesca could see that color had returned to Brooke's cheeks, though her countenance was falling.

Brooke said, "I gather he's not the one. Is that right?"

"He ain't the one by a long shot."

"Oh, well. I told Bernie that this may not work for you, but he persuaded me that Mark has such great credentials."

"In just a few days, I've grown beyond the person you knew at Joachim's birthday party last week. I live with my mother. I have no money, though I'm filthy rich in streetcar tickets that no one will buy." Francesca laughed. "An-n-nd, I have no man. But I'm way too busy to be bothered by such small concerns."

"You seem happy in spite of the heavy load you carry. Are you?"

Francesca tilted her head and rolled her eyes. "I think so. I'm unhappy when stymied by this investigation and think of poor Em, but only then."

"Well, let's change the subject. I'm so glad you're staying the night. Com'on up to the guest bedroom. I've got a surprise for you."

Brooke grabbed Francesca's hand. Francesca did not move, but gave Brooke a frowning look that wrinkled her nose.

Brooke stopped and looked into Francesca's face, her eyes darting in search of meaning. And then, she smiled. "No, silly! It's not another man!"

Both women laughed as they raced up the stairs.

"Oh, Brooke, it's gorgeous! And I love the color. It's so rare. Thank you so much."

Francesca held her hands clasped together in front of her chest as she moved around the bed inspecting the champagne gold dress spread out as if a ballroom dancer was wearing it. Moving closer, she stumbled over matching shoes. "Brooke, this is too much. You shouldn't have!"

"Nothing is too much for you, my friend."

"Where did you find it, and the shoes?"

"I found both in Tremé."

"How can that be? I've lived there for eons and know of no place in Tremé where there are such treasures."

"Well, there is such a place on St. Phillips Street near Villere, at Laura and Tony's."

"Oh, my God! My auntie and unk?"

Brooke beamed and nodded. "The same."

Tears welled in Francesca's eyes. "How can I ever repay you?"

"You can't. I won't allow it. But I'll be very happy to see you wear both to the big spring ball at the Orleans Ballroom two weeks from tonight."

When they had debated the purpose of octoroon and quadroon balls for two hours, Francesca asked for a truce. After Brooke agreed to an armistice, they made tea in the kitchen.

Francesca said, "I know it's late and ol' Bernie probably wants to put his thing in you before he sleeps, but I need to ask you about one more matter."

Brooke flushed and slapped Francesca's shoulder. "Ah, ha! Lady detective or not, you really *are* the same ol' Fran! And I'm so glad!"

Her quick smile vanished and with a serious stern look, Francesca asked, "Have you heard of Judge John G. Cocks?"

A scowl fell across Brooke's face. She said, "Yes! Damned be his bloody time! May he die a slow and painful death from torture and then rot in hell."

Chapter 14

General Butler had been writing notes of direction for over an hour to various staff members when Major Stone announced Francesca and Anna at eight o'clock sharp on Monday morning, May 5. He abandoned his writing chore and met them in the middle of his office.

Butler's second warm welcome after three days impressed Francesca. Butler shook hands with both. "Good morning, ladies! A beautiful new spring day is upon us and it is made all the better by your visit."

Mrs. Butler, General Shipley, and Captain Puffer joined the group. Butler took a seat in the circle of visitors with his back to his desk. When all had exchanged pleasantries, Francesca said, "General Butler, sir, I want you to know that I did a bit of asking around since we last met. As you recall, it was only last week that I met Mlle. Cocks. When I inquired about her father of two people who do not know each other, one colored and one white, I found that they both knew of this notorious man and his dastardly deeds."

General Shipley said, "General, this is going to be a short meeting. My inquiry, too, was made among disparate citizens and I met only one of seven people who did not know some degree of detail of Mlle. Cocks' story."

Francesca thought General Butler probably repeats this ritual of covering his moustache, mouth, and chin with his hand each time he goes into deep thought.

General Butler's gaze was fixed on Anna. Without turning from her, General Butler said, "Mr. Puffer, is this Cocks fellow the same deadbeat who refused to pay Major Anderson?"

"Yes, sir. He is the same person."

Mrs. Butler asked, "Do you mean our Major Anderson who was forced to surrender Fort Sumter?"

Captain Puffer nodded and said, "Yes, ma'am."

General Butler stood and paced before he spoke again. "First, I want to thank you, Mlle. Dumas and Mr. Shipley, for looking into this matter." He continued pacing, looking at the floor. No one spoke. Presently, he stopped in front of General Shipley. General Butler said, "I have made a decision. Mr. Shipley, see that an allowance is set up for Mlle. Cocks from the good judge's estate when we seize it."

"Yes, sir."

General Butler paced again. "Mr. Puffer, give Mlle. Cocks one of the judge's houses, preferably one large enough for her to let apartments." His pacing paused and he raised a forefinger toward the ceiling. "Oh, and manumit her."

Captain Puffer's grin was wide. "Yes, sir!"

Anna leapt from her chair and crashed into General Butler, embracing him in tears and kissing his bald head. Francesca thought General Butler's flailing arms made him look like a man trying to ward off angry bees about his head.

Francesca and the group laughed.

Anna released General Butler still repeating, "Thank you, sir! Thank you so much!"

* * *

Twenty minutes later, Francesca sat with Major Stone in his office. For a minute, he sat staring at papers on his desk that Francesca did not believe he was reading. She cleared her throat and said, "Major Stone, what was it you wanted to talk about?"

He stood and said, "I don't know how to say this, so I'll just start. You probably sense that I'm attracted to you."

Francesca kept her face neutral. "Yes, I know."

"I want you to understand that I'm setting aside my interest in you for two reasons. First, I'm married. Second, if you

122

agree, we want you to work with this staff as an agent. For both reasons, you and I can't have anything going on between us."

Francesca swallowed, hard. Blinking, she said, "Major Stone, I assumed you were married. And I understand that marriage vows have limited ability to harness one's lust for the flesh of another."

Major Stone started to speak, but Francesca waved him silent and continued. "Under different circumstances, I might have considered you a very eligible suitor.

"So, now, let's go on to this matter that I do not understand. Sir, did I hear you correctly? You wish to employ me? Doing what, exactly?"

Major Stone resumed his seat and spoke in what Francesca thought was his official voice. "Captain Puffer has been made the Deputy Provost-Marshall of New Orleans. In his new position, he has already heard about your investigation of a murder. Yes, he has met Detective Rousseau. And, yes, we want you to work for us as an agent. That means you would work undercover discovering and reporting on the activities of those in this city who are working for the Confederacy."

Startled, Francesca sat with her mouth agape, staring at Major Stone. Presently, she used both hands to push off her chair and stand. She felt her thoughts were crashing into each other and all being demolished before she could run one to ground. She thought *what about time I need to find Em? Lord, you know, I need the money. Francesca felt her fingers tremble, so she clasped her hands. Money or no, Em comes first. But, Mary Mother of God, please pray that I make the right decision.* She said, "G-give me a few m-minutes, please."

As Major Stone left the room, he said, "Sure. Take your time."

Twenty minutes later, Stone knocked at his office door.

Francesca smiled and said, "Oh, please come into *'my'* office. Let's discuss your offer and my requirements." She thought *I must sound like Mother's speech to Joachim's attorney last December, dictating the terms of our plaçage contract.*

He handed Francesca a folded note from Anna. Without reading it, she put it into her handbag.

Stone sat behind his desk and selected a pencil. "I'm ready. What is it you require?"

"Sir, please manumit me and my mother."

Momentarily speechless, Stone's fell mouth open and he dropped his pencil. He recovered and said, "You can't be a slave, you're white."

"That's what you said about Anna. She's white, but I'm not white. I'm a quadroon. My mother is a mulatto. You see, Major Stone, though we have many written and unwritten rules in New Orleans about race and sex, these rules have never applied to white men."

He frowned and smoothed his moustache. With a sigh, he raised his eyebrows and said, "I see I have much to learn about your city."

Francesca nodded and continued. "Next, please return my mother's house to her. I also need you to manumit my friend Edna Black who is owned by M. and Mme. Buisson of Citizens Bank. And last, this work you want me to do must not in any way impede my search for my friend, Emily."

"Is that all?"

"Yes, sir."

Stone looked up from his note taking. "Consider it done."

"All of my requirements?"

"Yes, all."

Water welled in her eyes. Francesca fought to hold her tears. "Then, I accept your offer. Mary, Mother of God, thank you! And thank you Major Stone."

He stood and offered his hand. "You are most welcome."

When they resumed their seats, Stone said, "Now, let's get back to business for a few minutes. I wouldn't be concerned about your investigation. Captain Puffer and Mr. Mahan have advanced a most interesting theory about your case. They believe the man you seek could be more than a Confederate sympathizer. Of course, that's one reason for their interest in you."

"What's another?"

"Mr. Mahan thinks a woman may be more successful than a man as a counterspy."

Francesca blinked. "Who is this Mr. Mahan?"

"John Mahan is General Butler's most trusted spy. Before the war, he was a detective. That's all I can tell you about him. Mr. Mahan will direct your work. Please return on Wednesday at eight o'clock sharp to meet him and start your training. By then, Captain Puffer will have the manumission papers ready for you, Anna, and the others."

They stood. Francesca wanted to embrace Stone and squeeze him, but thought *I'm not sure if I should risk stirring his emotions*, so she did not. Instead, she said, "Major Stone, thank you again, sir. Please convey my thanks to General and Mrs. Butler."

She turned to leave and Major Stone said, "Er, don't forget to read your note. Oh, and please keep your employment a very closely held secret."

"Yes, sir."

In the lobby, Francesca read Anna's note.

Dear Fran, you will always have a home with me and my children. Please join us as soon as you can at 192 Canal Street. Love, A.

Francesca sat by a window and wept.

* * *

While Francesca walked the two blocks along Royal Street from the St. Charles Hotel to Citizens Bank, she heard in the distance the bells at St. Patrick's Catholic Church and the St. Louis Cathedral signal twelve o'clock. She noted the bells were almost in sync, but were different by two chimes. Inside the bank she was greeted by the now familiar short man that she met on her first visit.

"As you have guessed, I am here to see M. Buisson."

"Mlle. Dumas, isn't it?"

"Yes, sir."

"Mademoiselle, I regret to inform you that M. Buisson is away in Baton Rouge on bank business. And I'm afraid I can't give you a good date to expect his return, what with the rumor that the Yankee fleet is sailing, as we speak, to capture Baton Rouge."

She sucked her teeth and opened her mouth to speak, but closed it again on the voice inside her head saying: merde. Francesca recovered and asked, "May I leave a note for him?"

"Why, of course, Mademoiselle, and I will see that he gets your note. Here, you may use my desk."

Francesca thought of all the rotten luck…. Then it dawned on her that she had forgotten to act on Edna's suggestion. *I must make more notes to me of what I need to do. I'm getting lost in the details.*

Excited, she dashed off her note to M. Buisson:

Dear M. Buisson,

I wish safe travels for you. Urgent. I need your answers to a few questions like these:

Who were Joachim's enemies?
What was he working on at the time of his death?
Did he do anything unusual in April?

Mlle. Francesca Dumas.

Francesca hurried away from the bank without saying farewell to the short man. Skipping her midday meal, she decided *I must go without delay*. She lifted the front of her ankle length dress and ran toward Tivoli Circle. Smiling, she thought how unladylike. What would Sister Juliette and Mére Henriette think? Three blocks on, she was panting and her stomach made noises. From that point, Francesca was forced to be content with walking briskly the remaining twelve blocks. She was already glowing. Aboard the Prytania Street line streetcar, she fidgeted on the hard oak seat and reread some of her investigation notes.

At Joachim's house, she found the key behind the usual brick and let herself inside. A small desk stood by the dining room window. In the desk, Francesca found papers related to the house and Joachim's personal bank account register. She laid these aside and kept them in a separate stack, papers and ledgers detailing Joachim's real estate holdings and stocks. At length, she thought this stuff is interesting but I have no way of connecting it to anything. Mary, Mother of God, please pray for me.

She sat at the desk rubbing her face with both hands and looking out the window. Then the thought hit her that all of the papers she had separated belonged to Joachim and really were connected in some way, but not obvious today. She decided to take both stacks with her. Now, I must get over my loathing of this place and enter the bedroom.

Upstairs, Francesca searched Joachim's wardrobe. The pockets of his clothes were empty. In the drawers, she discovered one paper, a hand drawn map of plantation properties downriver. Under the head of the bed on the side where Joachim had slept, she discovered the brown leather satchel that Edna had supposed existed. Inside the satchel, under letters and several documents, she found a small cloth bound ledger that Joachim had used as an appointment book. In the book, she found recent references to her name and a woman named Francine. Francesca sucked her teeth as her anger rose. So that's her name! Little wonder that the word 'Fran' rolled off his smooth silver tongue so easily. Bloody hell! She slammed the ledger closed and threw the book across the room, its pages fluttering before it crashed against the wall.

Francesca sat on the floor feeling betrayal anew. Her head hurt and her breathing was deep, causing her chest to heave. Her anger gradually gave way to hunger pains and a severe headache. When she struggled to her feet, she felt dizzy. Aloud, she said, "I'd best get out of here and find both food and water."

On the fourth step of the stairs, Francesca slipped and fell on her butt and slid feet first to the quarter landing. The satchel followed and crashed into her head. She lay on the quarter landing for several minutes checking damage to her body. Her head throbbed and her butt hurt. Then, she heard a noise from the back of the house. The effects of the bumps and possible contusions were set aside. She grabbed her bag and put her left hand on the handle of her pistol. The sound of two men talking was clear as they walked along the pathway between the house and Prytania Street. Dragging the satchel, she crawled back up the stairs to the bedroom and sat on the floor in a corner.

She listened until the voices faded completely. With a sigh, she thought *I am trespassing. Why didn't I think of that before? Here sits the klutzy girl detective on her sore butt with a massive headache and stolen papers and not a thought of getting caught until she hears passersby. Girl, get up now and get the hell outta here! If Em only knew, she would surely fire my sore bottom on the spot.*

When Francesca stood, she stepped on Joachim's appointment book. For a long moment, she looked down at his appointment book as if it were a new discovery. Then, she exhaled and decided *now I am a mature unemotional woman detective.* She picked up the appointment book and placed it in the satchel.

Chapter 15

At five minutes before eight o'clock Wednesday morning, May 7, Francesca was surprised to be met in the lobby of the St. Charles Hotel by a smiling Sarah Butler. "Good morning, Francesca. Oh, I just love your skirt and matching accessories. So tasteful. Walking in, you could be the belle of the ball."

Francesca glanced down at the opened lace collar on her ruffled front white blouse and blushed. "Oh, Mrs. Butler, you are so kind. Thank you and please call me 'Fran'."

"Thanks. I will, but only if you'll call me Sarah. So what if at forty-six, I'm old enough to be your mother."

After greetings, an embrace, and two minutes of chat about a tea Sarah would host in the afternoon for officers's wives, she presented Francesca with the cloth bag hanging from her arm. "Here are some clothes and things Mr. Mahan asked me to purchase for your new work."

"Thank you, Sarah."

Francesca took a quick look into the bag and up at Sarah's amused smile. In the bag, she saw a woman's blond wig, a black wooly minstrel wig, two front-lace small-cup corsets, men's shirts, and several pairs of men's trousers. She thought what have I gotten myself into? What surprises lurk in the bottom of this bag? Francesca made an exaggerated rising of her eyebrows and said, "Now, I'm not so sure I should have thanked you just yet."

Sarah laughed and took Francesca's elbow. "From what I've heard of your sleuth powers, I think you'll enjoy your work. Come with me. I'll take you to Mr. Mahan."

* * *

Separately, they boarded a St. Charles Avenue line streetcar headed downriver along Bourbon Street. As if they had never met, Francesca followed John Mahan aboard an Esplanade Street line streetcar after several passengers boarded between them. For the entire trip to the Fairgrounds Race Course, she listened from inside the car as John stood on the front platform with the mule driver laughing and swapping haint stories. From time to time, Francesca stole a glance at John. She had guessed his age as thirty, but he had told her before they left General Butler's headquarters that he was forty-three. She thought only children want to put their age up, so how does he stay in better shape than all the men she knew except Tony? No matter, she thought, *who is my mystery partner and what will he be like? And why are we meeting at a race track?*

As instructed, Francesca took the lead and walked the seven blocks from the Seventh Street streetcar stop to the race track. She paused to ostensibly look into the window of a grocer, but actually she wanted to learn how much distance John allowed between them. While she was stopped, she saw John, a block behind her, use a hand to shield his eyes from the morning sun as he pretended interest in a house on the east side of the street.

In the shade of the grandstand, John introduced Francesca to her teammate, Marcelle Dainez, a free Creole man of color and a former member of the Crescent City Native Guards. Again, she guessed the age wrong. She thought he was twenty or twenty-one, but he was twenty-nine. On the track, she learned why John and Marcelle's youthful appearance belied their ages. John explained that he would conduct some training while they walked the track, briskly. With her clothes bag and purse secured in a locker, Francesca, now wearing trousers with her hair tied up, was panting and glowing and unable to keep pace with her older comrades.

By noon, John had introduced them to matters they would need to master in the coming weeks though he would be available as a coach for only two more days. Among the topics were the Naval Colt .44 revolver, Spencer repeating carbine, a smaller sidearm of their choice, horsemanship, telegraph, physical conditioning, first aid, and hiding in plain sight. He explained that they needed to know how to use the larger weapons in an emergency.

John cooked their noon meal as a demonstration. From his haversack, he crumbled hardtack and fried it with bacon. He added dandelion greens gathered by Francesca and Marcelle to his frying pan. As Francesca watched the flickering flames of the cook fire, she thought *I was so tired; I had to gather dandelion greens on my knees. I can't remember when I was ever so tired. And I can't believe it's only noon.* As soon as she finished eating, Francesca fell fast asleep on the ground.

A half hour later, she was awakened by an ancient horse snorting as he grazed next to her head. Afraid that the horse may step on her, Francesca leapt to her feet and was immediately dizzy. Two hours later, she had learned to ride, using both a cavalry saddle and a side saddle.

On Thursday afternoon at the old Confederate Camp Walker, half mile from the fairgrounds, Francesca held her smile within, for she had more hits on targets than Marcelle, or even John. After her first success, she thought *I can do this. I'll be alright. It matters not that muscles I didn't know I have are hurting from my neck to my feet, I'll be alright.*

A courier arrived Friday afternoon with a telegram for John. He immediately announced to his two new recruits that Baton Rouge had surrendered during the day without a fight.

By the end of Friday, Francesca learned that she would hide in plain sight working as a clerk in Thomas F. Browne's Agency for Singer Sewing Machines, located one block on the riverside of General Butler's headquarters in the St. Charles Hotel and in the same block as the City Hotel. Marcelle would drive a delivery dray for the Browne Agency. Their new work address was 7 Camp Street.

In his last instructions, John said, "Check every day between noon and one o'clock in the St. Charles for telegram orders from me. Oh, by the way, what you earn at Browne's is yours to keep in addition to your $39 per month army salary."

Chapter 16

Francesca, Anna, Able, and Arianna set out early Sunday morning, May 11, for an unhurried walk to St. Augustine Catholic Church. Francesca and Anna wore identical thin white lace veils over their hair that draped nearly to their waists. They dressed in bright colors and Francesca smiled while she tried in vain to understand a nagging, but vague, feeling that several more clues had to be found to finally identify the murderer who stole Emily. Even so, her spirit was lifted by brilliant sunlight, a gentle breeze, and the smell of roses wafting from the trellises in front of shotgun houses lining Rampart Street. She looked furtively from the corner of her eye at several houses and thought *it's silly to think Anna can know what I'm thinking. Anyway, I wish Mother had insisted that Joachim build a house for me here in Tremé. Oh, well.*

"Fran, this is a gorgeous day! Thank you so much for inviting me to visit your church. I should have thought to come and give thanks to God for my freedom without prompting."

"Speaking of visiting, we're both visitors. It's sad, but true. I haven't been to mass since the spring of last year."

"Did your absence have anything to do with meeting Joachim?" Anna called to Able who was walking ahead of them. "Don't let go of Arianna's hand."

Francesca said, "Yes. It had everything to do with Joachim."

"How much further is the church? My shoes are pinching my toes."

Francesca pointed and said, "We turn left after that corner house onto Bayou Road. The church stands on the next corner at St. Claude Avenue. It'll be just a few minutes more."

"Whew. I'm thankful for that news.

"Able, turn left."

When they turned the corner, Francesca stopped to take in the sight of St. Augustine Catholic Church. The front had been recently whitewashed and from a block away, it gleamed in the morning sun. The belfry stood on the right as one faced the façade. Francesca smiled as her eyes settled on the beauty of the bell-shaped copper dome atop the belfry. The dome had an appealing aqua patina, showing its age of twenty years.

Anna's mouth dropped open as she drew a breath and then said, "It's beautiful!"

At St. Claude Avenue, a round black woman ran to meet them. She seized Francesca in a bear hug. Tears spilled from Francesca's eyes as she held the woman in her equally tight grip. The woman cried silent tears. Holding his sister's hand, Able looked on, mouth agape, wide-eyed.

At length, when Francesca could speak, she sniffed, held the woman's hand, and said, "Dear Edna, my friend, please allow me to introduce you to another of my friends. This is Annabelle Cocks. These are her children, Able and Arianna."

* * *

They occupied the entire front pew on the Gospel side of the nave. Francesca thought *I am in the middle of my family.* She reached over and held Ada's hand. Tony and Laura sat close to the center aisle. To Francesca's left sat Edna, Anna, and the children. Francesca blinked and looked again when she realized they were a rainbow of colors, their skin and their clothes. She also noted they were of three generations and that males, Tony and Able, anchored the ends of the pew. She smiled.

After most parishioners departed, Father J.B. Jobert led the "family" in a prayer of thanksgiving for the newly freed as they stood about him at the edge of the chancel.

When Rev. Jobert said, "Amen," Francesca recognized that in her joy, she had not included Emily in her prayers; Emily who was born free but now lived in captivity. Francesca hugged herself and raised her face to the stature of Mary. She muttered, "Mary, Mother of God, please pray for unworthy me. I need help to find Emily. Please...."

Moist-eyed, Laura draped an arm around Francesca's shoulders.

* * *

They convened for a mid-day impromptu celebratory meal at Laura and Tony's house. Ada and Edna prepared the food. Tony advised Laura. "Let the experts have the kitchen. You and me and the children can clean up after we eat."

Laura laughed. "Gladly!"

Having learned from Edna that M. Buisson had not returned from Baton Rouge, Francesca sat in Emily's small bedroom making notes about what she thought she needed to know from M. Buisson. Her notes turned into variations on one theme: Joachim's projects. Soon, she went to the kitchen and announced, "All of you know about my encounter with Mme. Buisson. As some of you know, there are not many things I dread more than ever seeing her again. Fitting examples include meeting an alligator or a snake."

When the adults and Able laughed, Arianna said, "Ha, ha!" That caused even more laughter.

Francesca said, "Nonetheless, before the sun sets today, I will call on Mme. Buisson."

Edna led the applause while she said, "Hear, hear! Hear, hear!"

* * *

Francesca and Edna rode a St. Charles Avenue Line streetcar to Louisiana Avenue and started the six block walk to the Buisson residence.

Aboard the streetcar, Edna was uncharacteristically quiet. Once on the ground she embraced Francesca and said, "I want you to know I have never experienced joy as I felt last Thursday when your messenger showed up and asked for me. I couldn't read all those big fancy words on that paper. But I could read your small note that said I's free! Chile, I screamed and shouted! Mme. Buisson come a runnin' askin' what was the matter. I did like your note said. I gave her my paper. Chile, she had to sit down. First, she turned as white as my paper. Then, she turned redder than a beet. Her natural color ain't come back 'til Friday!

"Friday, me and her could talk plain." Edna smiled as she explained, "In my new arrangement with Mme. Buisson, I will still sleep in the pantry room of the kitchen house and do the same work. Two things are different. First, my salary will be ten dollars per month. It ain't much. But, considerin' I won't have food and quarters expenses, I'll be fine. I'll save my money toward openin' up a little business."

"Edna, I'm so proud of you."

"Thank you. Thank you *very* much. I couldn't be happier if my own Rebecca had said it. That chile allus talked 'bout openin' up an inn and feedin' folks."

"So what's the second thing?"

"Oh, the second thing is I can quit whenever I see fit, and for any reason. And that holds even if the black codes return. I think I can trust her on that. M. Buisson was not there to give his word."

They had reached Coliseum Street. "Edna, I'm very happy for you. Let's slow our pace. For now, I need to talk to you about a matter that could mean life or death for me or those with whom I work."

Edna's smile vanished. "Something told me, it was strange for you to suddenly go to work in a sewin' machine store, 'specially with Em stolen and all. Hmmm. Life or death, eh? Well, okay. I'll not tell a soul anything you say. But, before you speak, let me remind you of an ol' sayin' I heard back in Mississippi: 'A body can't tell what he don't know.'"

Francesca thought about the warnings from Major George Stone and Agent John Mahan. For a long moment, she was silent. Edna waited as they plodded slowly ahead. Then, Francesca stopped, eyes cast down as if studying the vegetation about her feet.

Edna reached out and held Francesca's shoulder with one hand and asked, "Are you okay?"

Before she could answer, Francesca saw one of three white horsemen wheel his steed from Louisiana Avenue onto the pathway for pedestrians in front of them. She saw anger in his face. He said, "Nigger, get your filthy black hands off this woman! Who do you belong to? Your master will hear about this outrage!"

Edna's hand remained on Francesca's shoulder as she looked the man in the eye and said, "I's a free woman! I ain't got no master!"

The man snatched a whip from his saddle horn as he said, "Why you impudent black bitch, I'll teach...."

Francesca thought oh, mon Dieu! Then, what would Edmond Dantes do? In a flash, she stepped between the horseman and Edna. She used her right hand to keep Edna behind her. Francesca kept her eyes on the horseman's eyes as she shouted, "Sir, she's my friend. She was not harming me."

Two horsemen joined the first. The man with the whip paused, then frowned and said, "What?"

"This woman is my friend."

He looked around at his grinning comrades and flushed. He turned back to Francesca and said, "White people can't be friends with no ignorant animals. Don't you know niggers ain't people? Gal, ain't you got no sense of decency?"

Still holding Edna behind her, Francesca felt the muscles in Edna's arm tighten. Francesca made her grip on Edna's arm firmer. She said to the man with the whip, "Sir, please let us be. Enjoy your Sunday ride."

The man spat brown tobacco juice toward Francesca and returned his whip to his saddle horn. With disgust on his face, he turned his horse to rejoin his snickering fellows. Over his shoulder, he said, "And tonight, you and your nigger woman enjoy y'all's unholy girly orgy."

Francesca stood staring at the receding horsemen as they rode toward the river. Then she noticed her heart was pounding and her head ached at the temples. She turned to Edna and saw tears streaming down her face. But Edna made no sound. Francesca thought *in the year since I ventured beyond Tremé and Vieux Carré, I have, ever so slowly, come to realize that all the new people I meet see me as white. Even more slowly, this encounter and my investigation are raising questions I must answer: Who am I? Am I black or white? And why does it matter what or who I am? But I am beginning to understand why Brooke chose to be white. It appears there is some huge harassment factor that is eliminated from one's life by simply being white. I cannot fathom how huge this thing is. I cannot recall hearing it talked about. I don't know what it's called, but I now know it is as present as the air I breathe. The trouble is, after seeing that I've enjoyed this invisible freedom,*

I feel guilty that I have it. I know I've done nothing to earn it, nothing but have skin perceived as white.

Water welled in Francesca's eyes. A single tear spilled onto her right cheek. Without words, Francesca and Edna began walking again, hand in hand.

* * *

The Buisson's black butler, James, ushered Francesca into the parlor and announced her presence. She sat on the front edge of a chair and endeavored to take in the elegant and exquisite surroundings of the parlor before Mme. Buisson appeared. She thought one must feel enormously free from worry when one is rich.

Dressed in black, Maria swept into the room with her back arched and her chin held high. She said, "Bonjour, Mlle. Dumas. Bienvenue dans notre humble demeure."

Without smiling, Francesca stood and responded in English. "Good afternoon, Mme. Buisson. Your décor is magnificent. I particularly like your taste in art." Francesca's open palm gesture indicated two side by side wall mounted paintings. "I especially admire your Degas copies of original works by Michelangelo."

"Thank you. I try to support local artists. You know young Edgar has roots…."

"Yes. His mother was Mlle. Célestine Musson of New Orleans."

Maria cocked her head to one side and a faint smile appeared. She said, "Please sit and make yourself comfortable. James is making your favorite, sassafras tea. You know, I must cease my constant underestimation of you. Please forgive me. My upbringing is at fault. You are teaching me that the stereotypes I learned must be unlearned."

Eyes wide, Francesca was momentarily stunned. So she limited her response. "Thank you very much for tea.

"Now, Mme. Buisson, I am here on a rather urgent matter. In the absence of M. Buisson, I hope you will answer a few questions for me related to the murders of your step-son and M. Louis Laveau, plus the stealing of Mlle. Emily Jenkins."

Maria frowned and said, "My husband told me M. Laveau was wounded. Did the poor fellow succumb to his wounds?"

"No. Quite the contrary, he was on the mend. Then, he was murdered in his hospital bed in the middle of the night."

Maria's mouth fell open and her eyebrows rose. "I was amused when Edouard told me of your investigation. From this day forward, I want you to know that I respect your work and will do all I can to help."

Tea arrived.

"Please go ahead with your questions."

"First, I want you to know that I mean no disrespect by any of my questions. It is essential that my detective mentor in the Police Department and I get the answers we need to catch this murderer and thief of persons."

"I understand."

Francesca retrieved a new small ledger from her handbag and a pencil. "Do you recall any unusual topics Joachim may have discussed in your presence during the last several months?"

"No."

"How did the two of you get on?"

"Well, it's an open secret that we didn't see eye to eye on a number subjects, most notably, plaçage and the war. Oh, by the way, I thought it appalling that he kept putting off telling you he planned to marry another."

"Do you mean, Francine?"

Maria's face showed surprise. "Er, yes. My, you are thorough."

Francesca ignored her. "If you know of quarrels between Joachim and Francine, what were they about?"

"Yes. Time. Francine thought he was too obsessed with his work and not giving her enough of his time."

Francesca thought *that was the time he spent with me; he didn't work hard; he hardly worked.* "Tell me about his work."

Maria reached into a satchel she had brought into the parlor and retrieved a sheaf of papers. She held them at almost arm's length to read. "I have the note you left for Edouard. In your note, you wanted to know what projects he was working on at the time of his death. I have written a list of the ones I know about and the ones clerks at the bank told me about. He had three residential foreclosures underway in the city. You asked about enemies. I think he was too young to have enemies, except, of course, those people upon whom he foreclosed. He also worked with a client to finance the purchase of a plantation. Lastly, he was in a group working on analysis of contingent policies for expected currency changes."

Francesca made notes.

Maria said, "You may have my folder."

Francesca continued scribbling and without looking up. She said, "Thank you."

After a short silence, Maria asked, "Are you sure Joachim was murdered?"

"Yes. I'm sure of it."

"But who would want to kill a young unsung banker?"

"The man who did it is the one enemy Joachim had."

* * *

Francesca had supper with Brooke and Bernard and asked the same questions and took more notes. For the little they knew, their answers were the same as Maria's. After supper and a long debate deep into the night with Brooke, Francesca agreed to wear the gift champagne gold dress and attend the big spring ball on the next Saturday night with Brooke and Bernard. Again, they declared a truce in their ongoing argument about the role of class, race, and the place of women in New Orleans society.

With her investigation ledger in her hand, Francesca fell fast asleep with the lamp still lit in Brooke's guest bedroom.

Chapter 17

At half past eight, Friday morning, May 16, Troy Dodson wore his wide brimmed white hat low over his eyes and carried his long .44 in a new brown shoulder holster, butt forward, under the left side of his suit jacket. On his table in the City Hotel's restaurant lay two copies of the secessionist newspaper, *True Delta*, in which the current issue detailed General Butler's order that all use of Confederate currency end by "May 27 instant." Inside a piece of canvas secured by twine, Troy carried letters from city officials and his reports for General Lovell. The letters and reports, miniaturized and coded, were inside his shirt. In a prearranged signal, he read from the next to last issue of *Harper's Weekly*, dated May 3, 1862, featuring a front page that was recognizable from a distance; it displayed large likenesses of Generals Sherman, Grant, and nine other generals listed as "heroes of the Battle of Pittsburg Landing." Occasionally, Troy glanced past the paper toward the entrance, though he only had a vague description of the man he was to meet.

Presently, a dapper businessman wearing a thin dark closely cropped Van Dyke beard entered the room, waved off the maître d, and made straight for Troy's table. Troy thought, humph, a skinny mousy excuse of a man is he. The man said, "Bonjour. I'm Charles. Count De Mejan sent me."

Troy stood, looked Charles Camille Heidsieck level in the eye, and offered his hand. Charles appeared to relax when he heard Troy's confirming response: "Vive Napoléon III." Troy thought maybe he's not a mouse after all. His handshake is firm.

Breakfast was served and Charles looked up from inspecting his food and asked, "What is this creamy yellow-white cereal?"

With a bite of his blackberry jelly buttered biscuit in his mouth, Troy anticipated the next question and said, "Grits. It's made from corn."

Charles examined his brown-orange entrée and said, "Your American lobsters are exceedingly small."

Troy laughed and said, "They ain't lobsters. They're called crawfish and some of'em ain't as small these. They're freshwater critters. Watch me. I'll show you how to eat'em." Troy thought *damn, I can't remember the last time I laughed.*

Over the next several minutes, Troy decided he may use Charles as a courier after all. He thought being a mousy-looking Frenchman may contribute to his cover. He learned that forty year old Charles had only recently arrived in New Orleans and had come on an errand to collect debts owed Heidsieck & Company, sellers of champagne with high pinot noir content from the region about Reims in the north of France. Troy thought this fellow's knowledge and business makes for an excellent cover story. This could expand into something more.

In one of his many glances at people entering the restaurant, Troy spotted a comrade who worked for General Lovell and beckoned him to breakfast with them. Troy thought Richard Johnston appeared ill at ease from the moment he saw recognition in Richard's eyes. "So, Richard, my good fellow, I hear tell there's trouble on the horizon for our boys over there in Paris a courtin' government and businesses. What do you know about that?"

Richard's hand shook and he spilled grits from his spoon onto his shirt. With wide eyes, he said, "I'm afraid all I know is Butler's people..... Hey, is it okay to talk in front of him?" Richard had tilted his head toward Charles.

"Sure go ahead. I believe Charles is a trustworthy man."

Chewing his 'small lobster' Charles smiled and nodded.

Richard continued, "Well, all I know is that Butler works fast for a man new to New Orleans. What I heard was his folks seized the eight hundred thousand dollars in silver specie within days after we delivered it to the consul."

"Why, do tell. How do you think ol' droopy eye got on to all that silver so quickly?"

Richard's hands shook more. "I have no idea. All I can tell you is what I heard."

Ignoring Charles, Troy sat up to his full height, gave Richard an icy stare, and said, "You were responsible for getting the specie from Citizens Bank to the vault Count De Mejan had arranged for us. I want you to tell me what went wrong."

* * *

After their meal, Troy insisted that Richard accompany him with Charles to make good on his promise to assist in a debt collection. Charles carried the newspapers. They crossed Camp Street in front of the Thomas F. Browne Agency for Singer Sewing Machines and walked in silence three blocks to Tchoupitoulas Street. They turned upriver and six blocks on found Charles's debtor client, E.M. Rusha. The establishment was number 56 and faced Girod Street. An ad hung in the window that said, "Importer of Foreign Wines and Liquors."

Troy guided Charles and Richard to a stable behind the liquor store and across Commerce Street. Troy said, "Now, Richard, I want you to tell me how the operation you were responsible for turned into a Federal seizure of eight hundred thousand dollars."

"I-I-I d-didn't tell n-nobody." Sweating profusely, Richard backed away, looking for an escape route. Troy produced a short Bowie-style knife from his jacket, made a fast lunge toward his target. With his mouth open in the shape of an 'O',

Richard grabbed Troy's wrist, but underestimated the momentum behind Troy's thrust and his grip slipped up Troy's arm. Troy stabbed Richard in the center of his chest. Charles gasped, and then, with both hands over his mouth, murmured, "Oh, mon Dieu."

Troy leaned over the dying Richard, ruffled his clothes, took his purse, and used Richard's shirt to clean the blood from his knife. Troy stood, looked a trembling Charles in the eye, and said, "I know you saw the nigger who did this and stole poor Richard's purse." Pointing, he said, "See, he's running down that alley yonder."

Troy drew his .44. Charles cringed and backed away. Troy fired a round into the straw and manure covered ground inside the stable. Two mules began wild braying. Troy counted to five and fired again into the ground. Then, he said, "Bloody hell! Two misses! The damn nigger is getting away, running like a rabbit toward the river. Without a horse, no white man could hope to catch'em. Isn't that what you saw?"

Still trembling, Charles said, "Oui, Monsieur Dodson, oui."

* * *

Inside the E.M. Rusha Wine and Liquor Store, Troy made the introductions. The chief accountant received them on behalf of his absent boss, the owner. Standing at the sales counter, Troy put his left hand into the pocket of his trousers, causing his jacket's lapel to shift and reveal his revolver. The accountant blinked. Charles was silent. Troy said, "M. Heidsieck is here to collect the debt this house owes Heidsieck & Company of Reims. So here's what I want you do: pay up today."

The accountant began to perspire and his hands shook. He arrested his tremor by folding his arms and said, "Sir, I'll need

Mr. Rusha's approval to honor your request. He should be back from Mobile in a week, or ten days at the most."

Blinking, Charles shifted his weight from one foot to the other.

Troy rocked back on his heels and waited, his revolver still exposed.

After a minute of silence, the account wrung his hands and said, "S-sir, p-please understand. I-I-I…."

Troy said, "I'm not accustomed to repeating myself. So let me ask one final question." He leaned toward the accountant. "Did you not understand what I said?"

With his eyes darting to and fro, the accountant interlaced and unlaced his fingers several times before he spoke. At length, he said, "M. Heidsieck, will a payment today of one third of Mr. Rusha's debt be acceptable followed by payments of ten percent of the remaining balance per month until his debt is satisfied?"

Before Troy could speak, Charles put out his hand and said, "Yes. That will be fine."

The accountant exhaled, glanced at Troy, turned back to Charles, and said, "At half past two, please meet me at Union Bank. Please be prompt. The bank closes at three."

* * *

Inside Union Bank, the trio exchanged documents. Without a word, Troy handed Charles his canvas bound letters and reports. Once outside, they parted company with the accountant, M. Joseph Marks. Troy said, "Carry my dispatches and the two newspapers inside the diplomatic pouch Count De Mejan will provide. Deliver all to the French consul in Mobile. He'll know what to do and let you know when to make a return trip."

Charles asked, "Am I to always travel aboard the *Dick Keyes*?"

Troy laughed. "Yes. Our friend, the captain, has a pass approved by Butler to haul flour to New Orleans."

* * *

On the ferry to Slaughter House Point, Troy bought two more copies of the *True Delta*. He rode at a smart canter to Belle Chasse and found Theodore Packwood sitting in a large white wicker chair on the veranda of his main house facing the sunset. His boots were off and his feet rested on a pillow. At his side on a small wicker table was a pitcher of mint julep and pewter cups. Packwood hailed Troy and waved him over. A grinning livery boy, about twelve years old, ran out and grabbed Troy's reins as he dismounted then led the horse to the stable.

"Troy, m'boy, com'on and join me. Let's enjoy this great sunset before the rain gets here."

"Oh, that's what it is! I was glad to get off that horse because my leg was starting to hurt again."

"Now, I'm sure we'll get rain, what with this sunset and your leg telling us.

"Grab a chair and a drink. Let's toast the return of the mighty United States dollar to these here parts."

"I bought a paper for you. How'd you get the news so soon?"

"Zunts sent a messenger with a copy of today's *True Delta*. His note simply said, 'Read it and weep'. There ain't no need a weepin', yet. This thing ain't over."

"So you've changed your mind and now agree with me that we can still win the war?"

"Oh, hell no! This whole bloody war was a lost cause from the start. We're jes prolongin' our misery. Forget all the silly-ass rumors about France and England cozyin' up with us."

Troy thought this foolish old man ain't got good sense. *Why do I bother to argue with him?*

Packwood continued, "Alex Stephens got it right when he said the war is about the proper status of niggers. But he and the rest of Davis's crowd didn't think through the money part. We can't buy the manufacturing might the North has. Why, they make everything they need. We have to run their blockade twice each time we want to buy European manufactured materials for our soldiers. New Orleans fell 'cause we couldn't build warships fast enough to defend ourselves. Because we have good generals and soldiers it may take years, but we're gonna fail 'cause we ain't nobody's economic power. The thing on my mind is what then? The niggers are gonna be freed, you mark my words. Ol' Abe knows what the hell he's doing. Then, the question becomes; how will plantations like Belle Chasse fare in the new wage economy?

"Now, the thing that ain't over is the real-world matter of switching to United States currency. From my many years o' dealings with the banker crowd, I'm sure they're gonna try to pull a fast one and leave the holders of good ol' CSA paper, like you and me, high and dry."

"What? They can't do that! Bastards! It'll kill a little guy like me!"

"You mean like us. They will try, and fail. The thing that happens next, I predict, is Butler will step in to protect us and stiff the banks."

Troy thought what? *Butler protecting me?* Now, that's a hellava note and laughed. He frowned. "Why in bloody hell would Butler do that?"

"We're told he's our enemy, and in that blue uniform, he is. But Butler's actually a northern lawyer by trade and I believe he'll do it because he's fair and dislikes seein' the powerful run rough shod over ordinary folks. On a real and practical matter, if people can't buy bread, Butler doesn't have nearly enough troops in New Orleans, or in Louisiana for that matter, to quell an uprising by the masses. Fairness will take a hind seat to practical, if you ask me."

Troy poured another mint julep and stared gloomily into his cup. He thought *dammit, why did he have to start making sense now? The old codger is smarter'n I gave him credit for. New Orleans was done in without a fight. I know we can fight. But I'm beginning to see that our boys need more means to carry on a long and winning fight. Butler, damn his black soul, has snatched back big money Richmond had counted on using in France.* He pushed his hat back and held his forehead. He felt his thoughts were running in parallel lanes as if at Metairie Race Course, the war and buying Belle Chasse. Now, what about the planter class? Surely, the upper class will be left standing, no matter that the North wins. *Bloody hell! I can't believe I just thought it possible we could lose this war.* He shook his head and took a long pull on his mint julep.

Troy saw Packwood watching him. So he cast his eyes down and examined the planking in the floor. Packwood said, "Ain't you gonna tell me again 'bout how you and your boys whupped Lyons and sent his soldiers a runnin' helter-skelter? Or tell me 'bout how Beauregard and Bragg are gonna win down here and link up with Lee?"

Without looking at Packwood, he said, "No, sir, I ain't got it in me tonight. I'm tired. I think I'll git some supper and turn in."

* * *

While Emily and the cook cleared away the remains of their supper of dandelion greens, bacon, and cornbread, Troy leaned back in his chair and again appraised her. He thought she is a hellava good looking gal, what a great set o' tits and ass, nicely shaped full lips, and more intelligent than some white women to boot; if only her sandy hair was straight and she was a bit lighter....

Matt laughed and said, "Pa, I do believe Big Bro is love-struck. See the way he's eyeing his ol' yalla gal."

Troy responded with an icy stare.

"See, Pa, I told ya. See the way he's a lookin'? That's the way he used to do when me and the boys'd tease'im 'bout some ol' gal at school."

Paul said, "Boy, you hush that talk 'fore your ma and that gal hear."

Matt persisted. "But, Pa, it's true. If'n you don't believe me, ask'im how cum he won't let me put my thing in'er. He wants her all to himself." Matt pouted. "T'ain't fair, that's what!"

Paul shook his head. After a sigh, he said, "Matt, son, for crying out loud! You're twenty-nine years old and still behaving like a five year old. What's to become of you? I just don't know. Now, go on and git the hogs looked after. Me and your brother got some business to discuss."

Matt rolled his eyes at Troy and stood. "Yes, sir, Pa."

When Matt was out of earshot, Paul made another sigh and coughed. He glanced again at the copy of the *True Delta* on the table and said, "Son, promise me that when me and Ma are gone you'll look after Matt. You know he's never been too bright, but he's a good worker and could be a big help to you. I'm asking you again, have more patience with'im. He don't mean you no harm by his ribbin'. That's just the way he is."

Troy nodded. "Yes, sir. I understand. Sometimes at first, I forget and let him irritate me. Yes, sir. We're blood kin. I'll look after him."

"Son, I thank you. I don't need worryin' 'bout Matt on my mind these days."

"Yes, sir."

"Now, I'ma tell you right straight out, I think he's right. I believe you do like this gal, this Emily." Troy opened his mouth, but Paul held up a hand and continued. "Don't get me wrong. Ain't no harm in getting yourself a little brown sugar now and again. But I've seen the way you look at her. And I believe Matt is right. First off, you ain't renamed her. I know you remember that's an important part o' breaking a nigger new to service. Since she ain't never served before, you're gonna have to break her down from the ways of a free woman."

Paul paused for a bout of coughing. He took a sip of water. When he could continue, he said, "We can talk about her later. Right now, we need to pay attention to Butler and the banks. I agree with Theo about Butler ain't gonna allow the banks to stick it to the holders of Confederate paper."

"Oh, did y'all talk?"

"Yeah, I just left him ahead o' you ridin' in."

Troy pushed his chair back from the table and crossed his legs. "So, Pa, do you think we'll be able to go ahead with the Zunts and Union Bank offer to Packwood even after the currency change?"

The old man nodded. "I do. But I fear we're gonna need to close this thing 'fore the end o' next month."

"Why's that?"

"Soon, I don't know how soon, but all the niggers are gonna be free…."

153

With a troubled look and eyes cast down, Troy interrupted. "I understand."

"Okay."

Father and son sat in silence for minutes. At length, Paul said, "Are you still going to the Orleans Ballroom tomorrow night?"

Troy rubbed his chin and said, "Oops. I forgot all about that."

Paul chuckled and coughed. "Some Judah Benjamin you're gonna be. He had a classy looking treasure of a woman on his arm when he entertained. I know with the war and all, you ain't had much time for social stuff."

Reminded, Troy leaned back as he saw again in his mind's eye Benjamin enter the parlor for a Belle Chasse party with the beautiful Natalie St. Martin on his arm. He could hear again the jealous murmuring that went up from the women.

"Son, what with no Mardi Gras to speak of, I hear this ball will be the most elaborate of the season, due to the fact that New Orleans is now off war alert. I think you oughta short cut this thing and go to the ball and pick out one o' them octoroons that's itching to pass. Y'all could make something special outta this place. Your ma would be proud."

Grinning, Troy slapped both thighs and said, "Okay, Pa. It's settled. I'll go to the ball."

Chapter 18

As Saturday afternoon, May 17, wore on, the lightning and thunder ceased. But the sound of rain droned on against the foot square cobblestones of St. Louis Street and the tin roof of the awning on the front of Antoine's Restaurant. An occasional carriage stopped in front of the door and elegantly dressed white couples stepped out under the protection of umbrellas held by black valets. Many white men were at Antoine's that late afternoon to have an early supper before going to the evening's much anticipated spring ball.

Francesca wore a black dress and matching bonnet. Brooke's dress was gray with black buttons, cords, and lace. Bernard was already dressed for the ball in his white pique waistcoat, over a pleated white satin French cuffed shirt with a white cravat tie. His black tailcoat and breeches were wool. The lapels on Bernard's tailcoat were black satin. His white gloves and black top hat rested on the fourth chair at their table.

Their food arrived and as the waiters retired, Francesca reached for a spoon. Before she could dip into her crab, oyster, and shrimp gumbo, a chef appeared with a large salad bowl filled with five different greens covered with diced tomatoes and oregano.

It was Ada. She announced, "I found out what you young people ordered, mostly meat and bread." She smiled and put down three small bowls. "How're y'all gonna teach your young to eat if I still gotta watch y'all like a hawk to get everyone o' you to eat right?"

Francesca pretended to pout. "Aw, Ma. We wanted a light supper."

"Chile, I done been to many a ball in my day. Believe you me, y'all gonna need the energy on that ballroom floor. So eat up. "'Fore they blow out them candles tonight, y'all gonna thank lil' ol' me."

Grinning, Francesca took her mother's hand and said, "Ma, is it okay if we say thank you now?"

Ada squeezed Francesca's hand and said to Brooke and Bernard, "No matter that my favorite chile has mo' mouth than she needs, I still love her with all my might."

Laughter.

Ada stepped away saying, "Y'all have a good time tonight."

When Ada was gone, Brooke and Bernard started to speak at the same time. Brooke said, "You didn't tell us you have a sibling!"

Francesca laughed. "I don't. Ma always tells me I'm her favorite child."

* * *

They left Bernard in the restaurant and retired to Ada's room upstairs in Antoine's boarding house where Ada still maintained a room though she had her house back. Before supper, Bernard had deposited Brooke's trunk in Ada's room. The trunk contained all the clothing and accessories Francesca and Brooke would require for the ball.

Francesca reheated the two warm kettles atop the wood-burning stove. She poured steaming water into a copper tub that was shaped like a parlor chair with a wide high back and arm rests, but was without a seat in its circular bottom. Into the bottom, Francesca added cold water until she felt the water temperature was comfortable for her body.

She was removing her clothes behind a vertical unfolded floor standing screen when Brooke said, "Fran, wait. Try this stuff I ordered. It came in on a ship this week." Brooke handed Francesca a fancy bottle.

"Thank you.

"I think. What in heaven's name is this?"

"You're welcome. Put it in your bath."

"Not until you tell me what it is."

"Oh, alright." Pause. "Okay. It says here on the box that it's made in Paris by the house of Oriza L. LeGrand."

"I can see that much on the bottle."

"Just hold your horse. The box says it's a fragrant hygiene product and hair conditioner made from wormwood, lavender, rosemary, savory, sage, cinnamon, cloves, camphor, and garlic in apple cider vinegar."

"Whoa! All that! Are you sure this stuff won't take my skin off? I'd really be the talk of the ball then!"

Laughing, Brooke said, "I used it. And I still have all of my skin, and hair, too."

Before opening the bottle, Francesca sniffed Brooke's hair. "And you carry a pleasant scent. Hmmm. This stuff smells like you."

"No, silly. I smell like it."

Francesca relaxed in the fragrant water without moving for ten minutes wishing she knew where Emily was. After a sigh, she finished her bath. She pulled on all new clothing, beginning with calf-length yellow muslin pantaloons trimmed in white lace on each calf. Brooke laced up and tied Francesca's corset beneath her shoulder blades. Her corset was topped on the front by a three inch wide band of white lace. Francesca's yellow muslin corset cover matched her pantaloons. She tied the draw string of her petticoat so that the lace hem touched her ankles. And then, she pulled on the champagne gold dress. She looked at herself in the mirror and felt elegant and radiant. Francesca smiled.

Brooke said, "Okay, time to stop admiring the woman in the mirror and get your hair finished."

Francesca laughed and before she sat she arranged the dress to minimize wrinkles.

Brooke started with the front. She stopped and put her hands akimbo. "Fran, I didn't know you had pimples!"

"What? Me neither! Where?"

Brooke took Francesca's hand and placed the forefinger on a cluster of three pimples near the hairline on Francesca's right temple. "There."

Francesca said, "Oh, those are my little friends who show up every month about a week before my menses starts. And then, they disappear by the time my menses ends."

Rubbing her chin, Brooke studied the offending pimples. Finally, she said, "Okay, I'm going to hide your little friends. I'm determined to make you the belle of the ball this fine rainy night!"

Brooke's solution was a narrow length of yellow Spanish lace cut from her chemise placed across Francesca's forehead and tied in a bow behind her head. Next, Brooke used one of her chain necklaces to fit over the Spanish lace with a yellow sapphire hanging below the chain. The stone rested between Francesca's eyebrows.

"Dammit!"

"Now, what's wrong?"

"Your damn head is too big! The chain won't meet!"

Francesca laughed and said, "I think I need an even bigger head to understand the world we live in and...."

"Don't start. We don't have time to argue. Does your mother have any thread here?"

"I think she moved all her notions back to Tremé. Can't you use a tress?"

"Damn. Why didn't I think of that? You know what? Your big head is pretty smart!"

* * *

Holding her dress and petticoat up on both sides to mid-calf, Francesca stepped down from Bernard's coach and ran three steps to the shelter of umbrellas held by valets. Even in her hurry, she noticed that, unlike her last visit to the ballroom, the shutters over the arched large windows on the first floor of the building, the banquette for duels, were closed to the rain, which still fell in sheets. In spite of herself, she glanced up at the balcony over the sidewalk where she first kissed Joachim.

Inside, Francesca went directly to the curl in the bannister that began on the second riser of the stairs to the ballroom on the second floor. She reached out and touched the light colored polished wood with her elbow length white glove, stirring memories of the previous year. Brooke stood on the first riser inspecting the short train of Francesca's dress and the arrangement of her hair.

"Brooke, was that mirror up there last year?"

"Huh? Where?"

Francesca pointed. "There, the shield shaped mirror on the wall above the landing."

The ornate French mirror was surrounded by a frond and floral design carved in a gilt wood frame. Below the mirror, was a wall mounted marble table with two gilt wood legs barely large enough for the lone candle that stood upon it.

"Oh, that. Yes, it was there. Why?"

Francesca made a deep sigh. "I guess I'm now trying to remember what I promised myself I'd forget."

"That does not sound healthy at all. Now, snap out of it. Let's go so Bernie can take you in for your grand entrance. Remember; make him wait until the music starts for the next dance. I'll be inside to start a commotion so everyone will look at the entrance."

Francesca gave Brooke a big smile and their gloved hands touched as Brooke hurried up the stairs. Francesca waited for Bernard on the second landing, seated on a beige upholstered canapé. While she sat there smiling and greeting couples and unaccompanied white men, she remembered that John Mahan said, "Hide in plain sight." She made all of her greetings in English. She thought money does dress the body well. These fellows arriving solo are from Joachim's age to ancient. But they all dress well.

Standing back from the ballroom entrance with Bernard, Francesca fought off an attack of nerves. She thought *why I ever agreed to go along with Brooke's scheme to get me attention, I'll never know. I don't know if I like being the one looked at. It feels weird.* To distract herself, she poked Bernard in his ribs with her elbow and whispered, "Stop trembling. You're making me nervous."

Bernard coughed and caught his giggles in his glove. "You just can't stop being a troublemaker, can you? Uh-oh. There's our first cue. The next dance is starting." He held out his arm.

Francesca let her hand rest on his arm. She whispered again, "Wait for my signal." As Brooke had instructed, she counted to fifteen and then said, "Go!"

They stepped off together, beginning on with their left foot. Passing through the doorway, Francesca heard glass break followed by a gasp and Brooke's voice, "Oh, my, what a dress! Bravo! Bravo! I simply must have one!"

Startled by the sound of breaking glass, both Bernard and Francesca reacted, recovered, and sweep onto the dance floor, bowed to each other while holding hands, and began dancing.

Other female voices chimed in with approving and admiring words. Francesca saw past Bernard's shoulder as they whirled about the floor that she had the attention of every male eye in the room, even the men dancing. She smiled more broadly and thought damn that Brooke for being such a good friend. Before Bernard could find a seat for them, a French Navy officer was introducing himself and asking for the next dance.

And so it went for hours. On their fourth dance, she had forgotten his name and the naval officer had to repeat his introduction, "I am Alfonse Lemoine." This time, he add: "I come from Marseille and am the First Mate aboard the good ship, *Catinet*, moored at wharf number seven in your fair city. I humbly request the pleasure of your company at a party planned aboard the *Catinet* on Saturday evening next."

Francesca thought Marseille! Edmond Dantes! She stifled the big smile she felt, prompted by thoughts of *The Count of Monte Cristo* and its mulatto author, Alexandre Dumas. With a subdued smile, she said, "Oh, I don't know. Remember, I don't speak French."

"That will not matter. I shall be happy to translate for you!"

Though Francesca knew she would accept his invitation, she put him off. "Oh, thank you very much. You are so kind and gracious. I'll decide before Thursday and send you a note by messenger." She thought: John Mahan!

A tired Francesca sat drinking water with Brooke and Bernard. She kept her broad smile radiant while she turned away dance requests. Again, she noticed a man seated in the far corner of the room with his left leg stretched out straight. Francesca remembered he had been watching her. She tried, but could not recall seeing him dance. She made quick nod. "Bernie, do you know the man in the corner, the one with the melancholy eyes."

Bernard took a long swig from his mint julep cup, glanced, and said, "No. I can't say that I've ever seen him before."

Brooke overheard Francesca's question and added, "Me, either. Humph. If you ask me, he doesn't look so great. Don't tell me you're interested in *him*?"

Francesca laughed. "Okay. I won't."

Grinning and crossing his legs, Bernard said, "Brooke, not every bloke needs to be as handsome as I to spark a woman's interest. Besides, he's dressed as well as anyone here."

Brooke laughed and punched Bernard's shoulder. "I'll have you know, my friend isn't any ordinary.... Hey, Fran, where're you going?"

Francesca was making her way along the edge of the dance floor, turning down more dance requests as she moved closer to the end of the rectangular ballroom.

At length, she pointed to a chair and said to the man in the corner, "Hello. I'm Francesca. May I sit here?"

The man smiled and stood. He said, "It will be my pleasure to sit with you and make your acquaintance. My name is Troy Dodson."

* * *

With a few minutes of chat, Francesca decided Troy was a fish out of water and that he knew it. She thought he had no clue about how to change matters; he isn't ignorant, but he's far from smooth.

Francesca said, "Let's dance. It'll do you good."

Troy hesitated, blinked, and shifted in his chair. He drew his left leg up twice. Then, he said, "Why, thank you. I've never been asked to dance by a lady before. The pleasure is mine, Francesca."

She extended her hand. "You can call me Fran."

Troy stood and limped onto the floor with Francesca on his arm. "Thanks. But tell me. Are you feeling sorry for me, or what?"

They started to dance and she saw him wince. Francesca asked, "Did you have an accident and injure your leg?"

Troy laughed. "No. I'm pretty sure the Yankee who fired that artillery shell did so with purpose."

Francesca forced the smile to remain on her face as she thought merde, no surprise, another Secesh. "Sorry. Now, to answer your question, no, I don't think seeing one you believe to be in need of help and acting is feeling sorry. But, of course, you're free to have your own opinion about what feeling sorry means.

"So tell me. Why're you here this rainy night on that bad leg?"

Troy raised his eyebrows. "You are unusually direct to be so, so...."

She tilted her head and smiled. "So what?"

Troy flushed. "....Be so young and pretty."

Francesca turned on a beaming smile, put a dip in her step, and with flair, said, "Thank you, kind sir.

"Now, why're you here?" Pause. "I'm waiting. There're only a few possibilities: first, a quick lay, second, a placeé; third, a wife; and it can't be the fourth, to dance the night away. So which of the three is it?"

Troy flushed again, frowned, and lost his step. Francesca did a quick change of step and matched his step.

At length, he said, "You're way more'n I imagined looking at you from across the floor. You cut like a knife, like you know why I'm here and can see that I'm failing."

"Let me guess. You're looking for a woman pleasing to the eye for a long term monogamous arrangement. Am I right?"

Sweating, he hesitated, then nodded, and finally barely audible, said, "Yes."

"Okay. Stop kicking yourself because I see your purpose and progress. I noticed you in part because I saw you noticing me. Only then, did I decide to introduce myself and see if I can help."

The all-colored male dance orchestra, including a clarinet, three fiddles, two tambourines, and a bass drum, stopped playing and they sat. Francesca continued waving away pursuers, to which Troy reacted by moving his chair closer to her.

He said, "Fran, I'm not use to getting help. I don't ask for help, even when, in hindsight, I needed it."

Francesca looked him steady in the eye for a moment and then, said, "Well, it is my opinion that if you don't change your ways, the woman you will get you won't want. You're likely to end up with a childlike yes woman who is afraid of her shadow. If that's what you want, stay the course."

Now, she thought what does that puzzled expression on his face mean? He rubbed his stubble. The announcement was made: last dance. Troy put his hands on his knees. "What you've said is new to me, and troubling. What can I do?"

"We'll have to talk about that at another time. I see my friends are standing. I'll need to go with them."

Troy sounded hopeful. "Talk at another time? Good. I was hoping I'd see you again. Can it be soon?"

Francesca thought make him wait. She said, "I'm happy to help you. Perhaps, we can talk next month. I've received several offers tonight and I've learned to take time and reflect before deciding a course to follow."

Troy blinked behind a blank expression. "Listen, I've heard that men aren't supposed to...."

She laughed. "Ask a lady how old she is. I don't mind. I'll be nineteen in September."

Troy frowned. "Really? How in blazes did you become so mature and wise at such a young age?"

"Good night, Troy. I've enjoyed our chat."

"How will I find you again?"

"You won't. Send a note to Mr. Bernard Williams on Philip Street. I'll find you."

Chapter 19

192 Canal Street

Thursday, 22 May 1862

Dear M. Alfonse Lemoine of the *Catinet*, Wharf #7:

It was my great pleasure to meet you on Saturday last. I accept your invitation for Saturday next. I will arrive with my friends, Mr. & Mrs. Bernard Williams.

Francesca

"Anna, thank you so much for letting me wear your new brown skirt come Saturday."

"Oh, you're welcome. Anything I can do to help you land yourself a new fellow, I will. Oops. Sorry. Bad pun."

Washing breakfast dishes, Francesca laughed. "Don't worry. This one can remain at sea and return safely to Marseille. It's just a party."

"So I guess he's not the one. Is that why you're taking your chaperones?"

Able asked, "Auntie Fran, can I play with your chaperones when you go to work?"

Francesca and Anna broke into hysterical laughter. When she recovered, Francesca hugged Able and explained.

With an impish smile, she turned to Anna. "When I'm interested in a man, I'll leave my bodyguards at home. Okay, I've finished the kitchen. I'm off to the St. Charles to find a messenger."

"Fran, it's less than ten blocks to the river. You could deliver your note yourself and save money."

"Smart Alice."

"Ma, why does Auntie Fran sometimes call you 'Smart Alice'?"

Francesca laughed. "Good-bye. See you two at suppertime!"

* * *

At one o'clock, Francesca went back to the St. Charles Hotel as it was her turn to follow John Mahan's instructions to check daily for a telegram from him. Mahan's first telegram since Monday read:

Thu, 22 May

F. Dumas & M. Lainez: At 0800, F, 23 instant. Go to G. Stone for instructions. J.M.

Back at the Browne Agency, Francesca found Marcelle in the stockroom loading boxes onto a dolly. She gave him several pages of deliveries to be made on Friday and Saturday. The telegram was the second page. She thought hmmm. *Marcelle is here right under my nose and I've completely overlooked him. He has a quick mind, is strong and a handsome brown to boot. What was I thinking? Oh, and he's probably like me, near broke. Okay. He's still interesting. I'll think about all this later.*

* * *

The next morning, Francesca and Marcelle arrived separately at Major George Stone's office a few minutes before eight o'clock. Though Stone greeted them warmly, he appeared to be irritated and his manner was stern.

"John asked me to brief you for your next mission. By the way, Francesca, John sends his thanks for including the *Catinet* in your activity report."

Francesca nodded.

Stone continued. "Okay. Here's the situation: European consulates in New Orleans have strong Confederate leanings. Further, the French have demonstrated direct support and aid to our Confederate enemies by selling war materials to them and worse, receiving hundreds of thousands of dollars' worth of silver from Citizens Bank and attempting to spirit it to Richmond and Paris. Now, specifically, the *Catinet* is a French man-of-war that slipped past our quarantine point without stopping. Assume that her crew is well armed and hostile. The captain of the *Catinet* has violated international protocol, and possibly French neutrality, by not notifying the United States of his presence in our port. A squad of infantrymen will be at the foot of Girod Street should you need help to escape. However, they have strict orders not to board the *Catinet*.

"This is your mission: Francesca, tomorrow night, you are to attend the social event mentioned in your report. Take no action beyond observation or casual questions. Your objective is to learn with whom in New Orleans the crew is engaged. The commanding general will base his actions regarding the *Catinet* on information you acquire. Report your findings on Sunday. Marcelle, you are to conduct armed patrol of wharf number seven while Francesca is aboard, but do not attempt to board the *Catinet* unless you get a clear distress signal from Francesca. Arrive at the objective separately. Remember, neither of you is a member of the United States Military or Navy.

"Francesca, you will lead and control the operation. While all is well, wear your handbag on your left side. If you need help, appear on deck wearing it on your right side. Coordinate any further details with Marcelle on your own.

"Do you have any questions?"

They answered in unison, "No, sir."

* * *

The high thin clouds beyond Carrollton had changed from orange and red to purple by the time Francesca, Brooke, and Bernard arrived on Wharf Seven at the foot of Girod Street. Francesca felt the evening's warmth and humidity on her bare shoulders. The blouse she borrowed from Laura was white satin with a three inch lace cowl that draped and clung to the sides of her shoulders and across her chest above her corset. She wore Ada's small brimmed brown hat that matched her high-top shoes and handbag.

As they stepped down from their coach, Brooke said again, "Really, Fran, you do an incredible job of coordinating outfits borrowed in pieces from a host of women."

"The host only adds up to three women. Make it four if you count me; the shoes and handbag are mine."

"No. It's three...."

Bernard laughed and said, "Stop it, you two. Lieutenant Lemoine is coming to meet us."

He met them on the wharf well ahead of the warship, which was larger than Francesca expected. The party had already started on the main deck. Lemoine greeted them, bowed, and kissed Francesca's gloved right hand.

Aboard the ship, Lemoine strutted about with Francesca on his arm introducing her, repeating that she didn't speak French and that he would happily interpret for her. She thought *why he's showing me off like a prized ornament or perhaps as a great fish he has caught. He's going out of his way to make sure we're seen together by rich important looking people. She*

*shook her head. I guess I'm only beginning to learn the strange
ways of men.*

After she met the *Catinet's* captain, Lemoine tapped an
obvious aristocrat's shoulder and said, "Pardon me, sir. Your
Excellency, Consul General Count De Mejan, please allow me
to introduce Mademoiselle Francesca Dumas, a merchant of
machines here in your city of duty."

Francesca stifled the urge laugh aloud. She thought *so
quickly, I've risen from clerk to merchant. I wonder what kind
of machines Count De Mejan thinks I sell. Oh, well, I hope my
smile does not betray my amusement.*

De Mejan was gracious. He bowed and kissed her hand. In
this manner, she met all the officers of the ship and the New
Orleans French Consulate. Next, Lemonine introduced a
handsome well-dressed businessman. "Monsieur Charles
Heidsieck of Reims, please...."

He interrupted. "Mademoiselle, I am Charles Camille
Heidsieck. How are you this very beautiful evening?"

"I am well, sir. I do hope your fine champagne is aboard
this vessel. I have not seen it about New Orleans since the start
of this dreadful war."

Charles beamed and offered his arm. "Well, let's get some
for you straight away. It is quite gratifying to meet Americans
who are familiar with products of our house. This way please."

Francesca curtsied again and placed her free hand on
Charles's arm and in minutes, near the stern, the threesome was
toasting each other.

"Perhaps, you and your friends can find my products at
Rusha's Imported Wines and Liquor, one of my best American
vendors. The bartender tonight is the accountant there. Mlle.
Dumas, permit me to introduce M. Joseph Marks."

Marks nodded said, "You and you friends will be welcome
at Rusha's."

Francesca curtsied and said, "Thank you. I shall look forward to seeing you there."

While the Marks poured another round, Francesca caught the eye of Troy Dodson at amidships, who was walking without a limp. He smiled and waved. She smiled and nodded. She noticed that both Charles and Marks waved to Troy. She thought hmmm. It's a small world.

"Momentarily, an aide to Count De Mejan said in French, "M. Heidsieck, here is another late dispatch from a CSA agent. Please add it to the diplomatic pouch."

"Does this latest dispatch go to the Mobile Consul?"

"Everything in the pouch goes to him. He knows what to do."

"I have another question, why can't I just take any boat to Mobile?"

"Don't ask. Just get on the *Dick Keyes* every time. She sails Tuesday."

As the aide turned to leave, Lemoine was answering Francesca's question about the mast and their display of a plain blue flag with a single white star at its center beside the Stars and Bars." Minutes later, the party-goers were singing lusty renditions of 'Dixie' and Harry McCarthy's 'The Bonnie Blue Flag'."

* * *

Sunday, May 25, the family gathered at Ada's house for dinner that was traditionally served at about two o'clock. Ada and Edna prepared cornbread, red beans and rice, and gumbo made from crabs, crawfish, sausage, okra, tomatoes, and onions; while Francesca worked in her room to write her *Catinet* report for General Butler and review the material in Joachim's satchel for clues. Anna, Laura, and Tony sat in the kitchen within earshot discussing General Butler's orders #29 and #30. They expressed great pleasure in the fact that Butler, with order #30, restricted the actions the banks were wont to take.

Tony said, "The bank people have maligned Butler and called him everything but a child of God. Scream as they might, the banks will not leave the citizenry, rich or poor, with the short end of the stick as they did last September in the switch to Confederate notes."

Anna asked, "So my Confederate notes can be redeemed until Tuesday for silver?"

Laura said, "Yes, or for good ol' United States notes!"

Tony added, "I heard on the street that Butler's orders 29 and 30 are worth at least a reinforcement of twenty thousand troops. And I for one believe it."

Anna frowned. "What does that mean?"

"It means Butler has won the hearts of the vast majority of New Orleanians."

Laura said, "We need to remember that there is a minority who still want to make mischief, and, I'll wager there are Secesh sympathizers in what you called a majority. Why, just yesterday, that witch, Martha sends for me; wanting me to design a pattern so some Secesh heifers can make a flag for one o' Beauregard's regiments up at Corinth."

Tony teased, "Seems as if it's been a lil' while since you heard from yo' baby sis."

"Not long enough!"

Anna said, "Pardon me. But why do you call your little sister a witch?"

Francesca stood in the doorway and answered, "Martha Corlin is white and a daughter of Auntie Laura's mother's former owner. He manumitted her before Auntie was born. Martha calls herself Auntie Laura's foster sister because they were born a month apart and raised on breast milk from the same woman, Auntie Laura's mother.

"Auntie, after we eat, please fill me in on this flag business, including Martha's address."

Edna caught Francesca's eye with a knowing look.

Chapter 20

Wed, 28 May

F. Dumas: At 0800, Thu, 29 instant. Go to G. Stone for a further message. J.M.

Francesca said, "Good morning, sir."

Major Stone smiled, handed her an envelope, and said, "In this envelope is a twenty-five dollar bonus for your fine work Saturday last. Your report led to the arrest of M. Charles Heidsieck aboard the *Dick Keyes*. He was carrying Confederate dispatches and contraband information in a diplomatic pouch."

Francesca felt sad and her face showed it. She said, "What will happen to him?"

"Well, first off, General Butler sent him to be held at Fort Jackson. What is likely to happen next? He'll be tried. We usually hang spies."

She thought he seemed as though he was such a nice man, and handsome, too. On second thought, maybe he really is a good man, just working for the wrong side. *Yes, that's how I'll think of him.* "Oh."

"General Butler also issued an order banning the singing of rebel songs, including 'Dixie' and 'The Bonnie Blue Flag'. He will emphasize this when the captain of the *Catinet* responds to the general's written 'invitation' to come calling at headquarters.

"Good work, Francesca."

"Thank you, sir."

* * *

On Thursday, there were few clients entering the Browne Agency. Though she could not examine her notes, she sat staring out the window across Camp Street toward the City

Hotel, but not seeing passersby while trying to sort myriad notes in her head. Francesca thought *pride, get outta my way. I've got to see Detective Rousseau. I'm lost. Emily, where are you?*

At five sharp, Francesca bolted from Browne's and six minutes later was inside City Hall, five blocks away. The desk sergeant immediately waved her forward and ushered her into Rousseau's office. While waiting, she examined her ledger and scraps of paper.

Rousseau rushed in sweating, huffing, and puffing. As he stuffed papers into his satchel, he said, "Francesca, it's good to see you again. But please forgive me. I must run. General Butler has assigned a new provost-marshal, Colonel Jonas French, and a provost-judge by the name of Major Joseph Bell. Both officers are waiting to meet with me and other detectives."

"At this hour?"

Rousseau shook his head as he moved past Francesca for the open door. "Yes, dammit, at this hour. It's like this around here every day. I'm sorry, I've done nothing on your case since I last saw you. But I've been to many bloody meetings!"

Francesca was crestfallen. Her eyes brimmed with tears. "Sir, I'm in over my head. I need your advice. I'll try not to ask too much. When can I see you? Please, sir....?"

Rousseau stopped in the hallway and looked back at a dejected Francesca. After a moment, he said, "Meet me here at six sharp Monday morning."

Francesca shouted to an empty hallway, "Yes, sir! I'll be here!"

Chapter 21

At two minutes past six on Monday morning, June 2, Rousseau led Francesca from his office to a chalkboard equipped classroom in the tax collectors' area of City Hall. There, she munched her sausage and jelly biscuit, followed by an egg biscuit. Rousseau provided tea.

"Let's get started. Our time will pass before you can say Jack Frost. We'll have to vacate this room and I'll be off to another meeting. Where do you want to start?" Rousseau held his cup in one hand and erased the chalkboard with the other.

"Sir, I've made many notes on scraps of paper and in my ledger. I've tried many times to connect these notes and let them help me make conclusions. Worse, the documents I've collected since we last met have not helped me."

"Documents? What kind of documents?"

"A friend suggested I should find Joachim's satchel. I have his papers."

Rousseau dropped the eraser and walked toward Francesca. "This is great! Is your friend a detective or military officer?"

"Oh, no, sir. She's a slave. Er, only not anymore. She was manumitted a few weeks ago."

With a confused face, Rousseau stopped in his tracks. "Huh? I mean that's good. But, how…."

"Oh, she's a friend of mine. We go to the same church.

"Hmmm. Sir, are you thinking what I think you're thinking?"

Blank-faced, Rousseau nodded and said, "Probably."

"My friend and I were manumitted on the same day by General Butler."

Rubbing his chin and blinking rapidly, Rousseau sank onto a chair. "Oh, my, my. You're right. I thought you were white. Hmmm, I must re-order my thinking. First, the Yankees came.

Now, like I've been told, I just assumed nig...., ah, colored people to be unintelligent. You and your friend have squashed that lie in my head, but good. I must also tell you that some time ago; I told my wife if we had a daughter I'd want her to be like you..., still do...."

Francesca saw the old man's hand tremble as his words trailed off. "M. Rousseau, that's the kindest and most sincere thing anyone has said to me in a long while." She stood beside him with a hand on his shoulder. "Thanks, Pa."

Flushed, Rousseau looked up smiling and said, "I couldn't ask for a better daughter."

* * *

Half past seven was approaching and Rousseau had covered most of the space on the chalkboard with multicolored chalk. He had separate sections for his two types of maps. The first he called 'facts & items' where he included sources, objects, and documents, dating each. Second, he scribbled on the side: 'set priorities'." Third, Rousseau drew connecting lines with arrowheads between selected facts and items. Fourth, he used dashed lines to avoid repeating ground already covered or dead leads. To further illustrate his method, he listed several items from Francesca's notes and they worked together to connect them.

His second type of map was for locations and the events that occurred there. Francesca made a miniature sketch in her ledger of the area between the levee, ambush site, and hospital. Rousseau ended by describing two cases he had solved and repeated, "Please remember, this is just my method. I hope you can use bits of it. Further, I've not seen two cases that were exactly alike in all my years of police work."

"I see. I also see my task as more daunting."

Rousseau took a quick look at his pocket watch and gave the stem a wind. "Fran, your case is complex by any standard. It will take some time. But you can solve it by applying some organization and method."

"I must. I will."

Stepping toward the door at ten minutes before eight, Rousseau said, "Now, you're talking. You can, in time.

"Okay. I hope this helps."

"Oh, I see tremendous progress in less than two hours. Pa, thank you very much."

Again, Rousseau flushed. "Welcome." Then, smiling, he exited and mumbled, "D-daughter...."

* * *

Mon, 2 June

F. Dumas:

At 1000, Tu, 3 instant. Go to G. Stone for instructions.

J.M.

The door was ajar in the small office adjoining General Butler's office where Francesca sat with Major Stone. Stone whispered, "Any minute now, a woman the general sent an orderly to fetch will enter. You're to provide facts to the general if need be."

"Yes, sir."

Momentarily, an orderly knocked and was admitted with the woman. General Butler lifted Francesca's report from his desk and glanced at it. He said to the woman, "Is this Mrs. Martha Corlin?"

"Yes, General."

"Living at Race and Coliseum Streets?"

"Yes."

"Well, Mrs. Corlin, my information is that in your recent sewing bees, you have made a flag to be sent to one of Beauregard's regiments. I'd like to have that flag for some folks in my home town, for they have never seen a Confederate flag. Won't you please go with my orderly and get that flag and bring it here?"

Martha's jaw dropped. She gasped and said, "General, you must be mistaken; you've been misinformed as to the person."

Francesca sat up in her chair. Major Stone placed a finger across his lips.

"You and I both know you had that flag made. Let's not have a fuss made about it and have me require a party of soldiers to go and take your house apart. As you will recall, the flag is hidden under your pillow.

"Orderly, take Mrs. Corlin to the house from which you brought her and return her with the flag.

"You can go, madam."

"May I ask you a question, General?"

"Oh, certainly; I will do my best to answer."

"Which one of those girls gave information about the flag?"

"Oh, I can't tell you that, madam. I must protect my sources."

"I know, I know. One of them has been seen walking with a Yankee officer."

With an amused voice, Butler said, "Oh, but you may falsely accuse her. It may be one of your servants."

Francesca flinched and held her breath. Again, Stone put a finger to his lips.

"No, it was not one of my servants, General; that won't do. The only one of my family that knows anything about it is my foster sister, the daughter of my nurse brought up with me from the same breast. She would never tell."

"Oh, well, I am glad you have such faithful servants."

With both hands over her mouth, Francesca held her giggles.

Chapter 22

At half past six on Sunday afternoon, June 8, Troy sat on the lower Belle Chasse veranda facing west with Theodore Packwood smoking long Cuban cigars. Packwood had just insisted that not enough time had passed for Louisiana markets to adjust and give a clear picture of real estate values. Now, the two men were quiet for a time watching Packwood's grandchildren play in the waning sunlight.

Troy broke the silence. "Why the hell didn't Droopy Eye pardon William Mumford?"

Packwood looked at Troy. "Weren't you in town most of last week?"

"Yeah. But I don't claim to know Yankee ways."

"Instead of testing your knowledge of Yankee ways, let's apply some logic and see where we come out."

"Okay by me. Shoot."

"Let's go back a bit and look at ol' Butler's behavior last week. Why didn't he let the bankers fuck the people in the currency change over?"

Tugging at his mustache, Troy hesitated, and then said, "I guess he hates bankers as much as the next man."

"That may well be. In addition, I think he knew in his gut that there'd be hell to pay if the people got shafted again in another currency switch in eight months. My guess is he, like me, could see in his mind's eye blood running in the streets. Then, his ol' goose woulda really been cooked, well done to crispy."

Troy smiled as Packwood laughed at his own words. Troy crossed his legs and said, "I like it. But what in blazes does that have to do with hanging Mumford? I see no connection."

Packwood pitched forward in his rocker and pointed to Troy with his cigar and said, "I think Butler's second currency edict was more to do with maintaining order among the citizenry than about the bankers. Order, my man, public order.

"Now, recall last night when you gave me a rundown on the actions of the mob present in the hours leading up to Mumford's execution."

Nodding, Troy said, "Yeah, they were a rough armed bunch, cussing and threatening ol' Droop."

"As I recall, you named several gamblers, like Mumford himself, enforcers, and some known criminals all yelling for Butler to pardon Mumford – or else."

"Why not pardon? Day before yesterday, he pardoned six fellows sentenced to death."

"Pardoning the six minions who broke their parole 'cause they didn't know any better shows the man ain't no dummy. I see it as a good use of mercy."

"What?"

Packwood ignored Troy. "Now, on the other hand, if he pardoned Mumford, a man who ripped down the United States flag off the United States Mint and dared the government to arrest him, was tried, convicted, and sentenced to death; Butler's words and orders wouldn't be worth the paper they're written on. That stupid showman, crowd pleasing, drunkard Mumford, oughta have had good sense enough to know he'd be hung. Now, this is the thing: if Butler backed down and pardoned the stupid sonovabitch, speaking as a son of the Confederacy myself, I predict Butler woulda had mob rule in the streets, starting yesterday afternoon. That was all about public order, my man, public order."

Troy lit another cigar. He thought the ol' man is only a borderline patriot. *Though he makes Butler look good, I can't find fault with his logic.* Blast him. "Okay. Makes sense. So, Butler's saving his own skin, huh?"

"In a manner o' speaking, yes."

No matter how true, Troy was tired of the Butler-Mumford debate. He blew blue smoke toward the ceiling and said, "By the way, I need a favor."

"Shoot."

"I met a fine lady at the ball a coupla weeks ago."

Packwood turned and offered his hand. "Well, congratulations, my man!"

"No. Not like you think. She probably wouldn't have me. But I think she'll try to help me so's I can find the right gal."

Packwood shook ashes from his cigar. "What's wrong with this one, ugly? Puny? Both?"

"Oh, no! She's beautiful and quite healthy. What's wrong is she's too damn smart and independent for me. Even if she went for me, I have no doubt; we wouldn't last a month."

Packwood began rocking again. "So, how can I help?"

"I wanna make a good impression on her. Will you let your kitchen and serving niggers help me entertain her and two of her friends for a one o'clock dinner in your house on the third Friday instant?"

"O'course."

Chapter 23

Edna returned her blackberry beignet to her plate and touched Francesca's hand. "Fran, I'm so sorry to hear about your loss."

They sat in their usual corner at Café Du Monde for a midday Saturday meal. Edna had stopped at the Browne Agency at noon and the friends had walked to the French Market enjoying singing birds and the blossoms of late spring along their way. After their food arrived, Francesca had broken the news that François was found dead in the empty kitchen of his defunct restaurant.

Francesca dabbed her favorite apple beignet in brown sugar sprinkled on her plate. She could feel sadness on her face. The news had come to her at the agency in a note from Ada on Friday, June 13. Now, a day later, she was still trying, without success, to gather good memories of François. Lost in thought, her hand stopped moving but still held a corner of her beignet against the sugar.

At length, her eyes focused on Edna. She said, "Thank you, my friend. You're kind and caring. I so appreciate your friendship. But as I told Ma last night; I'm having a difficult time feeling sorrow for my father. I can barely remember him being where I needed him when I needed him, not at Christmas, or my first day of school, or my confirmation, or my first ballroom dance. Staring into space and dry-eyed, Ma just nodded and stroked my hand. I have a feeling that she, too, was searching her memory for the rare moments of happiness with Pa. I'm sure she had such moments with him when they were young. That'd be before gambling and binge drinking took him away from us. He'd lose which was most of the time, and then, according to Ma, drink himself into oblivion even before I was born. Growing up, I saw it for myself the few times he'd come around. Ma said it got worse last year, and still worse this year. She said if he'd lived he'd be homeless, for today the new owner of the restaurant is taking possession. Such a wasted life.... I think my sadness is about what could have been; what I missed, not what I miss.....

"Ma claims that Pa died on purpose, probably drank himself to death. But how can that be? Can one do such? Why would he do that?"

"Fran, I don't know. Perhaps he simply saw no reason to live and willed himself to die...."

"Aided and abetted by alcohol from the empty bottles found scattered about his body."

"Fran, I'm very sorry. What can I do to help?"

"Oh, I think there is nothing to be....

"Wait!" Francesca's face brightened. "You can help me celebrate a new man in my life. I'm not to live a life of tragedy. I'm sure of it!"

Edna folded her arms and frowned. "I know bein' peeved at Joachim helped you get over his two-timing self really quick. But ain't it still too early to be talkin' about bein' in love again?"

With an impish grin, Francesca said, "He's an older fellow, and very wise. I'm very happy to have him in my life. I can't wait for you to meet him."

"At your age, I have to ask how old is old. Over thirty, like me, could be considered old by folks like you."

Francesca ignored Edna; she said, "Edna, he's the smartest and most patient man I ever met."

"Most of'em seem that way when you first meet'em. Stop yo' gushin'. Who is the ol' buzzard?"

"And he's already told his wife about me!"

Edna's face showed abject horror and she covered both ears. She mumbled, "Oh, my Lawd..."

Francesca was grinning from ear to ear. "I've known him for a few weeks and Monday of last week, we came to a deep and mutual understanding." She looked about and then said, "He is Detective Philipe Rousseau!"

Edna's eyes went wide. Louder, she repeated, "Oh, my Lawd!"

Still grinning, Francesca said, "Detective Rousseau is my new *Pa!*"

At first, Edna's face showed confusion, and then she smiled. Next, she tucked her lower lip under her upper teeth, made a ball of her cotton napkin, and hurled at Francesca. Laughing, Francesca caught the napkin before it struck her face.

"Chile, you nearly gave me a heart attack or stroke or somethin'! Enough o' yo' jokes at the expense o' ol' peoples like me."

"Oh, stop it. You're not even forty, yet."

Edna was settling back into her seat and looking her regular self again. She said, "Seriously, is there some new development with Philipe?"

"Yes! He told me he had said to his wife if they had a daughter, he'd want her to be like me! I was deeply touched. So, since last week, I call him 'Pa' and he calls me 'Daughter'. Then, my natural pa up and dies. Ain't that something?"

* * *

Three streetcars later, the bell at St. Patrick's Catholic Church rang out four o'clock. They stood with Edna's purchases at St. Charles and Canal Streets waiting to say good-bye as Edna would board a Prytania Street Line streetcar for the long leg of her journey back to the Buissons.

"You're quiet and melancholy. Is it yo' pa?"

Francesca sighed. "No. It's Em. I'm doing a poor job of finding her. Soon, it will be two months since I last saw her."

"I'm doing bad for Emily, too." Edna rummaged through her cloth handbag and fished out an envelope bearing Francesca's name. "I almost forgot. Mme. Buisson asked me to give you this. I think it has to do with your investigation."

Francesca stuffed the envelope into her handbag and sighed. "Detective Rousseau, I mean, Pa took two hours of his day to teach me how to organize my investigation. Every time I start, I hit a roadblock. And this is after he gave me this great talk and created a large diagram for me to follow on a chalkboard. Some days, I think I'm back in Sister Juliette's Algebra class where I was never any good. Like then, this investigation strains my pea brain. It actually makes my head feel as if parts in one side are straining against parts in the opposite side."

Edna said, "Stop kickin' yourself. These things take time."

"Yeah, but I can't even make my notes into the structure he suggested on that chalkboard."

"What are you usin' for a board?"

"I'm trying to piece together sheets of paper from a writing tablet…."

"Humph! I can fix that small problem. You'll hafta make dem notes work. That's your part. Come with me."

"Where're we going?"

As they walked, Edna laughed. "As folks in Mississippi say, 'we're going to see a man about a horse'."

* * *

Several blocks later, they arrived at an office on number 70 Camp Street with lettered front windows that read: *New Orleans Daily Crescent*. Edna opened the door and a small bell announced their presence. A man emerged from a back room wiping his ink stained fingers on a long dirty apron. "Good afternoon. I'm James Nixon. May I help you?"

Smiling, Edna said, "Good afternoon, Mr. Nixon, sir. Why you sho' can. You may not 'member me. Sir, I'm Edna Black and I know you likes your steaks well done. You and me met at the Buissons."

Nixon's face brightened. "Oh, yes. Of course, I remember. How are Edouard and Maria?"

"Oh, dey's all fine. Mr. Nixon, sir, dis heah is a family friend, Mlle. Francesca Dumas. I'd be much obliged if you can spare a few o' yo' misprinted pages with a blank side for a lil' project Mlle. Dumas is workin' on."

Chapter 24

On Friday morning, June 20, Anna served sassafras tea, first to Brooke, then Bernard, and finally to Francesca in the parlor of her three story urban house. She poured tea for herself and sat next to Francesca.

Brooke said, "I really like this dress and I think it's appropriate for the dinner this afternoon."

Bernard gestured with both hands as he said, "Brooke, don't you see? Fran's advice is not about whether your dress is appropriate for this engagement or not. I understand her reasoning and, frankly I want to follow her advice and err on the side of caution. Had I known this morning that this is the same dress you wore the day the killer may have seen you, I would have burned it."

Brooke laughed with the women. Then, she said, "Now Bernie, why would you burn a perfectly good dress that I paid your good money for?"

"Because, I love you."

Brooke flushed and beamed. Francesca applauded. Anna's grin displayed teeth and delight. She clasped her hands together in front of her chin.

Francesca pointed to the clock above the mantle and said, "So, Brooke, it's settled at twenty past eight. We'd best quick find something for you to wear. As Anna said, you can chose from her clothes and mine to make an outfit. It's time we get busy. You know how I hate being late."

* * *

At nine o'clock, Francesca announced from the stairs, "M. Williams, we present Mme. Williams!"

Francesca and Anna stood on either side of the stairs applauding. Brooke gracefully descended the stairs like a woman at the center of attention. She wore Anna's brown skirt, Ada's brown small brim hat still on loan to Francesca, and Francesca's white ruffle front blouse with Anna's white and orange silk scarf about her waist as a sash. The scarf hid gathers in the skirt where they had raised it, for Brooke was two inches shorter than Anna or Francesca. Brooke had added one of Able's brown wild turkey feathers to Ada's hat.

Bernard applauded. "Bravo! Bravo!"

* * *

The *Atlantic,* a sternwheeler, got underway at ten past ten from wharf number six for the short river trip to Belle Chasse. Bernard had chartered the small steamer for the day.

Francesca stood alone near the bow, far from the smoke belched aft by the *Atlantic's* steam engine. She thought the *Atlantic* had seen its best days and ought to be refurbished or scrapped as soon as Monday. She hoped it would last the day. Approaching Slaughterhouse Bend, she was reminded of her first riverboat trip the previous spring at age seventeen to Mobile and the end of her virginity. Francesca thought having money would mean having small pleasures like a day off from one's regular routine without worrying about making ends meet. She sighed. *That's what I had with Joachim, though eventually I would have had to get my head around the fact that I'd have to share him with Francine.* She looked over her shoulder for Brooke though she did not expect her to emerge from her cabin. Francesca turned back to face the wide brown waters of the Mississippi River. She *thought if she could hear my mind, Brooke would say, 'you have two fish on your hooks; girl decide, Alfonse or Troy, and then throw one back, either one will do. It doesn't matter much which you keep. Then, live like me.' I guess she has a point. But, if I had to choose today from among the men I know now, I would choose none. I know only one I'd consider. But I don't know nearly enough about Marcelle to be sure because I purposely ignore him. I'm certain we would fail in our work if, as Mr. Mahan and Major Stone would say, 'we got mixed up together.' Yes, I know they're right. And I certainly don't need to get fired, not now. So I'll continue ignoring Marcelle and think about all that later. Wait a minute, fool. Choosing Marcelle would be too stupid. Can't you see already he ain't got a damn cent to his name? She sighed. But, it's clear to me, he has good sense.*

Brooke called from the stair to the second deck. "Hey, Fran. Com'ere."

* * *

At fifteen minutes before one o'clock, the *Atlantic* set down its gangplank on Belle Chasse's west bank landing. Troy had sent a carriage to fetch them. Twenty minutes later, they were seated at Packwood's dining room table. Troy brought Packwood in for a quick introduction. Packwood briefly glad-handed each guest and said upon exiting the dining room, "Bon appetite! Y'all hollow if ol' Troy ain't treatin' ya right. Y'all younguns go 'head and enjoy your stay at Belle Chasse."

The Williams and Francesca laughed. Francesca thought Troy was nervous and struggling to smile. She thought hmmm. He really is wound tight.

After dinner, Troy arranged for a servant to give the Williams a tour of the house. He also gave the servant strict orders to venture no further than the grounds of the big house. He sat alone with Francesca on a shaded side of the lower veranda. When he asked if it was okay to smoke, Francesca said, "Yes. But let's swap chairs so I'm up wind."

While Troy lit his cigar, Francesca asked, "How long since you sat here with a woman?"

Troy hesitated, puffing his cigar, and then said, "Last time was before I joined the army last spring."

"Where is she?"

"She got married last summer."

"If she's what you're looking for, describe her personality for me."

"To tell the truth, I don't know what I'm looking for, except I want a wife who can be the gracious hostess once I own Belle Chasse."

Francesca thought *I don't think I'll mention this to Brooke. She'd deliver me to Belle Chasse hogtied and gaged and ask Troy to 'sign here!'* She smiled, "If you're not careful, you could finish your search by midnight tomorrow."

Troy bolted upright, eyes wide, spilling cigar ashes on his suit. "What? How?"

"If what you told me is all you want, I could find for you a number of candidates who'd jump at the chance to be your wife and hostess here."

Troy was still on the edge of his seat, frowning. "That quickly?"

"Yes. Are you sure that's all you want?"

"W-w-well, er, ah, I-I don't actually know. What I mean is I don't understand what you're asking me."

Francesca sat up and placed her hands together on her lap. She spoke slowly and quietly. "Troy, a quadroon, like me, or an octoroon, has no chance in New Orleans life except to attract, by whatever means necessary, a white man who will support her and her offsprings. Why? Free men of color don't want the trouble of a wife who looks white and can cause him to be shot, hung, or beaten to death. She would not have money enough to buy an enslaved man. He would have no education plus she would own him, so you can imagine the rest. Such a woman would find you to be a dream come true. She would be all yours for the taking that is if you don't mind having a woman who only wants what you have and not want you for the man you are."

Francesca leaned back in her chair as did Troy. They sat in silence until his cigar burned his fingers.

At length, he said, "You've made plain for me what I had no eyes to see." He went silent again. Francesca thought for sure, he's hatching a scheme to seek out a sister who will gladly cross over, become white, and do his bidding. *I could do this – not with him, but a man like him, like that Mark Donohue. Or can I? Why don't I know the answer to this question after all I've been through? Merde. I tire me. Dammit.*

Francesca answered a few more questions for Troy before she and the Williams left for the landing and their four o'clock rendezvous with the *Atlantic*.

Chapter 25

When Francesca and Edna finished their dinner at Café du Monde on Saturday, June 21, Edna said, "As teens, I hope Rebecca and Rachel don't have to make decisions about questions as difficult as the ones you face. I commend you for your perseverance. And I pray for you. Yesterday, while you were at Belle Chasse giving advice, I thought perhaps it would benefit you to hear some advice yourself. I have a friend who helped me adjust to my new life, a life I didn't choose; a life without my daughters and husband. She is a wise elder and compassionate beyond her years. Over time, I learned her story and it reminds me a great deal of where you are in your life. I think she can connect with you in a way far different from me or Anna."

Francesca thought oh, no. Edna wants to help, but has really missed the mark this time. The old woman is probably wise, but is surely outta touch with my kind of problems. But I can't hurt Edna's feelings. Perhaps, in time she'll forget about this. "Well, maybe later, I can go see her."

"Though she's sick, she agreed to see you this afternoon. I think talking to a quadroon like her...."

Francesca leapt from her chair. "What? She's a quadroon? Let's go! I wanna meet this woman!"

Edna grinned and collected her empty shopping basket and bags. "Okay."

Moving toward the door, Francesca turned and asked, "What's her name?"

"Mother Henriette."

Francesca stopped and held her head with both hands. "Oh, mon Dieu! Mère Henriette Delille!"

"What, chile? What's the matter?"

"She was my schoolmistress! It never occurred to me that she would know what plaçage was! Why, of course, she would! Oh, my God...."

* * *

Aboard the Esplanade Street streetcar, Edna asked, "By the way, is Mr. Nixon's paper of any use?"

"Oh, yes. Thanks again. Mr. Nixon's big pages save me from having to remember scattered notes or trying to find some little scrap of paper. Why, already, I've organized and transferred all the notes and started on documents. Best of all, I can see many puzzle pieces at the same time. I feel hopeful again. The problem now is time. With this job, I only get to work on it nights and weekends. For example, I'll have to interview folks on Sundays who were foreclosed upon.

"You're the solution lady. Do you have a solution for time?"

They laughed and Edna said, "Not now, but soon's I do, I'ma have to keep it for myself!"

* * *

From the Plauché Street streetcar stop, they walked briskly to St. Bernard Avenue and turned left. When Francesca saw the old house where she studied Religion, English, French, Rhetoric, and tried to learn Algebra, she stopped and let her memories flood back. She tilted her head and said, "Now, the house looks so much smaller than it appeared when I was last here."

"At your age, five years is a very long time. You were only fourteen and your legs were shorter."

"And I thought I was so smart but didn't know diddley."

They were laughing when the front door opened and Sister Juliette Gaudin stepped outside to greet them. "Sister Black, it's always good to see you. Now, who is this little stranger with you? Wait, wait, and don't tell me." Sister Gaudin tilted her head from side to side. "She looks vaguely familiar. Oh, my, it's my favorite Algebra student! Francesca, darling, I welcome you back to the scene of the crime!"

Francesca thought her own smile was that of a school girl trying to please a teacher. She didn't feel grown up at all. She felt odd. "Yes, Sister Julie, it's me."

Sister Gaudin smiled and corrected Francesca. "It is I."

Francesca thought, *I knew that. Am I reverting to the child I was....? Am? Oh, Phooey!* "Yes, ma'am. By the way, Sister Julie, you may be happy to know that one of your students, Annabelle Cocks, still remembers how to solve for the missing side of a right triangle."

"Oh, my. It's always good to learn that some of the seeds one plants yield fruit. Thank you for letting me know."

And then, Sister Gaudin took each woman under an arm. Her warm smile disappeared and she lowered her voice. "Sister Black, as you recall from last Sunday, I reported that my dear friend, Henriette, was doing poorly. She seems even worse since yesterday."

Edna said, "We can come back at another time."

Sister Gaudin shook her head. "I told Henriette the same thing. But she insists on seeing Francesca today. Considering this, please let me ask you to make your stay brief and not tax her."

* * *

Inside, Francesca did not recognize her schoolmistress. Francesca thought the gaunt pale woman sitting by the window in a rocking chair pruning a potted plant could not be the energetic Mother Delille she remembered; a woman being everywhere at once correcting or cajoling as necessary. Though it was early June, Mother Delille wore long sleeves with a wool shawl about her shoulders. Her lap and legs were covered by a colorful quilt. Her habit covered most of her brunette hair. She thought Mother Delille looked much older than her fifty years, and that hacking dry cough.... *Maybe we should go.* She looked back for Edna, but Edna was closing the door and remaining in the hallway with Sister Gaudin.

Mother Delille made a small wave of her frail hand and said, "Come, my child. Sit with me and let's enjoy the afternoon sun."

"Yes, ma'am. My name is Francesca...."

Interrupting, Mother Delille smiled and said, "Mademoiselle Dumas, I know perfectly well who you are. You were in my initial class to prepare for Holy Communion back in '53. And I'm praying for poor François's soul. I offer my sincere condolences to you. How's Ada?"

Francesca stopped in her tracks. Her eyes widened as she thought whatever her sickness, it surely has not affected her head! Momentarily, Francesca dragged a chair from a desk and sat before Mother Delille's knees. She said, "Thank you for the class, for your prayers for my father's soul, and thank you for inquiring about my mother. My mother is very well, thank you. Now, how about you? Are you feeling up to my visit?"

"Mme. Black asked me to see you. I am happy to do God's will as well as He will give me strength to do so."

Francesca blinked and sat up straight. She thought *where shall I begin?* Before she could collect her thoughts, Mother Delille said, "I learned last year that you had entered into a plaçage agreement with the young banker, a M. Buisson. Mme. Black tells me he tragically just lost his life. Where does his demise leave you?"

Francesca thought *I guess I can just start with now.* She made a sigh and said, "Mother Delille, I have a temporary reprieve from destitution, I have a job. My first thought was I had lost the man who would someday be my husband. You see, I thought he loved me. After his death, his step-mother let me know where I stood."

Mother Delille said, "That is not unusual, that is, in the beginning, perhaps he did love you. But then, his family and social circles point out that he needs natural heirs and he reasons that he must marry a white woman, no matter whether he loved you or not. But, of course, you know this now. Do you believe in the sacrament of marriage?"

Francesca thought *do I?* Then, convinced, she said, "Yes, Mother. I do. I would like to have a husband. But now, I cannot see how that can happen. I feel trapped...."

"Before you look for a husband, Francesca, know who you are. Knowing who you are is an important first step in life. Then, decide your principles and live by them. You are young, yet, and you have time."

"One of my greatest troubles is trying to figure out what or who I am. Only lately, I've noticed that I'm perceived as white."

"Are you?"

Francesca thought, *Uh-oh, I never should have mentioned that. What do I say now?*

Mother Delille took a deep labored breath and coughed several times into a cloth on her lap. At length, she said, "Well, are you white? You cannot give a wrong answer. You are white, black, both, or something else. What do you feel? Who are your friends? But, more important, who are your personal role models? You need not tell me your answer. But I believe when you prayerfully answer these questions within yourself you will know who you are. From that point forward, I expect you'll be able to set a course and follow it."

Astounded by Mother Delille's calm manner and easy forthrightness, Francesca thought *why didn't I think to come here long ago?* "Mother, how did you decide when you were my age?"

"Child, my path took some of the same twists and turns yours has taken. I met a young white man and danced with him and others at quadroon balls." Mother Delille laughed and continued, "Why do you have that incredulous look on your face?" Mother laughed again and, holding up a hand, fell into a spasm of coughs. She took a sip of water and said, "I was not born into this religious community. I fell in love as young women do. First, I had to find out who I was. Only then did I learn that God had planned for me a life of service to the poor and to slaves. Second came the matter of principle: I had to decide that a plaçage arrangement was not for me, and more important, why."

"Mother, can you tell me your reason why?"

"I will, but my guess is you'll need to reach your own why. My why was my strong belief in the sacrament of marriage, period. I fervently believe plaçage is a system of bondage for quadroons and octoroons."

Mother Delille fell silent, her chin resting on her collar bone. Francesca waited. She thought *I have much to think about. My role model, I know, is Auntie Laura. Sorry, Ma. Why is that? Auntie is strong, a great mother, runs a business, and is a partner with her black husband. I will follow in her footsteps. She is more black than white. Now, I realize that I never felt white. I should have known that when I realized I didn't know how to be white. I feel relieved. I've decided something. I am black with no fear of whites, nor do I have illusions about them.*

Mother Delille raised her head.

Francesca stood. "Mother, thank you so very much for your counsel. You have led me to answer one important question and raised more that I had failed to ask myself. Your candid sharing of your path has helped me. Again, I thank you."

Francesca saw a radiant and peaceful smile. Mother Delille said, "Francesca, you should thank God. I am only his instrument. Go in peace, my child."

Chapter 26

Francesca was finishing the last of Ada's catfish and Edna's biscuits leftover from Sunday dinner when Marcelle returned to the agency and dropped a sheaf of papers on the table in front of her. She thought day old cold catfish ain't half bad with vinegar, pepper, and salt as she reached for the papers. She thumbed through the pages searching for the telegram she knew must be there.

Mon, 23 Jun.

F. Dumas and M. Lainez:

At 0800, Tu, 24 Jun meet me and G. Stone.

J.M.

* * *

At breakfast the next morning, Anna said, "Don't worry, too much. Fran, you've come so far. I just know you're going to find Emily soon, probably before dog days are here."

Francesca rearranged her crawfish atop her grits for the third time. She bit an apple jelly biscuit and, while chewing, said, "Yeah, but the right time is now. Try to imagine being in her place while trying to keep hope alive."

"Aren't there any more foreclosed people to interview?"

"Alas, I interviewed the last one Sunday. Now, I'm trying to figure what to do next. True, they are a most unhappy lot. But my guess is none of them murdered their mortgagor."

"Did you look again for any of those scraps of paper you call notes that may have fallen somewhere?"

"Smart Alice…. Oh, my! Look at the time! Girl, I gotta git!" Francesca began shoveling grits into her mouth at a furious pace.

* * *

When Francesca arrived at Major Stone's office, she was surprised by the presence of Sarah Butler who gave her a warm greeting. She was the last to enter the office as the bell at St. Patrick's Catholic Church began the first of eight chimes.

Walking past Major Stone's desk, John Mahan tapped it with his pencil and said, "Let's get started. Francesca and Marcelle, this briefing is high confidential. Nonetheless, you can decide not to undertake this assignment after you hear the details.

"Here's the situation: Secesh General Earl Van Dorn was appointed by Jeff Davis as commander of what Davis calls his Trans-Mississippi District. In plain English, that means Arkansas, Mississippi, and Louisiana. Van Dorn was once one of ours, a West Point grad. Knowing him, as soon as we fail in our foolhardy attempt to divert the Mississippi River's flow away from Vicksburg with a damn canal, I expect he will make a move to retake Baton Rouge as a stepping stone back to New Orleans. Van Dorn needs a victory. He's still smarting after we defeated him at Pea Ridge and he needs to get back into Davis's good graces. Getting New Orleans back would make him a hero."

Francesca shuddered. She thought *Oh, merde! We're not safe? Have I made a premature dismissal of the Secesh? Can we go back into slavery? My home, my family…. Oh, mon, Dieu!*

She was focused now; Emily was out of her mind for the moment. She paid close attention as John said, "On our side, soon's the fiasco at Vicksburg is over, General Butler will order General Williams back downriver to defend Baton Rouge.

"Okay. This is our mission: find out and report at the earliest possible time Van Dorn orders the movement of troops by his generals, primarily Breckenridge and Ruggles. We will accomplish this objective by establishing a telegraph intercept and listening post, or LP, on the plantation of a friendly Unionist by the name of David Carpenter. His plantation is near Brookhaven, Mississippi. We will begin construction of our LP by this Friday night and remain in place until the situation clears."

Francesca and Marcelle looked at each other for a long moment, then at Major Stone who pulled on his cigar and blew blue smoke at the ceiling.

John smiled, but otherwise ignored them. He continued, "Let me be clear, we are to give the earliest and most complete alarm possible to Generals Butler and Williams.

"Now, this is my outline for how we go about this mission. I will take both of you to the Carpenter Plantation as newly purchased slaves. My disguise will be that of an agent buying from Thomas Foster's New Orleans Slave Depot and making a delivery. Francesca, we'll need to make you into a colored man by Friday. Why Friday? We'll have a new moon come Friday. That'll give us several dark nights to establish our LP inside one of Carpenter's cabins near the railroad and the telegraph lines. By the end of next week, we'll be back to a rustler's moon.

"The army will outfit us with our needs before we depart. Let me speak plain. That means rations for the first few days of what could be two months in the field. We will live off Carpenter's gardens, weeds, and small game."

Stone said, "In addition to initial rations, we'll provide weapons and ammunition, but no support personnel. You'll be on your own."

Francesca was staring at Major Stone. She had never been away from New Orleans for more than a weekend. She thought *make me colored?* How? Be a slave? Two months on a plantation? What is game?

Sarah interrupted John. "I will help Francesca appear as a young colored man; that is, if she agrees to go on this mission. But there are other considerations. In the field, her body will work the same as it does here. We'll need to assume the maximum time possible for her to be in the field and plan accordingly. You need to be clear so she can know what to expect."

Francesca was startled. She thought *oh, my. In my excitement, I'd forgotten my menses.*

She smiled at Sarah and whispered, "Thank you."

Oblivious, Major Stone dusted his cigar. "Much of what happens in the field can't be planned for. Soldiers cope as situations arise."

John nodded and resumed his seat between Sarah and Stone. "Sarah, you're the makeup expert. I'm counting on you to help Francesca anticipate and prepare. To complicate matters even further, Sarah, I'll need you to teach our colored 'slave Frank Carpenter', a.k.a., Francesca how to change into white 'cousin Frances Carpenter' and back again."

Sarah said, "The only difficulty I see is repeated application of chemicals to her skin, not the wigs or clothing. It will be better if she can remain 'Frank' for the duration."

John lifted his notes again and said, "Okay. The operation will dictate whether we'll need 'Frances' or not. Let's continue. I will accompany you to the Carpenter Plantation and leave you there after the LP is set up.

"I expect you to work out listening shifts. Candidly, this is a boring and tedious assignment, unless you're discovered and need to escape."

Francesca asked, "So I should have plenty of time to work on my investigation. But what about progress with interviews? Two months is double the time poor Emily has already been away. I don't like the idea of adding another day of delay."

John said, "I'll be in and out of New Orleans. If you have a lead you want run to ground, send me a note by way of David Carpenter. I expected that; I'll do the foot work for you. Speaking of notes, let's go over our communications. Here're your code words for June and July." John gave each, Francesca and Marcelle, a page. "For June, the off-set is the second letter of the code word. In July, it'll be the third letter."

Marcelle wanted to know, "Why do we need a code word for each day? Isn't one for each month enough?"

Stone said, "Yeah, I was thinking the same thing. Isn't this overkill and unnecessarily complicated?"

John paused and rubbed his chin. "I've never had an agent compromised or allowed the enemy to learn that my people listened to their communications."

Marcelle looked at Francesca and said, "You know what? Overkill sounds really good."

Laughter.

John handed out two more pages. "These are stolen Secesh code words and offsets. As you see, there is only one word per week. Memorize these before Friday and burn the paper.

"Last instructions: you'll be listening for one message in particular. This will be a telegram from Van Dorn to Breckinridge directing the latter to attack Baton Rouge. Then, and only then, are you to encode and send your alarm telegram to me, including the number of troops and dates. As Major Stone would attest, things don't always go according to plan.

So send any additional telegrams, but only if it's critical knowledge needed by General Butler. I'll trust your judgment.

"Okay. That's it. Let me know by noon if you accept this mission or have more questions."

Francesca was holding the sides of her face with both hands trying to concentrate and recall the questions that had come to mind while John talked.

Marcelle asked, "What do you advise in case of discovery?"

John pointed to his head and said, "I recommend wit over weaponry."

Stone added, "Remember, you'll get no help from the army. Oh, by the way, the Secesh will hang spies."

Though she tried to avoid it, Francesca gulped and put her hands over her mouth.

* * *

It was a Friday like no other in Francesca's memory. She walked in lockstep with Marcelle through the grand ornate rotunda of the St. Louis Hotel at the intersection of St. Louis and Chartres Streets at one o'clock, June 27, just two blocks from the St. Louis Cathedral, three from the Orleans Ballroom, one from François's defunct restaurant, and one and a half from Antoine's. The spacious room was occupied by merchants with goods ranging from bottled remedies for this and that ailment to pictures by this artist or the other to farm implements to people sold as slaves. Each sales person or auctioneer was attempting to out bellow the competition. The din was deafening.

She thought a man was inspecting her. He spoke, not to her, but to the man behind her. He said, "Good afternoon, sir. I'm in need of fine specimens like these. My good fellow, could we forego the block and fix a price here on the side." Francesca thought the man speaking to John Mahan was among the best dressed New Orleans aristocrats she had seen.

John said, "Good afternoon, indeed, sir. I'm Albert Morris in the employ of an out of town buyer. Sorry, but these two are already spoken for. I just concluded the purchase with Mr. Thomas Foster. My task now is to deliver the new owner's merchandise. Perhaps, Mr. Foster may yet have something that will fit your needs."

Francesca stood with her left ankle tied to Marcelle's right; both had their hands tied behind their backs. John held rope leashes connected to their tied hands. In her role, she kept her eyes cast downward and had stopped beside Marcelle when John pulled her leash taunt. Thus began Francesca's life as the black slave boy, Frank Carpenter, age fourteen. She thought oh, my Dieu. Is this what Edna heard? And she must've heard it in this very room. '*Something* that will fit your needs'? *Merchandise? Marcelle and me?* Merde! *This gives me the creeps.*

I thought Sarah's burnt cork, nitrate of silver, lanolin, wooly black minstrel wig, and a modified corset transformed me into black 'Frank', but now I'm beginning to understand what I look like on the outside today has no more meaning than it did last week as to who I am inside. I'm still the same person, but I feel completely different today because of how I'm treated, not seen; unintelligent, deaf and dumb. Though I'd never say so, last week, I felt beautiful and optimistic. Now, I feel less than the 'Frank' I thought I'd be; I'm trying to imagine what animal I really am, certainly not human. No, not a dog for dogs are made to feel companionship. A pig? No, that's food. Hmmm. I've got it! I'm regarded as a work animal like the ones that pulled me so many miles over the years in streetcars. Yes, that's it. I feel like a long eared mule, owned as property and used as a tool to enrich my owner; in short, a bred offspring of an ass. But what do I know? This is only my first day as Frank. Edna's stories could never convey to me the indignity suffered by her soul. Not even close…. I suspect at this moment, I'm being spared lustful eyes, or worse, because I look like a teenage boy. No, I'm beyond speculating; I'm sure of it.

A grim gallows smile momentarily tugged at one corner of Francesca's lower lip. She thought ironic: *nitrate of silver is white; it made my skin black.*

* * *

Francesca thought what if this decrepit contraption of a locomotive breaks down here in the middle of alligator-infested Maurepas Swamp? It did not. The New Orleans, Jackson and Great Northern Railroad's rusty dilapidated steam engine that pulled a passenger car and two freights out of the railhead at New Orleans made a stop at Camp Moore. Several Confederate officers boarded for the trip north to Jackson, Mississippi and beyond. Francesca glanced out the window at Camp Moore with the thought that she may by chance spot General Lovell walking past.

The train arrived in Brookhaven, Mississippi near sunset, forty-seven miles due north of Camp Moore, Louisiana and one hundred thirty-four miles from New Orleans. Albert Morris was told to get his niggers off the depot platform and that they could not use the sidewalk. Further, they were told get out of town by dark. From one of the train's freight cars, they unloaded their supplies, contained in wooden boxes and kegs, and boarded the two wagons driven by David Carpenter's enslaved overseers for the three mile ride south to the plantation. In the dark, they settled into an unoccupied cabin at the end of a row of small unpainted houses for enslaved people closest to the railroad. The cabin's windows were mere openings that could be closed only by the hinged shutters mounted on the outside wall. Lying on her pallet with a haversack as her pillow that Friday night, Francesca saw several stars through the places in the roof where shingles were missing. The cabin had no ceiling. She thought *Mary, Mother of God, I need you to please pray for me in this strange place; oh, and please forgive me for wearing trousers again.*

* * *

Saturday morning, Francesca learned that Major Stone's rations meant bacon, beans, coffee, and hardtack at every meal. She thought I'm sure one can break a tooth trying to eat hardtack. She followed John and soaked hardtack in her tin cup of coffee.

They repaired the roof with shingles provided by David Carpenter. Francesca learned that she could climb the crude sap oozing pine slab ladder and stand on the roof of the cabin. She brought the shingles up while John and Marcelle nailed them in place. They finished the roof at noon and went on a reconnaissance to the railroad and telegraph line beside it, some one hundred feet to the west as the crow flies.

They were eating dinner at one o'clock when John said, "Soon's we finish, let's get started with laying the wire."

Francesca looked at Marcelle, who said, "Okay."

Chewing, Francesca said, "I heard there's an old Mississippi saying that may apply here. 'A body can't tell what he doesn't know.' I believe being seen laying wire can lead to big problems."

John said, "Hmmm. The hands are all off this afternoon and tending their gardens. You're right. I've noticed that we're objects of curiosity. Good point. So when do we string the wire?"

Francesca thought hmmm; of course, Edna would say the hands are only potted plants.

Marcelle said, "Well, the new moon can help conceal us."

John rubbed his chin. "Work in the dark?"

Francesca looked at her dirty hand and reached for another piece of bacon. "Sure, night will hide us from prying eyes."

John said, "We could wait until Monday when the hands all go to the fields."

"The small children will be here and will make it their business to play as close to us as they can. These little pigeons have big ears and even bigger eyes. Believe you me, they will run, not walk, to break the big news of their discovery to the nearest adult. And, if the adult is white, all the better. You can see the cascade from there."

Marcelle laughed. "Yeah, I'm reminded of when my little brother would run and tell everything he knew. Pa would hear my latest escapades and smoke my britches."

John joined the tales. "Uh-huh, your pa must've known my pa. Same thing happened to me when my big sister told the news. Okay, Fran, tell me when and how we lay this wire."

"Well, I haven't given this much thought, except, I'll tell you straight from the shoulder: I'm scared of discovery. Okay. Let's see. So far, not even the overseers that brought us here know we have wire. I feel real comfort in knowing the people here don't know. Let's get some white cloth and make strips about yea long. Once we decide where to lay the wire, these can be our bread crumbs until we're done."

John leapt to his feet. "Brilliant, Gretel!"

"Thanks, Hansel."

Marcelle hunched his shoulders and held his hands up, palms facing up. "Huh? What? Who?"

John was off in a trot toward the cotton weighing shed. He yelled over his shoulder, "Tell Marcelle the story!"

They spent the afternoon following several routes to and from the telegraph line on the east side of the tracks. The Bogue Chitto's two branches converged on the west side of the tracks. Francesca thought some bogue; this thing is a small river. John and Marcelle discovered a steep slope that led to a tributary of Bogue Chitto less than a hundred feet south of their cabin.

John said, "If Confederate scouts discover our wire, they'll be forced to follow it along a path that does not lead directly to the cabin. The bank and bluff will cause them to dismount and make noise climbing giving us warning."

Marcelle said, "Us who? My ass, sir! You'll be long gone!"

John laughed. "True enough."

Francesca followed their chosen route marking the way with materials John found in the shed, scraps of cotton balls left over from the last season, a burlap bag cut into strips, and a ball of twine.

At eleven o'clock Saturday night, the sky was clear. Francesca was happy to learn that John had had the foresight to paint the gutta-percha coated wire brown. Francesca was surprised that she could see by starlight, which she had never experienced on New Orleans's gas lighted streets. They assembled their weapons and armed with Spencer carbines, Francesca and Marcelle took up guard positions about five hundred feet north and south of the pole John climbed to make the interconnect. John used a combination seizing-wire splice at the junction of the mainline and its blue glass insulator mounted on a wooden wedge attached to the pole. In this method, he attached his wire without cutting and having to reconnect the mainline. He wrapped the exposed seizing-wire with Chatterton-Compound tape and hammered staples to hold his invading wire in place down the east side of the pole.

John and Marcelle buried the wire, while Francesca stood watch from a guard position nearby. After fifteen feet or so, Francesca was surprised to see John bury the wire in the bed of the Bogue Chitto tributary. She asked, "John is this wire going to work underwater?"

"This is gutta-percha wrapped twenty-two gauge wire I bought from Western Union. It's even worked for several years on telegraph cables under the sea without leaking electric current. And my guess is the average Secesh patrol will not spot the wire or our camouflaged spade work."

* * *

On Monday, John conducted a refresher class in Morse Code using live telegraph traffic as it occurred. He departed for New Orleans after breakfast the next day, July 1. Over the next several days, Francesca and Marcelle settled into a routine by sharing the chores of chopping wood for the cook fire, drawing water, gathering dandelion greens and blackberries, trips to the vegetable garden, and minding the telegraph concealed and muffed under a quilt. Francesca learned the small children minder was an ancient woman named Aunt Deb. Marcelle and Francesca cut extra firewood and left it to cure in the afternoon sun stacked against Aunt Deb's cabin. They communicated in grunts and nods and never lingered more than two minutes.

Francesca sectioned their cabin with two burlap cotton picker's sacks cut open and hung on a twine line, giving her the privacy of one corner. Both maintained a gruff scowl that kept the plantation children away, and adults, too. Hunting became Francesca's job. After his first turn in the woods, Marcelle said, "Damned if we ain't gonna starve 'fore Van Dorn says the word. We need meat on the table and I can't shoot worth a shit. So, Frank, I'm holding my hat in my hand asking you to *please* go shoot us some dinner."

Francesca returned an hour later with two squirrels.

Marcelle was ecstatic. "You kill'em; I'll clean'em and cook'em!"

* * *

A week after John departed, Marcelle said, "Frank, I see you carefully spread out your papers every day and pour over them for hours. I know you're keen to find your Emily. Now, this is none of my biznis, but are you making any progress?"

They were eating their noon meal. Francesca had in her mouth a bite from the crispy hind leg of a rabbit. She stopped chewing and sighed. Water welled in her eyes as she said, "No."

"I see you work at this day after day. You seem to lay out those large sheets in the same order followed by fewer and fewer scraps of paper. Am I right?"

Francesca was surprised that he had paid attention. She said, "Why, yes. You're right."

Grinning, Marcelle said, "Well, let me put my nose in your biznis and say maybe you should try starting at the far end of your puzzle and work backwards. It could cut down some on your cussing."

She blinked, tilted her head, and said, "Hmmm. I never noticed that I had a set pattern. Perhaps that's what leads me to the same rut every day." She smiled. "That's when I cuss. I think I dread the pieces I seldom look at because I doubt I'll know how to make sense of them."

"I don't know, but taking a look at it from the other end may surprise you. From your study of the front, it could be you know more'n you think you know. Just a thought...."

"Marcelle, thank you. I'll try out your suggestion soon's I finish my dinner."

* * *

At half past one o'clock, Francesca folded her newsprint sheets and laid them aside on the rough plank floor. In their place, she drew from her keg envelopes, ledgers, a register, and a calendar. When she had read all the entries in Joachim's ledgers for March and April, she said, "Merde! *I'm lost....*"

Marcelle was out foraging for firewood. It was Francesca's watch. The clatter of the telegraph started. She heard a short message from Camp Moore to Confederates at Jackson asking for rations. As usual, she struggled to decipher the message. Because he was better at it, she wished Marcelle would take over monitoring the dots and dashes.

Francesca stood and stretched. The cabin was hot even with both doors and both windows open. When she looked down, her eyes settled on Maria's folder. She thought *why have I avoided touching most of what Maria gave me? Do I still dislike her that much or have I for too long relied on my notes from interviewing her? This is not responsible behavior. I have allowed personal bias into my work. Worse, I've been slow to see it. So stop it.* She went to the window and faced the gentle breeze.

After rolling her pallet and using it as a cushion, Francesca began with Maria's folder. An envelope fell from among the papers. The envelope was from Maria, delivered by Edna sometime after the interview. Francesca had used the foreclosure pages, for they included a list of names and addresses for individuals upon whom Joachim had foreclosed. The last page, which she had not previously reached, had only a single entry: Financing application for proposed acquisition of Belle Chasse Plantation in Plaquemines Parish. Current owner: Theodore Packwood.

Francesca leapt from her seat. "Oh, my Dieu!" Then, remembering to avoid using her natural voice, thought *how could I have been so stupid and not see this page until now? I must stop calling myself an investigator. I am a fraud. She began pacing. So Troy did say someday he'd own Belle Chasse. Could he be the one asking Citizens Bank for financing?*

Disgusted, she snatched the envelope bearing her name written in Maria's hand from the floor. Inside was a letter on bank stationary, dated April 2, 1862, from Edouard Buisson to Troy Dodson confirming an appointment requested by Troy to meet with an officer of the bank to discuss financing the purchase of Belle Chasse Plantation. Edouard confirmed the meeting for ten o'clock, the morning of Thursday, April 10. She sank to her pallet-cushion and whispered, "Merde! I need to be in New Orleans…."

Francesca sat holding the letter and staring out the rear door. After many minutes, she thought *I've wasted precious time that I can't recover. I've got to move on…. Edna would tell me to stop kicking myself. Okay. Get to work.* She began by making new entries and connections on her newsprint sheets. A new set of connections centered on Joachim's map, potential relationship to Edouard's letter to Troy, Belle Chasse Plantation, and Joachim. Then, she looked at nagging places where connectors were missing: no direct link between Joachim and Troy, or between Troy and motive. *Who does Troy know that I know? Charles Heidsieck and Joseph Marks.* She was able to connect Troy and Joachim when she discovered in Joachim's calendar that the two met at the bank April 11. Still, no motive loomed but the calendar turned up another entry related to Belle Chasse; Joachim had out of the bank meetings with a James E. Zunts. Francesca searched for new combinations of links until suppertime.

Marcelle returned. "Did you make any progress today?"

A beaming Francesca folded and stored her papers. "Oh, I surely did! Thank you so much for noising into my business! Thanks to you, I've identified four people for new high priority interviews."

Chapter 27

Two days later, Francesca and Marcelle debated whether or not to let John Mahan know they had intercepted a wire from General Ruggles at Camp Moore to General Van Dorn advising the latter that he would need upwards of five thousand additional troops to retake Baton Rouge. No date was given. They decided to send an encoded letter instead of a telegram.

The same day, Francesca sent a plain letter to John by David Carpenter:

Thu, 10 Jul

J.M.:

Please ask T.J. Packwood to identify persons submitting proposals dated between April 10 and July 1 instant to purchase his Belle Chasse Plantation. Where is Charles Heidsieck?

Thanks.

F.D.

John's reply arrived two weeks later:

Thu, 24 Jul

F.D.:

Packwood received two bids: 21 Apr, J. Buisson & J.E. Zunts; 2 May, T. Dodson & J.E. Zunts. Heidsieck is incarcerated at Ft. Jackson for spying.

J.M.

With the letter clinched in her fist, Francesca leapt into the air and clicked her heels while shouting, "Yes! Yes!"

Marcelle said, "A body'd think you won something big. Did you?"

"At long last, I've established a motive for murder and have a prime suspect."

"Congratulations, Constable."

"Not so fast there, comrade. I owe big thanks to you for this breakthrough. Now, I've gotta get home and find ol' Em!"

"You did the work and I'm proud to know you." Marcelle blinked and lowered his voice. With a steady gaze, he said, "You're one hellava woman...."

Francesca stopped exuding and stood still for a long moment as they stared into each other's eyes. She thought *I feel too euphoric right now to trust my judgment. I've grown to like this man, but I'm not ready to test my feelings any time soon.* Priorities: One, bring Em home. Two, prove murder and capture the perpetrator, Three, then and only then, begin a slow scout for a business or a man. Francesca crossed her arms over her chest and smiled. She said, "Sir, my name is Frank."

Both laughed.

The next day, Marcelle was on hand to capture the text of an encoded wire in which General Van Horn told Generals Breckinridge and Ruggles that he would entrain four thousand soldiers at Vicksburg bound for Camp Moore. Expect arrival end of day, Monday, 27 July. Attack by 5 August.

Together, Francesca and Marcelle worked for hours wording, rewording, and encoding their alarm message to John. They realized a strong need to get the urgent message right and clear on their first attempt. At half past midnight, Saturday morning, July 26, Marcelle transmitted their encoded telegram to John.

After sunrise, John's encoded reply said:

Sat, 26 Jul

Ack. Remain in place.

J.M.

Saturday night, Aunt Deb knocked softly on their door. Both Francesca and Marcelle slept fully clothed, wearing their shoes. Marcelle stood by the door only after Francesca was in place to cover him with her Spencer carbine. With a trembling hand, Francesca waved and nodded she was ready. Marcelle snatched the door open, nearly extinguishing their lone candle with the breeze he created.

Aunt Deb entered leaning on her cane and sat upon a keg. With mouths agape, neither Francesca nor Marcelle said a word. Panting, Aunt Deb said, "Wait. Lemme cotch me breathin'."

At length she said, "I know y'alls a wonderin' what dis ol' 'oman wants. I come ta tell ya, de 'Cesh done found out somebody done sont sompin ober dey wire. Deys mad, too. Dey been out a lookin' fer who so never done it."

With wide eyes, Francesca and Marcelle looked at each other and nodded. Francesca decided in an instant to chance trusting Aunt Deb. In her disguised voice, Francesca said, "Aunt Deb, how do you know all this and why are you telling us?"

"Chile, y'all de talk o' de country. I knowed y'all was in heah doin' sompin de 'Cesh ain't gone lak. I also knows a 'oman when I sees one." Without displaying emotion, she touched her throat and pointed to Francesca.

Francesca was startled and it showed on her face. Involuntarily, her hand covered her throat.

Aunt Deb continued. "How do I know what I knows? Why, we niggers habs our own wire. Runs word o' mout', plantation ta plantation. Slow but sho'. So now y'all knows to be on watch 'til y'all can 'scape. Okay, I takes me leave. Gawd bress y'all."

As Aunt Deb left, Francesca said in her natural voice, "Thank you."

Aunt Deb did not look back, but said, "Y'alls welcome."

* * *

Francesca and Marcelle sat for almost a half hour without talking.

Finally, Marcelle said, "We haven't exactly been discovered, but I think it's time we put our 'discovered escape plan' into action."

Francesca nodded and said, "I agree."

"Well, it's eleven o'clock already. So let's get crackin'."

Somber, Francesca stood and said, "First, we need a plan to do the plan."

Marcelle laughed. "Sorry. I know this is serious, but what you said struck me as funny."

She smiled. "In a way, it is. Let's start with these little details. I'll encode our abort telegram. Please send it to John. But before that, please let ol' Mr. and Mrs. Carpenter know that 'Cousin Frances' will arrive in about an hour for a bath and bed. Let them know Frances will need to be on the first southbound train come morning."

"You're right. We do need to coordinate duties and avoid missing an item, like burning code sheets, encoded drafts, and Frank's clothes...."

"And most of yours...."

"And burying equipment and cutting the wire down from that pole."

"What about the buried wire?"

220

"Leave it. Okay. I'll get the fireplace going again and let the Carpenters know to expect Frances."

* * *

Two hours later, Francesca sighed and announced, "Well, it's just like Cousin Frances, to be an hour late! Why, I'll bet the second-line will be back in Tremé by the time she gets to her own funeral!"

Marcelle slammed his hand over his mouth so no sound escaped his lips and laughed until he cried. While he recovered, Francesca retrieved the fancy travel satchel and dress within plus accessories from the last of the wooden crates John used to conceal their supplies. Francesca thought Sarah really has great taste, and she didn't scrimp with money provided by my United States Government.

She set the crate in the fire atop another crate already ablaze and stuffed her papers into the satchel. Hands akimbo, she looked at Marcelle sitting on the floor still laughing while wiping his eyes and thought this is a good man. *I could do much worse. I'm almost sure that in time I could love him as much as or maybe more, than I loved that rat, Joachim.*

"Marcelle, I never liked your escape plan. Now, I hate it with passion. It will take *weeks* walking only at night for you to get home. You're talking about walking through enemy territory."

Marcelle nodded. "Fran, that's not new. As a black man in this country, I've always walked in enemy territory."

Upon hearing what she accepted as a simple truth, Francesca nodded and dropped her hands. She thought *I have so much to learn.* She held out both hands and helped Marcelle to his feet. Francesca took a step and reached to embrace him. When she felt his strong arms about her, she knew she was at least right by thinking this could be the man. Though she felt warmth inside and secure in the embrace of a man in the middle of great danger, she held back her feelings, kissed his cheek, and slipped from his arms.

Still Frank, she picked up her satchel and handbag. At the door, she turned and took a long look into what she could see of his eyes by the glow from the fireplace. Remembering the touch of Marcelle's hands when he blackened spots on her face and neck she had missed with burnt cork, Francesca was glad he could not see water welling in her eyes. She pulled the door saying, "Marcelle, fare thee well. See you in Tremé."

* * *

During her long bath at the big house, Francesca remembered Sarah's warning: "When you want it off, silver nitrate will not wash off right away. Use the burnt cork and lanolin on your face; put the silver nitrate only on your hands and wrists. Make sure you do not lose your gloves; else, when you're Frances you'll have a white face and black hands." She smiled and thought Sarah didn't imagine the gloves would hide her blistered hands and broken nails. When her bath was finished, she lay awake upon a feather bed wearing one of Mrs. Carpenter's night gowns. Francesca tried to picture Marcelle beginning his walk toward New Orleans while she was so comfortable. She fell asleep at about five o'clock Sunday morning; then slept for only one hour.

At the station, the blond wigged Frances learned that the first train south was to be a special troop carrier and that the depot master knew of no other scheduled train until Tuesday. With John's money, Francesca purchased a ticket and later bribed the silver haired conductor to board the train. Once aboard the officer's car, she sat with an elderly couple, the only other civilian occupants.

Chapter 28

Instead of going to work at the Browne Agency Tuesday morning, July 29, Francesca was waiting on the steps at City Hall for Detective Philipe Rousseau. Looking down at her familiar long dress that almost touched the ground; she took a deep breath and thought it is great to feel like a woman again. Sorry Frank. When she saw Philipe, Francesca dropped her satchel, ran, and embraced him. She said, "Bonjour! Papa, would you believe it? I found the motive! I have a suspect!"

"W-what? Who? How? Wait." Amused, Philipe held up a hand. "Hold it. Let's start over. Bonjour. Now, let's go inside and you tell me all about your discoveries, from the beginning."

Grinning, she hunched her shoulders and said, "Okay, Papa."

Two hours later, Francesca had walked Philipe through her charts and answered his questions. Beaming, he said, "I'm impressed and very proud of you. I knew you could do it."

"Thank you."

Philipe held his chin, elbow in the other hand. "So, you've met your suspect socially, this Dodson fellow. Interesting, and you tried to help him?"

"Yes, sir. I guess I'm a poor judge of character. I had no idea he could be a murderer and a thief of persons."

"Humph. I've arrested pretty and cultured women in my time. But, tell me, how did you feel when you discovered he was your best suspect?"

"Please allow me to correct you, sir, my only suspect. To answer your question, I was chilled to the point that I can still feel the shudder that ran down my spine. My first thought was of Edna telling me to be prepared to meet the devil himself.

But never would I have dreamed it'd be a man who looks like Troy – the spitting image of a successful businessman."

Philipe shrugged and picked up his notebook. "I nabbed a few of those, too. I had some foot work to follow up this morning, but I'm putting that off and joining you. Let's go find your Mr. Zunts. I'll get the desk sergeant to arrange a little steamboat trip for us this afternoon down to Fort Jackson with the guys from the provost-marshal's office. We'll see how M. Heidsieck is getting on in his confinement. Ready?"

Francesca leapt from her chair. "Yes, sir! I'm ready!"

* * *

Using the 1860 City Directory, they learned James E. Zunts was a partner in the ownership of the City Hotel, located six blocks from City Hall. Mr. Zunts, in his early fifties with an ample belly, was affable and welcomed them to his office. Francesca noticed a marked change in Zunts's demeanor when Philipe's questioning reached the subject of Belle Chasse Plantation.

Philipe said, "M. Zunts, we have it on good authority that you are party to, not one, but two, proposals for the purchase of Belle Chasse. We know the details of both proposals. Now, I'm not a businessman like you, but tell me, is this your usual practice?"

Zunts coughed and blinked. "Well, er, ah, no, to be perfectly candid."

"So, why did you sign on to that second bid dated Wednesday, April 23?"

Francesca made a note that upon hearing this question, Zunts flushed and beads of sweat appeared on his forehead.

Zunts held onto the arms of his chair and said, "A-a-ah, d-do I have to answer that?"

"Sir, your cooperation will be greatly appreciated. Your answers during this interview will be held in strict confidence."

Zunts struggled from his chair and paced with his hands behind his back. Philipe and Francesca remained silent. After three passes in front of his desk, he stopped before Philipe and said, "Er, are you sure what I say won't be repeated to anyone outside this room?" Zunts glanced at Francesca, and then returned his attention to Philipe. "I need assurances from both of you that you will not repeat what I tell you."

Philipe said, "You have our assurance."

Zunts turned to Francesca and said, "Mlle. Dumas, I need to hear it from your lips."

Francesca cleared her throat and said, "Sir, I promise not to repeat what you say."

Zunts sighed and returned to his chair. After a moment, he said, "To be perfectly honest, I'm scared. Mr. Dodson has a way of intimidating without actually threatening a body. Yes, he coerced me into signing onto that second bid. To answer your previous question again, never in my career have I aligned myself with two proposals to purchase the same property." Zunts, looking at the floor, fell silent. No one spoke. Finally, he said, "That's the long and the short of it, except for the fact that I heard within a week of signing with Mr. Dodson my partner in the first bid was dead. A fine young man is gone...."

After a short silence, Philipe stood and offered his hand. "M. Zunts, you have been very helpful. Thank you very much for speaking in spite of your fears."

Francesca thought *what can I say to a man who has the courage to say he's scared?* She curtsied and said, "Thank you, sir. Your secret is safe."

* * *

Outside on the walk in front of the hotel, Francesca glanced across the street at the Browne Agency and thought *I hope Marcelle is asleep in a cool shady spot by a brook.* Then she asked, "Papa, after hearing M. Zunts, do we still need to go to Fort Jackson?"

"If you mean, is it time to go arrest M. Dodson, the answer is no. Why?"

Francesca was waiting for Philipe to continue when she realized his question was not rhetorical. She blurred, "Er, because he'd deny everything?"

"That's a part of it. Our real challenge now is to establish opportunity in the murder of M. Buisson, the shooting of M. Laveau, and the thief of Mlle. Jenkins. We have not yet placed him at the scene of any crime. I agree with you, though we will eventually prove he shot M. Laveau, it will be next to impossible to pin M. Laveau's murder on M. Dodson.

"Since I subscribe to the theory that knowing as much as possible about one's adversary before confrontation is essential to keeping body and soul together, I'm off to see your next candidates for interviews – the good M. Marks, and then M. Heidsieck. Coming?"

"Oh, yes, sir! Please add to my list a final interview candidate."

Walking toward the United States Customs House on Canal Street, Philipe said, "Who is your final candidate?"

In her best business-like voice, Francesca said, "Her name is Mademoiselle Emily Jenkins."

* * *

They found Joseph Marks by a window at E.M. Rusha Imported Wine & Liquors pouring over his account ledgers. He told them, "Mr. Dodson came in here with M. Heidsieck and acted as the enforcer. With his jacket open to reveal a huge revolver, he bullied me into making concessions on behalf of my boss, Mr. Rusha. Though M. Heidsieck was clearly scared of him, I see why he would hire such a fellow; we were a bit arrears. I, too, was afraid, so I made a payment though our accounts suffered."

* * *

At Fort Jackson, immediately after introduction to Philipe, Heidsieck asked, "If I agree to talk, will you let me leave for home? I mean, return to France?"

Philipe said, "My questions are about a local police matter and aren't related to General Butler's reasons for holding you."

"Well, I'm afraid I have nothing to say. I bid good day to you sir and Mademoiselle Dumas."

"Sir, I have men in my employ that can persuade you to talk. Shall I fetch one of them or can we begin?"

Heidsieck blinked, swallowed, and his hands trembled. "Oui, Monsieur. What do you want to know?"

Francesca said, "The night we met aboard the *Catinet*, along with M. Marks, we hailed M. Troy Dodson. Did you fear M. Dodson?"

Heidsieck took a deep breath and said, "Yes."

"Why?"

Heidsieck hesitated.

Francesca pressed. "He can't get at you in here."

Heidsieck looked at Francesca and shook his head. "Oh, but I must differ. The man is ruthless and is an agent of the Confederate Government. Since he is local, I'm sure if he wanted to harm someone within these walls, he'd find a way to do it."

Francesca's mouth dropped open and she stared at Philipe and then Heidsieck.

Philipe said, "Why were you afraid of him the day you went to Rusha's?"

Heidsieck took a deep breath and said, "Yes, I was a bit shaken when I met M. Marks. I know it was he who told you. What Marks didn't know was why. Minutes before we entered Rusha's, I saw Dodson summarily execute one of his fellow agents. He stabbed the man to death for a failed mission."

Francesca thought oh, my Dieu! Edna was right!

Chapter 29

During their return trip from Fort Jackson, Francesca and Philipe sat near the stern out of earshot of crew and passengers exploring alternative methods of rescuing Emily. As the rear paddlewheel steamer neared English Turn, Francesca tearfully pointed out the landing for Belle Chasse Plantation. Drying her face with her knuckles, she said, "I just know that's where she is." Francesca thought *I'm glad he didn't correct me and say 'likely where she is'.*

She took Philipe into her confidence and revealed why she was on the *Catinet* in May and her recent espionage mission at Brookhaven. Philipe whistled. "So that's why I didn't see you for a month."

"Yes, sir. Now that you've reminded me that Baton Rouge has General Butler and the Union Navy's full attention, I understand why resources are in short supply to help me fetch Em. Looks as if I should've remembered General Williams will be getting plenty of help, leaving none for rescuing Em. And who knows what'll happen after the battle at Baton Rouge?

"Sir, I know since Belle Chasse is in Plaquemines Parish; it's outside your jurisdiction. But I'm asking anyway; will you help me get Em outta Belle Chasse, sooner than later?"

Philipe took a deep breath and said, "Yes."

Francesca hugged Philipe. "Sir, you won't regret this."

"I'll live to regret it if we don't concoct and execute the perfect plan. We're talking about a coldblooded killer here. Otherwise, neither of us may live to tell."

By the time they arrived in New Orleans, it was close to nine o'clock and the glow of gas lighted streets greeted them. They had agreed on the primary objectives of their plan: first, snatch Emily, and then, second, lure Troy to New Orleans where police could arrest him. Philipe pointed out the details would be painstaking and require days to work out. They agreed to finish a plan by the following Monday, August 4.

Chapter 30

At noon on Monday, Philipe sent a messenger to Belle Chasse with Francesca's note:

Monday, August 4, 1862

T. Dodson:

Meet me at the Orleans Ballroom at eight o'clock Saturday evening, August 9. Brooke and I have found the girl of your dreams.

F. Dumas.

An hour before sunset the same day, Frank Carpenter went aboard the decrepit *Atlantic* with his new owners, Mr. and Mrs. Bernard Williams. As soon as Francesca had asked, Bernard agreed to charter the *Atlantic* for the evening of August 4. In her knapsack, Francesca carried a pair of shoes, knee stockings, trousers, a shirt, a wooly minstrel wig, bacon, and her trusty Allen and Wheelock .31 revolver. In her pocket, she carried five 1860 silver dollars tied in the corner of a red bandanna.

Approaching the riverbank below English Turn was slow tricky business. With the paddle wheel turning slowly in reverse against the current, the captain sent two crewmen to the bow with long poles probing for debris. Bernard and Philipe put Francesca ashore at first dark about fifteen hundred feet above the landing at Belle Chasse. Here she paused, trembling, and said aloud, "Mother Mary of God, please convey my thanks for the journey so far and pray that ol' Em will get home tonight."

She followed the trail that ran along the west bank to the edge of the plantation. Francesca looked about for some kind of landmark to know where she should turn and go through the woods to the bank, but found nothing in the flat terrain that stood out. To her, all the trees looked alike. At length, she decided to build a marker from sticks and fallen tree branches. Once her marker was built in the middle of the trail, she made her approach unseen to the kitchen house located only a short distance from the rear of the big house. It was suppertime.

At the rear of the kitchen house, Francesca could not prevent her hands from shaking. She paused again knowing for her plan to succeed she needed to move with dispatch. She crouched and forced herself to breathe deeply several times. After two minutes that felt like fifteen, she stood and went to the door with a silver dollar in her hand.

As she had hoped, the kitchen crew was in their supper service. She waited until a large matronly server she had seen on her previous visit was the only person who could see the door. Francesca tapped the door frame with the coin and waved it, beckoning the woman. With a finger over her lips, she motioned again for the woman to come to her. The woman hesitated and Francesca felt sweat rise on her forehead and her temples felt as if an August sun was upon them. Desperate for the coin to work, she held it up again and twisted it in the dim light. Frowning, the woman glanced over her shoulder and then walked to the door.

Once outside, Francesca pressed the silver dollar into the woman's palm. The surprised woman looked about in all directions and stepped out of the light, pulling Francesca with her. She whispered, "Boy, who're you? I knows you ain't from round heah. What ju want?"

Francesca said in her natural voice, "What I want is the girl called Emily that Troy Dodson stole a few months back."

The woman put her hand over her mouth and said, "My Gawd! You's a 'oman!"

"Shhh!"

The woman whispered, "Okay, okay. How we goes 'bout dis?"

Francesca thought the sound of the word 'we' was sweet and it calmed her. She breathed a sigh of relief. She said, "Go to the Dodson house and tell'em something they'll believe and send Emily with you to fetch some treat or something from the kitchen house. Will that work?" Francesca pressed another silver dollar into the woman's hand.

The woman smiled and said, "My name is Sadie. I'm on my way. I'll think o' sompin 'fore

I gits there."

Francesca sat behind a tree. In five minutes, the woman returned. "She a comin'. Sit tight."

Emily appeared on the path carrying a basket. Francesca felt her heart pounding. She leapt to her feet and seized Emily, putting a bandanna over her mouth. Emily struggled. Then, Francesca whispered, "Em, it's me, Fran!"

Emily bit down on the bandanna, dropped the basket, and more clutched than embraced Francesca. The two women fell to the ground rolling over and holding each other as if their very lives depended on their fierce grip.

With hands clasped, Sadie watched smiling and alternately glancing for any one approaching.

At length, Francesca whispered, "We've no time to lose. Hurry! Strip and give Sadie your clothes."

"Huh?"

"Don't ask questions, move. No talking."

By the time Emily's dress went over her head, Francesca handed her a pair of knee stockings, then trousers.

Francesca gave Sadie the dress and another coin. She said, "Quick, put these in your cook fire."

Holding Emily's dress to her chest, Sadie said, "I fear y'all best run nigh! Gwon! Git 'fore you's cotched!"

Francesca said, "Okay. When they ask, you say Emily never showed."

While Emily tied the shoes sitting on the ground, Francesca pulled the minstrel wig onto Emily's head and tucked in her sandy braids. Once on, she pulled Emily to her feet, handed her a shirt to wear over her waist-length chemise, and said, "This way!"

They ran from the kitchen house to a path that led from the first row of cabins to the barns and the cane fields beyond. At the path, Francesca held up a hand and said, "Walk." Francesca knew they could be seen along this stretch, but hoped no one would pay particular attention to two 'boys' walking along the path.

The dog was ten feet away when it made a low growl and barked once.

Emily said, "That's one of Dodson's damn dogs."

Francesca pushed Emily ahead and jerked a piece of bacon from her knapsack. She whistled softly and said, "Come dog and eat." She waved the bacon in the air hoping the dog would smell it. Sniffing, the dog wagged its tail, advanced with caution, and took the bacon. While the dog ate the treat, the two 'boys' walked past the barns where the only sound made was one of the mules braying. The cows and pigs were busy with their supper.

They began running again over the way Francesca had entered the plantation, along a wagon track beside a cane field. They were half way to the riverbank trail when a rapid clanging of the plantation bell began.

Startled, Francesca said, "What's that?"

"That's the alarm for a runaway's on the loose. It means they've missed me and know I'm running."

"Well, let's run!"

Running, Emily said, "It's best to run clever; not just run. I'll follow you for now, and then when I pass you, you follow me."

They made the turn onto the riverbank trail. Three hundred feet or so on, they heard the horses and dogs. Emily shouted, "They've got our trail. Follow me!" She led into the woods making a trail for the dogs under the trees with the lowest branches possible while zigzagging parallel to the wagon track.

Francesca felt herself tiring and slowing. She was gasping for breath. She smiled as she thought *ol' Em sure is motivated tonight. I remember she couldn't keep up with me when we were children running through the streets of Tremé.* Then, Francesca heard the horses crashing through the woods after the baying hounds and men cussing the tree branches. The first quarter moon was rising over the trees. She split off to look for her marker and saw it in the distance. The sound of the dogs was closer and closing.

"Em, turn to the trail!"

They ran past the marker and Francesca said, "Follow me." They went into the narrow wood between the trail and the river. Francesca could hear the *Atlantic's* steam engine. She also heard the dogs closing on Emily. She stopped, pointed, and said, "Em, the boat is just there! Get on board!"

Francesca pushed her shoulder against a tree, aimed her revolver with both hands, fired, and brought down the lead dog. That stopped the charge of the dogs. In the distance she heard a voice say, "Oh, shit! The damn nigger's got a gun! Slow down, boys. Don't get yourself bushwhacked!"

Francesca ran again and found Emily at the water's edge waiting for the gangplank.

The dogs regrouped and followed a new leader through the trees. Francesca did not have anything to lean against and steady her aim. She felt it foolhardy, but she put her left knee on the ground and used her right knee, elbow, and hand to support her shooting hand. She knew she had less than three seconds. Francesca saw the large bloodhound's coat glisten in the light of the quarter moon. She aimed and fired at the white teeth flashing like flickering candlelight. The dog yelped and went down. The pack stopped again. Francesca ran across the gangplank and the *Atlantic's* paddlewheel turned as soon as her feet hit the deck. They got underway while the crew was pulling in the gangplank.

Chapter 31

Emily, Francesca, Brooke, and Bernard celebrated as the *Atlantic* struggled upstream for safe harbor in New Orleans. Bernard surprised them with Heidsieck & Company champagne he had the crew store onboard during the afternoon. They enjoyed the cool breeze on the main deck, making their own music by singing, drumming against the wall, and stomping on the deck. Philipe and a few crew members joined the singing.

The *Atlantic* was putting in beside wharf number thirty at the head of Esplanade Street well before the last run of the Esplanade Street Line streetcar when Emily asked, "How's ol' Louie? Has his shoulder healed? In my excitement, I forgot to ask before now."

The revelers avert their eyes. The only sound was the *Atlantic's* engine. After a moment, Francesca released her lower lip from the grip of her upper teeth and said, "Em, I'm sorry. Louie passed away."

Francesca put an arm about Emily's shoulders. Emily raised her cup in salute. She sniffed and said, "Louie, you were a good friend!" She took a swallow and handed the cup to Francesca. Emily's mezzo-soprano voice brought the crew out to hear her sing. They removed their hats and stood silent.

Should *old* acquaintance be forgot,
and never brought to mind ?
Should *old* acquaintance be forgot,
and *old* lang syne ?

She sang the chorus and skipped to the fifth verse.

And there's a hand my trusty *friend* Louie!
And *give me* a hand o' thine !

And we'll *take* a right *good-will draught*,
for auld lang syne.

Emily sang the chorus again. When she finished, Francesca noticed people had gathered on the wharf to listen. Sustained applause came from all directions. Francesca hugged Emily again as both cried.

* * *

On the wharf, Philipe said, "Mlle. Jenkins, I'm sorry, but I do need to ask you just three questions before the streetcar gets here. I'll save my other questions until another time."

Emily and Francesca were holding hands. Emily said, "It's okay, sir. I understand."

"Did M. Dodson shoot M. Laveau?"

"Yes, sir."

Did M. Dodson steal you?"

"Yes, sir."

Did M. Dodson harm you in any way?"

"No, sir."

Philipe made notes. "Okay. Thank you and goodnight to both of you. Fran, I'm proud to call you my daughter."

"Thank you, Papa."

With eyebrows raised, Emily looked at Francesca and then Philipe's receding back and said, "Daughter? Papa?"

Francesca laughed. "We've got a lot of catching up to do. Right now, let's not let that streetcar get away."

* * *

Francesca and Emily disembarked at the Rocheblave Street streetcar stop, four blocks from Emily's home. Grinning, Emily said, "Last one home is a rotten egg!" And then, before

Francesca could reply, Emily ran. Emily stopped at her corner, Ursulines Street, and waited for Francesca.

She said, "Fran, do you know those women and children on my veranda with my folks and your ma? Oh, and there's a man coming outta my house."

Smiling, Francesca said, "Yes. I know them; I invited them. I'm so glad you could make it to your party!"

Walking again, they hugged and laughed. The people on the veranda took no notice of them in the light of the rustler's moon until Emily opened the low gate and they stepped into the yard.

Tony walked to the step and asked, "What can I do for you, boys?"

Emily's mouth formed an 'O'. And then, she looked down at her clothes and laughed. She raised her arms and ran toward Tony saying, "Papa, it's me, Em!"

Upon hearing Emily's voice, Tony nearly ripped his pockets getting his hands out to catch his daughter. Laura tore her way past Edna, Rev. Jobert, Ada, Anna, Able, and Arianna and bounded down the two steps to the walk and crashed into the embrace of Emily and Tony. The two pulled Laura into their silent embrace. The tears streaming on their cheeks shone silver in the first quarter moonlight. Laura continued repeating, "Thanks be to God for my child!" Much sniffing and many amens followed from all assembled.

While still in a tight embrace on the walk, Rev. Jobert laid hands on Emily, Laura, and Tony, offering a prayer of thanksgiving that was punctuated by shouts of "Praise God!" from the gathering. As soon as Rev. Jobert said, "Amen," Emily raised her voice and others followed:

> "Praise God, from whom all blessings flow;
> Praise Him, all creatures here below;

Praise Him above, ye heav'nly host;
Praise Father, Son, and Holy Ghost. "

And then, Francesca led her mother and friends as loud as she could sing in "For She's a Jolly Good Fellow." On the second time through the song with the family of three still embraced, neighbors left their verandas and stood on the street singing. Able moved his hands in the air, directing the impromptu choir.

One woman asked, "What're we celebratin'?"

A man said, "I don't know. But I'm a shut up and sing."

Before they finished, another man ran back into his house and returned with his horn. When the applause died, he broke into "When the Saints Go Marching In." More neighbors joined and sang in the street. Brooke and Bernard arrived in their coach with the coat of arms on the door.

Francesca said to Ada, "Ma, I could not have imagined, much less, organized such a party."

Ada hugged her daughter, "Never mind, dear. You did what nobody else could do."

* * *

The celebration continued while Emily took a bath and returned to more applause in her best dress and lace. At about two o'clock Tuesday morning, August 5, Ada and Edna made a breakfast of shrimp, bacon, crawfish, grits, and whatever neighbors brought for the pot. Francesca emerged from her bath in a favorite dress. Tony made a toast. "Here's to my two daughters, Emily and Francesca!"

As the neighborhood revelers made their way home, Brooke stood beside Francesca and said, "I'm very happy for you and ol' Em."

"Thanks."

"I'm also glad your face is white again."

Somber, Francesca turned and faced Brooke. "My face may look white, but in my heart, I've heard the call of my African roots. At last, I know who I am."

Chapter 32

Thursday afternoon, August 7, Francesca took Emily to meet Sarah Butler and Major Stone. Emily thanked Sarah for her makeup artistry and role in her rescue. Major Stone had celebratory beignets and real coffee brought in and toasted the Union victory at Baton Rouge on Tuesday. He informed Francesca that John Mahan was still in the field, but had set up an account for her at Citizens Bank with a one thousand dollar bonus for her 'recent contributions.' Flushed, Francesca was astonished. Sarah and Emily applauded. The mood turned sour when he announced that General Williams died in battle at Baton Rouge and that the Union suffered almost five hundred casualties.

* * *

While Emily visited nearby with Anna and her children, Philipe and Francesca conducted a post mortem on the Monday night rescue operation. They reviewed and made tweaks to their plan for the coming Saturday night operation to apprehend Troy Dodson.

As Francesca stood to leave his office, Philipe asked, "Are you armed?"

Perplexed, Francesca frowned and said, "No, sir."

Philipe shook a finger at her and said, "You're to remain armed at all times, until I give you the word to stand down. Understood?"

Still perplexed, she decided not to ask why, but said, "Yes, sir."

* * *

With Tony, Emily, and Laura, Francesca began preparing after the noon meal on Saturday, August 9, for the operation at the Orleans Ballroom. Tony was in his backyard workshop making new balls for Francesca's revolver, cleaning, and reloading it. In her sewing room, Laura worked with Francesca to fit her tiny revolver in a cushioned sleeve that she then stitched inside Francesca's corset. They double checked to be sure the sleeve would point the revolver's handle to the wearer's left. When Francesca tried it on, Emily laced and tied the corset's strings. Francesca laughed and said, "This would never work if my little mamelles were as large as y'all's."

Covering her mouth, Emily giggled. Laura smiled and said, "You're right. But it looks like your toy gun will fit where you can reach it in a hurry. How does it feel?"

"Like a third mamelle!"

The three women broke into hysterical laughter.

* * *

At six o'clock, Francesca glided into the ballroom in her dazzling champagne gold dress on Tony's arm and met with Philipe and his team of old plain clothes policemen dressed for a ball. Philipe said, "Tell me again, how we will recognize M. Dodson?"

"When I dance with him, I will tilt my head to my left."

"Okay. You men clear on that?"

Four men said, "Yes, sir."

One said, "Then, Gregory and I will approach and arrest him, right?"

With his eyes searching the face of each man, Philipe held up a fist and said, "Hell, no! I'm only going to say this one more time. I don't want you to arrest him as we normally would. This is no ordinary suspect. Dodson has killed three men that we know of. He will not go quietly. I want you and

Gregory to *seize* him from behind, pinning his arms. You're to assume Dodson will have a long .44 under his jacket and that he will not hesitate to use it on your ass. Am I clear this time?"

"Again, four men said, "Yes, sir!"

"Okay. Now, go fill your lemonade cups and chat up those four women actors I hired."

Another man spoke. "When Mlle. Dumas identifies him, me and Carlos will assume our backup positions downstairs, right?"

Philipe nodded and said, "That's right. I'm the backup on this floor."

* * *

From her post at the entrance to the ladies parlor, Francesca saw Troy arrive early. Tony had already taken a position downstairs as an Orleans Ballroom greeter. The time was only seven thirty. Francesca decided to make Troy wait alone and she retreated further into the parlor. She relaxed when the all-colored eight man orchestra finished its tune up and started the first dance number at seven forty five.

The chimes at St. Louis Cathedral, one block away, sounded eight times. Francesca walked briskly into the ballroom and pretended to search for someone even after she had spotted Troy sitting in the same corner where she first met him. She saw that he was staring at her. Once she ascertained that the three policemen were in their designated places, Francesca turned her face toward Troy and pretended to recognize him for the first time with the best alluring smile she could make. He met her half way across the floor.

"Good evening, Monsieur Dodson. It's so good to see you again! I'm so glad you could accept my invitation."

He kissed her gloved hand. "Well, er, I didn't w-want to let this chance pass me by."

"Why, Monsieur Dodson…."

"Call me Troy."

"Troy, you look a bit peaked. Is there something the matter?"

"Well, er, to tell you the truth, my stomach is a fluttering a bit. Nothing serious."

Francesca maintained her radiant smile, her eyes only on his. "Why, Troy, she's only a woman. You'll be fine. Let's sit you down for a few minutes. Then later, we can dance while we wait for Brooke and your girl. Is that okay?"

"S-sure."

While Francesca distracted Troy with questions about sugar cane, she curled a tress with her left hand to calm her nerves. When she could stand it no longer, the orchestra started a beloved number. With elbow length gloves, she slapped her lap and said, "This one of my favorite tunes. Sir, may I be so bold as to ask you for this dance?"

Grinning, Troy stood and offered his arm. "Why, certainly, Mademoiselle Dumas. I'm sorry I didn't ask first."

In the middle of the floor, they bowed to each other, and then each with one hand up holding the partner's hand and the other on the partner's waist, Francesca and Troy began to dance. She smiled and held her head tilted to her left.

Two minutes later, a policeman seized Troy's arm extended to Francesca's waist, but the second policeman was late reaching for Troy's right arm. The startled, but agile, former soldier saw the second policeman in his peripheral vision and met him by sending his elbow into the man's Adam's apple. The second policeman crashed to the floor in agony, gasping. Women nearby screamed. Francesca decided to scream, too. But she did not run as the other women did. And as their men retreated, the floor was cleared around Francesca and Troy. Meanwhile, Troy jerked his left arm forward, causing the first policeman to stumble. Troy hit the man's neck with the butt of his right fist and the man crumbled to the floor.

He saw Philipe, the only person in the room moving toward him. Philipe reached for his revolver. With blinding speed, Troy drew his .44. He reached out and grabbed Francesca about her waist, pinning her left arm to her body, and lifted her off the floor. Startled, she screamed again. Troy pulled Francesca against his body and leveled his revolver at Philipe. He said, "Not another bloody step, old man. Drop your gun and move over there with the crowd." He jerked his head to indicate direction.

To Francesca, Philipe looked utterly defeated standing before her. She remembered Major Stone's words, "Things don't always go according to plan. Soldiers have to adapt."

Philipe dropped his revolver on the floor with a clank and walked backwards to the crowd huddled on one side of the room.

Troy said, "Everybody, sit on the floor."

The people, including the orchestra, rushed to sit on the floor.

Troy held Francesca in front of him and walked to the door, pointing his .44 in one direction then another. He reached the stairs, and saw two men make the turn on the landing running up the stairs, revolvers in hand. He shot both before either could fire.

Going down the stair, Francesca said, "Put me down. I can walk. Hold my arm, if you want. I can't run in this dress."

Troy looked at her and she saw his hate. He hissed, "Okay. Any trouble outta you and I'll kill you now instead of later. Bitch, I know you did this to me." He put her down on her feet.

Francesca thought *I'm scared, but if this is my end, I want to go down fighting.* What would Edmond Dantes do? First, he would remain calm; adapt. She said, "Yes, you're right. At least I have Emily back."

Troy jerked her arm so she faced him. He said, "Was that your op Monday night? And you know Emily?"

She looked up into his eyes and said, "Yes. And yes, Emily is my best friend."

Troy shook his head and said, "Good job. I admire your work. Too bad you didn't work for me. I'm still gonna kill you soon's we're outta town. Now, let's go."

They walked past Tony and out into the silver light of a full moon. Troy commandeered a coach and standing beside the open door, he said, "Get in."

Francesca said, "Let go of my arm. I need both hands to pull my dress up and reach the step."

Troy released her arm. Francesca removed her gloves and with both hands pulled the front of her dress up to her knees. She made a quick turn and kicked Troy in the spot on his left leg where he had told her his battle wound was. Startled, Troy gasped and both knees buckled. Francesca heard onlookers gulp as she grabbed her revolver from its hiding place. Without aiming, she pointed and fired. Troy saw her move and tried to duck and lost his balance. The ball hit his left arm as he fell. Shuffing her feet, Francesca moved to her right, away from his gun hand. On the ground, Troy tried to level his .44 at a moving target. This time, Francesca took a one handed aim and fired a ball into the center of Troy's chest. She saw his teeth clench and heard the loud explosion of his .44 firing a ball past her and toward the entrance of the Orleans Ballroom.

Troy's revolver fell from his hand and he lay still in his blood. Scared stiff, Francesca waited, holding her aim at the dead man's chest.

Chapter 33

Sunday afternoon, August 10, was hot. Francesca used one of Anna's folding fans to help Philipe's wife keep him as comfortable as possible. Philipe's bed was near a window in the men's ward of Dr. Stone's Infirmary. Philipe sat atop his sheets, propped up by three pillows. His bandaged left leg was resting on two more pillows. Philipe said, "The good doctor told me I didn't have much more'n a flesh wound. I'm here to tell you, as much as this thing hurts, I don't want to feel what he calls one of his regular 'Saturday night specials'."

Mme. Rousseau, Emily, and Francesca laughed.

Francesca asked, "Did Dr. Stone give you the ball?"

"The ball passed through; there was nothing for doc to dig out."

Mme. Rousseau said, "If you were upstairs when the shooting was going on, how did you get shot?"

Grinning, Philipe said, "Oh, it was easy. I retrieved my gun and ran downstairs and out the door just in time to catch Dodson's last dying shot. I should've known Fran didn't need help from an ol' fart like me."

John Mahan walked in and joined the laughter. Francesca thought he looked older. After an exchange of pleasantries and introductions to Emily and Mme. Rousseau, John said, "Mlle. Dumas, I've just left the provost-marshal's office. All they talked about was you. Tomorrow morning, I'll go over to Citizens and double your account."

Francesca gasped and covered her mouth. She said, "Oh mon, Dieu! But why?"

"I learned this morning from Major Stone that Dodson was a Confederate agent. Stone learned that from you.

"And now, I'm afraid I have bad news. Your notoriety will end your service to the United States. You're too well known.

248

Worse, I have heard that you may become a primary revenge target of the Secesh. This is typical Secesh behavior. Plus, the Dodson family has lost a favorite son. I don't know what they'll do."

Emily said, "I know. Matt Dodson isn't very bright but he's meaner than a snake. From the day I set foot on Belle Chasse, only his fear of his brother, Troy, kept Matt off me." Emily turned to Francesca. "That was Matt's voice we heard chasing us last Monday night. I fear he'll want revenge and take pleasure in getting it."

Emily sniffed and Francesca hugged her.

John put his hand on Francesca's shoulder and said, "I'm sorry. I have more bad news. Marcelle was captured near Baton Rouge by retreating Confederates and hung as a spy. I'm really sorry."

Francesca looked at John's eyes in disbelief. Her knees felt weak and the room spun. She awoke in the men's ward on the bed next to Philipe to the smell of ammonia. Her temples throbbed and her tears wet her ears. She though Mary, Mother of God, was he the one? Why is he gone from me? *I have not forgotten the prayers that were answered, and I'm grateful, but I still grieve for this man who was not yet mine....* Francesca tried to smile at Dr. Stone, Emily, and Mme. Rousseau, all of whom were fanning her vigorously.

She sat up. Emily held her hand.

John's face was somber. He said, "Fran, I think our last op together is to get you outta New Orleans."

Emily said, "What?"

* * *

On Monday morning, August 25, 1862, the family said their fare thee wells at Anna's house on Canal Street. Francesca and Emily had hidden there from the potential

Confederate threat. The blond Frances Carpenter emerged dressed as an aristocratic slave owner with her two charges, Edna and Emily. After two weeks of heated debate among family members, agreement for Francesca and Emily to leave New Orleans was reached only when Edna volunteered to accompany them.

With fake slave deeds provided by Captain Puffer from the provost-marshal's office to facilitate travel through Confederate held territory, John Mahan put them aboard a New Orleans, Jackson and Great Northern Railroad train bound for Memphis, Tennessee. At Memphis, the trio boarded a steamboat for St. Louis, Missouri.

Using a letter of introduction from General Butler, they established a contract laundry service for the new Western Sanitation Commission Hospital being built on the Jefferson Barracks army post near St. Louis.

In 1871, Francesca, still in the laundry business with Emily and Edna, met and fell in love with a colored soldier, Sergeant Isaac Rice of Company A, Tenth United States Cavalry, at Camp Supply, Indian Territory. Francesca and Isaac later moved to Fort Sill, Indian Territory.

Partial List of Nonfiction Characters Appearing in *The Laced Chameleon*

Benjamin, Judah P., US Senator; Confederate Secretary of State

Browne, Thomas, Owner of the Singer Sewing Machine Agency

Hildreth-Butler, Sarah, Actress, wife of General Butler

Butler, Benjamin F., Major General, US Army

Casanave, Pierre, Founder of Undertaking Service

Casanave, Peter, Son of Pierre, Undertaking Service

*Cocks, Arianna, Daughter of Annabelle

*Cocks, Annabelle, Daughter of John G. Cocks

Cocks, John G., New Orleans Judge

*Cocks, Able, Son of Annabelle

*Corlin, Martha, Confederate Sympathizer

Delille, Henriette, Founder and Mother Superior, Sisters of Holy Family

Dumas, Alexandre, Author of *The Count of Monte Cristo*

Foster, Thomas, Owner of a New Orleans slave sales depot

Heidiseck, Charles Camille, Owner of Heidiseck & Company Wines, Reims, France

Jobert, Rev. J.B., Pastor, St. Augustine Catholic Church

Kendall, George W, Surgeon, Confederate States Army

Lille, Sarpy, Officer, Union Bank of New Orleans

Lovell, Mansfield, Major General, Confederate States Army

Mahan, John, General Butler's most trusted Spy

Nixon, James, Owner/Publisher, *New Orleans Daily Crescent*

Packwood, Theodore, Owner of Belle Chasse Plantation

Rusha, E.M., Owner of EM Rusha. Importer of Fine Wines & Liquors

Stone, Doctor, Physician and Founder, Dr. Stone's Infirmary

Strong, George B., US Army, Major, General Butler's Chief of Staff

**Tunnard, William H., Confederate Army Sergeant, 3rd Louisiana Infantry Regiment

Zunts, James E., Investor and Co-owner of the City Hotel

*First names assigned by author. See bibliography at: http://bobrogers.biz

**This character appears in the novel, *First Dark*.

Partial List of Fiction Characters appearing in *The Laced Chameleon*

*Black, Edna, Francesca's Friend and Servant in the Buisson Residence

Bouffard-Williams, Brooke, Francesca's Friend and Wife of Bernard Williams

Buisson, Edouard, Joachim's Father and Officer at Citizens Bank

Buisson, Joachim, Plaçage partner ("Husband") of Francesca, Son of Edouard

Buisson, Maria, Wife of Edouard, Stepmother of Joachim

Carpenter, David, Plantation owner, Brookhaven, Mississippi

Carpenter, Frances, Francesca's female alias

Carpenter, Frank, Francesca's male alias

Carpenter, Marcelle, Marcelle's alias

De Mortie, Ada, Francesca's Mother

Dodson, Matt, Brother of Troy

Dodson, Paul, Father of Troy and Matt

Dodson, Tory, Confederate soldier and spy

Donohue, Mark, Plantation owner and investor, Suitor of Francesca

*Dumas, Francesca, Plaçage partner of Joachim Buisson

Dumas, François, Father of Francesca, Restaurant Owner

Jenkins, Anthony, (Tony), Emily's father, Shoemaker

*Jenkins, Emily, Francesca's best friend

Jenkins, Laura, Francesca's mother, Seamstress

Johnston, Richard, Confederate spy

Lainez, Marcelle, Francesca's spy partner

Laveau, Louis, Joachim's friend

Lemoine, Alfonse, French naval officer, Suitor of Francesca

Marks, Joseph, Accountant at E.M. Rusha Importer of Wines and Liquors

Morris, Albert, John Mahan's alias

*Pierre, Jean, Confederate soldier, 3rd Louisiana Infantry Regiment

Rousseau, Philipe, New Orleans Homicide Detective

Williams, Bernard, Brooke Bouffard's husband

See bibliography at: http://bobrogers.biz.

*These characters appear in the novel, *First Dark*.

CPSIA information can be obtained at www.ICGtesting.com
Printed in the USA
BVOW01s1708090614

355706BV00001B/2/P